ABOUT THE AUTHOR

Colin Bostock-Smith was raised in a remote Devonshire village but made his way to London where he was first a journalist on the London Evening Standard, then turned to writing comedy scripts for the likes of the Two Ronnies, Rowan Atkinson, Tim Brooke-Taylor, Basil Brush and President Ronald Reagan.

Today he lives in deepest East Sussex with his partner Ruth, and writes novels about crime and passion in a remote Devonshire village.

Published in Great Britain in 2025
By Diamond Crime

ISBN 978-1-915649-53-9

DIAMOND
BOOKS

Diamond Crime is an imprint of Diamond Books Ltd.

Book Cover Design by Kathleen Harryman
https://www.kathleenharryman.co.uk

For information about Diamond Crime authors
and their books, visit:
www.diamondbooks.co.uk

For:

Jennifer and Robin, who lived it with me

The Man who Walked with Goats

Colin Bostock-Smith

Prologue

The Reverend Doctor Donald Simpson had often, in idle moments when not ministering to his human flock or attending to his spirited pair of pet goats, contemplated the circumstances of his own death. Don't we all?

His demise would, the Reverend Doctor knew, be a cataclysmic blow to the village. As the elected non-conformist chapel minister for North Tawe, in the heart of the West Devon countryside, Simpson stood tall – indeed, so tall, so proud, so upright, that wicked voices would sometimes wonder why he didn't topple over backwards. He ignored such comments. He stood for something. Rectitude. Decency.

When, some eighteen years ago, he had settled in the quiet West Devon village of North Tawe, he had by his stance, both moral and physical, not to mention highly audible, established himself as a natural community leader. The local vicar, elderly and near retirement, was no competition. Simpson had no wife to muddy the waters. And his assumed title of "Reverend Doctor" led him to inherit, almost by default, the leadership of the chapel community.

His Doctorate of Divinity had helped. It had arrived by post from the Jed Sherman Evangelical University of Maysville, Mississippi (No Coloureds, no Catholics, no Jews), and Simpson had hung it in the vestibule of the village Chapel, slightly too high on the wall to allow the occasional visiting non-conformist bigwig to inspect it too closely.

(To give him his due, Simpson, locally, preferred to omit the title "Doctor", thus avoiding the irritating task of turning away villagers who wanted him to look at their warts.)

So now, in this New Elizabethan year of 1952, when the Rev Simpson contemplated his end on this earth, he trusted that God would give him a good one. Perhaps he might be allowed to go at the height of one of his inspiring sermons about damnation. He was good at them. Or perhaps he would pass away when contentedly leading his other flock, his two beloved goats, for their daily roadside breakfast. Either death would be acceptable.

Of course he would have to leave the final decision to God. But he had faith. He had, as he frequently announced to his congregation, been washed in the blood of the lamb. God wouldn't let him down.

The one form of death that the Minister never contemplated was this: that he might be struck down by a long-bladed shining silver knife, plunged ferociously and repeatedly into his ribs, his heart, his stomach. That his blood would spurt, his vital organs rupture, his midriff be sliced open, its contents falling in ribbons to his knees, and that he would writhe in a long and final agony, sprawling obscenely across his elevated Minister's seat in his own chapel, while his killer watched him die, and smiled.

And when that exact death did envelop him, and he was so uncomfortably translated to glory, one could imagine that the Almighty would never hear the last of it.

CHAPTER ONE

Police Constable Derek Martin was knee-deep in hens. All around him, in the huge barn that served as a "deep litter" henhouse, there scratched, pecked and clucked what he estimated to be at least 50, perhaps more, chicken.

"And you're telling me one's gone missing?" he asked.

"Not gone missing. Thieved," said Joshua Voden, his face solemn and regretful, perhaps even with just a tinge of grief in his eyes.

Derek looked around. The barn stank, of course. Chickens have their own distinctive whiff. The atmosphere was almost feral. Outside a cold wind off the Atlantic was sweeping across the West Devon fields on this grim December day in 1952. But in here, in with the dozens of little brown bodies clucking their chorus of gossip, it was almost warm. Smelly, but almost cosy.

"Not a fox then?" Derek queried.

"Fox never get in here." The barn did indeed look impregnable. "Anyhow, if a fox get in, the bugger would kill 'em all."

True enough, Derek thought to himself. That's what foxes did. And with devastating results, too. Even his nature-loving wife Mary had to admit that.

There was a flurry, a series of squawks, and feathers flew. Two of the multitude had quarrelled, probably over some nameless bug they had found in the dank and blackened straw that carpeted the barn. Their sisters pecked on, regardless.

"Joshua, how do you know?"

"How do I know what?"

"How do you know one's missing? All right, thieved?"

"Counted them."

"You counted..." Derek indicated the swirl of brown fowl "...this lot?"

"Count 'em every day, don't I?" Joshua was a squat little man of about forty, a cheerful soul who Derek knew to be a stalwart of North Tawe's Green Dragon pub darts team. His appearance was typical of many a small-time West Devon farmer. He wore gumboots, old cords, an even older tweed jacket under which was a suspiciously grey collarless shirt, plus what might have once been a farmer's wife's warm woollen cardigan. He'd evaded call-up during the war, on the grounds of being a farmer, and therefore vital to the war effort, something which caused raucous amusement amongst those who knew him and his efforts at meaningful agriculture. That was in 1940. Now, in the last days of 1952, it would be even more difficult to describe him as a farmer, or his establishment as a farm. Of its fifteen rolling West Devon acres, ten were rented out for grazing. The farm yard itself was littered with the remains of half-hearted attempts at husbandry – a rusting tractor on three wheels, broken gates, ancient and overgrown rubber tyres – and the only sign of any successful agricultural enterprise was right here, in this old barn amongst its feathered multi-occupancy.

Derek turned to the man, looking him squarely in the face. "You're telling me you count this lot?" he asked, loading his tone with sarcastic disbelief.

"Told you. Every day.

"How?"

"On me fingers. And one of 'em's been took."

Was that a tear glinting in Joshua's rheumy eye? Or was it a spark of mischief? Was this another example of the ancient and rural Devonshire art of leg-pulling? Derek felt his suspicions coming on strong. He decided to call the man's bluff.

"Okay," he said equably. "Which one? Which one did they thieve?"

"Esmerelda."

"What?"

"Esmerelda. They've thieved her."

"Esmerelda. Are you saying the missing hen had a name?"

"Course. They all got names, son."

"All of them?"

"Course all of them. That one, by your feet, that's Marilyn. Next to her, that's Jeannie."

"Oh yeah?" Derek made one last attempt to challenge the man, to make him admit he was talking nonsense. He pointed wildly to the far side of the barn, where featureless hens wandered in pointless but crowded paths. "That one, what's her name?"

"You mean either June or Janet?"

"So you can't tell those apart then?"

"Them two is identical twins. Double-yolker."

Derek gave up. Any dregs of solemn legal police authority were now, he felt, lying in tatters in the straw at his feet. These bloody jokers of North Tawe, they'd done it again. He'd been caught again. He'd been fooled. The country bumpkins had won, the townie had lost. He'd been made to feel a simpleton. Most of the village would hear about it in 24 hours, and giggle. He felt a familiar sense of frustration, and humiliation, and even reluctant amusement.

* * *

It wasn't the first time he'd been made to feel like a credulous twit. They'd been doing it throughout the eighteen months he'd spent as North Tawe's resident village copper. Pulling his leg until he was lame, with their tales of how the village well, from which some residents still drew their drinking water, was a bottomless pit, or how gold had once been discovered in the Tawe river, or how the elderly Scotsman in the cottage at the foot of the hill would walk the streets at a full moon, bare-chested, kilted, and waving a naked sword. On and on until Derek sometimes imagined that he was followed down the village streets by spectral sniggers

The infuriating thing about this example of local culture – the routine of making a fool out of their townie tyro copper – was that, sometimes the stories were true. Take the case of the half-naked sword-waving Scotsman. Derek hadn't believed that one until he came face to face with the gentleman one November afternoon. The sword was real, the kilt was real, even the greying and rather sunken bare Scottish chest was real. And so were the wild Celtic cries of revenge and retribution that echoed around the village streets. No-one was hurt. Many were mildly amused. They understood that the man was another victim of the stress of the War, and the enemies he slew with his sword were ghostly Waffen SS warriors. Since he joined the force Derek had encountered several such cases of war damage to the nervous system – indeed, his good friend Colonel Critchley still battled with his own demonic memories. Now this reincarnation of Rob Roy in remote West Devon was, his neighbours assured Derek, quite harmless, and would soon retire to his cottage and his understanding wife in peace, leaving the shadowy German corpses to rot in the North Tawe street. Until the next full moon...

So that story, which he had first dismissed as mischievous local fantasy, had proved undeniably true. How the locals laughed, God rot them.

And now they were at it again. Here he was, up to his knees in poultry, and listening to that pint-sized apology for a farmer spinning him a load of garbage about his ability to count a milling multitude of the things, and even know them individually by name. Derek sighed to himself and watched the chickens. Smelly bloody birds. And why was he even listening to this grubby little man? Why was he, a properly uniformed, intelligent and clean officer of the law, the target of so much ludicrous leg-pulling?

"It's because you're new, and a townie." His wife Mary had told him. "They'll stop soon enough."

"When?"

"Oh, give it ten years. Grin and bear it."

Good advice, he knew. But he couldn't bring himself to grin at Joshua. The man might grin back, and he had already demonstrated that he had a repellent mouthful of black and cracked teeth which would, together with the stench of the chicken shed, put Derek off his lunch and quite possibly his supper. So instead he took refuge in correct police procedure.

He extracted his notebook and pencil. "Right," he told Joshua. "This will be reported. Theft of one hen, property of Mr. Joshua Voden of North Tawe." He paused then went through with it. "Answers to the name of Esmerelda."

He snapped the book shut, nodded to Joshua, and stepped back out into the cold and unambiguously fresh air. He straddled his police motorcycle, adjusted his helmet over his flaming red hair, and kicked the starter. For once the engine didn't catch. Dampness in the wind, he concluded. He was about to give it a second kick when Joshua shouted something from the barn door.

"Them beatniks, I reckon."

"What?"

"Them tribe of beatniks, them what moved into the old tumbledown chapel at Fursdon. Thought I saw one hanging around. I reckon they took Esmerelda."

The engine caught, and Derek roared out of the yard. The chill wind bit at his face.

"Beatniks", he muttered through his teeth. "That's all I need."

CHAPTER TWO

Just a couple of days later, Derek had forgotten about beatniks, or missing hens, and would have forgotten about Joshua himself, had he not caught the man's rheumy eye across the Dragon's big and crowded public bar. Joshua had grinned, his blackened teeth found a way to be seen through the smoky atmosphere, and Derek buried his face in his second pint.

It was Christmas Eve, celebrations in the Green Dragon were well underway, and, God help him, the jokers were at it again. Telling him fantastic stories and watching his face. On this occasion the story was, appropriately, about the local Silver Band, and what it would do, later that night. And this one stung. Partly because it had the virtue of all good West Devon stories, in that it just might be true. And partly because it was told to him, right there and then, by the people he believed he could trust - his own wife and a couple of his best friends, all of whom kept perfectly straight faces as they told him the story.

But Derek was wary. He took another good pull at his pint, and scrabbled in a near-empty packet of Smith's Crisps for the last decent sliver. He listened with apparent attention to the story of the Village Silver Band, of how they would behave at midnight that very evening. And then, perhaps on the strength of one too many salty crisps he had denounced the story. It was, he declared, just another leg-pull. Total fiction, he told them. Who on earth would behave like that? And what kind of fool would believe it?

"You're pulling my leg," he concluded.

"No, honestly, we're not!" Mary's face was bland and emotionless, which usually meant she was supressing a smirk.

"You are. You're winding me up, as they say these days. You've done it before, and you're doing it again. And this time I'm not falling for it."

Derek took yet another deep draft of his St Anne's Well brewery best bitter, and glared around at his companions bullishly. In turn they giggled back at him. They knew exactly what they were doing, the evil bunch. The vicar, the Reverend Hugh Shelley, who had been the latest to assure him of the truth of the matter, turned away to hide his grin in the rim of his glass of Bells-with-just-a-splash. His own wife Mary now sniggered at him openly. And the Colonel – Colonel Critchley in his gentleman-farmer outfit of knee-high boots, jodhpurs, and Jersey sweater with leather elbow and shoulder patches; he simply laughed openly and loudly.

"It's not funny," Derek told them all, as severely as he could, given the fact that actually he knew it was funny. He was being teased, of course, and he knew in his heart that there's only one thing worse than your friends teasing you, and that's when they don't. That last thought rang a faint bell. Had someone said something like that somewhere, in some school book or other?

"This is nearly 1953," he said pugnaciously. "People don't behave like that anymore. What sort of credulous twit do you think I am?"

This last remark was met with a meaningful and disrespectful silence. "It's like when they tried to tell me that the well was bottomless," he went on. "Absolute rubbish. Of course it's got a bloody bottom."

Derek realised that he had raised his voice with the words "bloody bottom", and a woman at the next table turned and looked at him curiously.

"I checked up on that one," he continued more quietly. "The County Surveyor put me right. When he came to talk about the drainage. He was still laughing when he left, I might tell you."

The woman at the next table lost interest. And, as the pub filled up, conversation became more difficult. It was, after all, Christmas Eve, and on Christmas Eve a large proportion of the local population of North Tawe heaved themselves out of their comfy chairs and went to the pub. There was nowhere else to go, not in 1952, not in a remote village topping a hill above the tangled coombes and by-ways of West Devon. The Green Dragon had successfully applied for an extension until after midnight, and John the landlord was busily taking full advantage of the burgeoning crowd, passing drinks across the bar like a demented poker dealer and rattling his cash drawer with the ever-welcome income. He'd even broken his own rule, and allowed his 17-year-old daughter Sandy to stand at the bar sink and rinse the empties.

"So," Derek had demanded. "When will the alleged extraordinary behaviour of the North Tawe Silver Band take place? Or rather not take place."

"Midnight," Mary told him. "You know- shortly after when the vicar has to slip off for Midnight Mass, and the rest of us sit here and get sozzled."

"Yes, "the vicar agreed. "Sadly I shall have to miss the Silver Band moment."

"How can you tell such whoppers?" Derek asked him. "For heaven's sake, you're a man of God."

"I'm a sporting man of God," the vicar replied. "Care to put a fiver on it?"

"You're on!" Derek told him.

The vicar smiled, bade them farewell, and disappeared to his duties. And it was only then that Derek's brain briefly resisted the effects of alcohol, and he calculated that the vicar, on his stipend, could afford to lose five pounds even less than he could.

Which meant the story had to be true.

"Bugger," he muttered. "Five pounds."

Mary smirked at him. "It's not coming out of the housekeeping," she told him.

After that there was nothing to do except pile into another pint.

* * *

The Non-Conformist Reverend Simpson was writing his Christmas sermon. He did not celebrate Christmas Eve. Christmas Day itself at the village chapel would, of course, entail a full service, including his major sermon in which he would continue to exhort his sober-suited congregation to follow him in the paths of righteousness.

But the night before Christmas should, he felt, be one spent in quiet contemplation within the bosom of the family. He himself didn't have a family bosom within which to contemplate. But he did have his animals. His goats.

The Rev. Simpson kept the smallest of small holdings – just the one field, rented and adjoining the Manse, as his home was known, plus a well-maintained shed. Simpson liked his goats, perhaps he loved them. There was a simplicity about them, a steadfastness that mirrored his own. They didn't argue, or repeat rubbish they read in the Daily Mirror.

Now, at his kitchen table, he wrote the last words of the exhortation which would send his flock home for their teetotal Christmas lunch, then lit a small Tilley Lamp and stepped outside his cottage to make a final check on the livestock. It was a cloudy and cheerless night, but he was able to ensure that the goats had bedded down nicely in their warm and draught-excluded home, and were murmuring to each other in quiet bleats.

Then he stood for a few moments, listening in the dark. Faintly he could hear laughter and voices on the wind. The pub of course – that alcohol-fuelled jamboree that would inevitably lead to beaten wives, desperate husbands, abused children...

But then, with midnight approaching, the sounds of revelry faded. The church bell sounded once. A solitary ringer getting ready for the 12 o'clock peal, he assumed.

Clouds shifted on a soft breeze, and the stars were out once more. From his shed came a louder, more plaintive bleat from the nanny goat. The image of the nativity invaded his mind. The stable. The smell of the farm animals. The shining light from heaven. But the light did not shine on him. Instead, from nowhere a black, unheralded and overpowering sense of guilt swept over Simpson. His heart heaved. Those terrible questions were being asked of him once again. Was he truly a good man? Everything that had occurred in his past was suddenly back, vivid and frightening. Was he a fraud? Was he cruel? Was he a sinner? Was he, God help him, a bad man?

No! With a huge mental effort, he fought back at the demons that threatened to possess him. He pushed at the dreadful weight of guilt, forced it to retreat, to go back to where it came from. This had happened before, and he had beaten it then, and he would beat it now.

And he did. He swallowed, panted for breath, stood even more erect than normal, and mercifully his brow cleared. And it was gone. And now he knew he was blessed. Despite everything that might have happened long ago, in another time. Now today he was saved.

He had been washed in the blood of the lamb.

Another bleat from the goats, this time the big Billy. The Reverend Simpson decided he better get to bed. In the morning his congregation would be waiting for his talk, and his goats would be waiting for their walk.

* * *

It was while Derek was getting the drinks in and handing more hard-earned cash across the Dragon's stained wooden counter, that something notably unusual occurred.

The pub door opened, and a palpable shock spread through the bar. A woman was entering on her own. That was rare enough. Women simply didn't go into pubs on their own, especially during a rowdy night like this. But this woman was different. She drew all eyes to her, she silenced every tipsy shout, she brought the darts match to a halt. In effect, she brought the entire pub to a standstill.

She was perhaps in her mid-twenties, and tall. Quite possibly over six feet. She wore a black garment – a cloak, perhaps, or something more expansive, tied with a scarlet ribbon at the neck, and covering her from her shoulders to the floor. It had a hood, which sparkled with raindrops – it was an evening of showers – but as she stood just inside the door, she swept the hood back, and bushels of black hair cascaded onto her shoulders. Her face was equally impressive – long, lean, expressionless, devoid of makeup. She wasn't pretty, Derek decided, not pretty as Mary was pretty. The nose was too big – almost hooked – for a start. But there was something calm and controlled about the way she looked around the big room. Something that made a man look at her, speechless and probably with his mouth half-open.

She paused, even posed, for a moment, then she moved to go to the bar, and those in her way quickly made her way clear.

At the bar a bare arm emerged from the cloak, clutching a large flagon. John reached for it, and an understanding glance and a nod passed between them, before he turned to a cider barrel – the one that dispensed the roughest of rough cider, the sort that visiting townies called 'scrumpy', thinking mistakenly that they were sounding authentic – and filled the flagon.

Money passed, John not even checking it. The woman had to carry the loaded flagon with both hands, and when she reached the now-closed entrance two of the local lads almost fell over each other in their efforts to open it for her.

Then she was gone, and the pub racket gradually ground itself back up towards full volume, like an ancient Fordson tractor with a crash gearbox slowly getting back up to its very slow speed. From the conversation that now ensued around Derek, as he made his way back with his tray of drinks, he guessed that half the customers knew who the woman was, if only vaguely, and the other half didn't and were demanding to know.

"Don't you know?" was Mary's reply to his question.

"No I don't."

She grinned at him with a mixture of malice and affection.

"I thought the local bobby would know about everyone on his 'patch'" she said, mocking the police term.

Colonel Critchley came to Derek's rescue. "I don't know for sure, but I think she was one of our beatniks."

"One of our what?"

"Beatniks. You know," Mary told him. "Weirdos. They've invaded that old chapel up at Fursdon."

"Oh. Right. Old Joshua was on about them. I forgot." Derek admitted. "Beatniks, eh? I thought you only got them in America,".

"Well we've got them here now." The Colonel pulled a military type of disapproving face. "Can't say I approve. Not the sort of type we want around here, I should have thought."

"Oh don't be like that, Colonel. It's not like they're tinkers or gypsies," Mary told him.

"I should hope not." Then, with an abrupt change of attitude, he went on: "I thought she looked rather splendid in that cloak and everything – almost medieval."

"I thought she looked great," Derek blurted, and then immediately wished he hadn't, because Mary visibly reacted, and gave him one of those wifely looks that any man comes to know quite early in a connubial relationship.

"Oh did you? "She loaded her voice with dangerous sarcasm. "Did you really? You thought she looked great, did you? Great, eh?"

If he'd been only recently engaged, or even just married, Derek would now be reduced to a spluttering of excuses, denials, explanations. But, on the basis of two years of wedded bliss, he rallied.

"Yes," he told Mary. "I though she looked great. Very attractive. And I'll tell you this," he went on, over-riding Mary's attempt to speak, "if you ask me, she's the second prettiest girl in the pub tonight."

He nearly caught her out. Mary had almost begun to say "And just who is the...?" but stopped herself just in time. He grinned at her. She grinned back, and contented herself by whacking him across the face with a half-empty packet of Smith's Crisps. As ever, it was no effort to tell Mary how lovely she was, because she was.

John the landlord came by, doing his usual busy-night impression of a whirling dervish-cum-street-crockery-vendor, as he collected empties for rinsing and re-charging, taking a snatched break from actually pouring the stuff out. As he passed Derek's table, with the harassed smile of a man who's making enough cash in one night to see him through to February, the Colonel laid a gentleman's restraining hand on his arm.

"Tell us, John. Who was your mystery woman customer?"

"Her? One of them lot up at the Fursdon chapel."

"A beatnik, eh? I was right. Are you sure you want to encourage that type of customer in the Dragon?"

"Her money's as good as yours, Colonel. And she's very polite. Speaks well. Nice girl, actually."

"And very pretty?" Mary suggested slyly.

"Oh yes. Cracker." John winked at her. "Second prettiest girl in the pub, I'd say."

Derek choked on his beer.

CHAPTER THREE

The Colonel had left the pub by eleven, draining his glass with a flourish. "That's my limit. I shouldn't even be here, but Ellen is spending time doing good at the hospital in Exeter. If I'm not back by the time she is, I'll be skinned alive. See you two in the New Year, I expect. Happy Christmas."

"And to you," Mary told him. "Hey! You two are not alone tomorrow, are you?"

"No, no. My brother, his wife, their grown-up son, they're all on their way. Which reminds me, I better get the turkey in the Aga. What are you two doing?"

"Oh, my mum would never forgive me if we didn't turn up. There'll be cousins, kids, big family do as ever, games, singing; a real family do." Mary said.

"Oh Lord!" He turned to Derek, with mock solemnity and pity. "Derek, my friend. My thoughts, my blessings, go with you."

When he had gone, Mary reached across the table, and took Derek's hand. "You don't mind about going to Mum and Dad's tomorrow, do you?"

"Course not."

"And you'll bring your helmet? For the kids to play cops and robbers?"

"Oh God, yes. But not the handcuffs. Not after what happened last time."

She smiled. "Heavens no. Listen, I know we said we'd see the night through, but we could go now. If you like. Make it an early late night. Or a late early night? Whichever."

There was a promise lurking somewhere in her words, but for once Derek was having none of it.

"Oh no you don't. We're staying. We're staying until that bloody silver band gets here, and then I'm going to see them do it. Or not! Remember, I've got a fiver riding on this. Not to mention my self-respect."

"And you're going to lose both. Because they're going to do it. I promise you."

"We'll see." Derek tried to instil some confidence in his voice, but he knew he was on a loser. The band would come. And, against all the rules of common sense, they would do it.

* * *

Someone else in the bar was also beginning to suspect he was on a loser. He was Neville Parsons, at 19 the eldest child - or the youngest adult - of the Parsons clan of doubtful repute. Neville had become something of a local hero since helping rescue PC Martin and his wife from the clutches of a gang of people-traffickers. But tonight he had other things on his mind.

He stood with his mates, apparently absorbed in a darts match. But in fact he was absorbed in the appearance of Sandy, John's daughter, as she bent over the sink behind the bar, in her skimpy sweater and those tight black jeans of hers.

Neville kept hoping Sandy would look up, and he could catch her eye. And, what do you know, she did!

Suddenly she lifted her gaze from the bar sink, straightened up to tighten her sweater across her chest, and looked straight at him.

Neville swallowed, and gave her a little wave, with his hand holding his darts. His other hand held a valuable half-finished pint of bitter.

Sandy responded with a minimal and non-committal grimace. And at that moment one of Neville's playing partners reminded him of the match with a nudge, and he dropped his darts and spilled beer down his trousers.

When he looked back, Sandy was busy rinsing glasses again.

* * *

Midnight came. The Silver Band came. And, as Derek watched with the sickening emotion of a man losing a bet, they did it. Exactly as he had been told.

"It" was, as Mary had laboriously explained to Derek, a much-cherished North Tawe seasonal tradition. The village silver band would yearly tour the local villages on Christmas Eve, playing carols and raising funds. Their last stop, a few minutes before midnight, was the Green Dragon, North Tawe.

However, since the War or even before it, no-one could quite remember which, a problem had arisen. This being the final stop of the night, and the band having spent the last three hours vibrating their lips into their silver mouth-pieces, the musicians were by now, to say the least, thirsty. So where better to slake that thirst than in the spacious bar of the Dragon, before playing their last carol of the night to the celebrating customers? Especially as the current landlord always stood the band a round.

Yet now the problem arose. About half the band were members of non-conformist families. Their lives were lived soberly under the watchful eye of their formidable Minister, the Reverend Doctor Simpson. They were Temperance, with a capital T. And they had each promised the minister and their mothers that they would never ever set foot on licenced premises. What to do? Half the band wanted in, the other half dared not enter for fear of Simpson's hell fire and damnation, and their mothers' tearful disappointment. Impasse!

Well no, no impasse at all, when set against West Devon enterprise. As Derek watched, the pub door was wedged open. Six of the band – two cornets, a euphonium, a flugelhorn and two tenor horns - entered enthusiastically into the rowdy secular atmosphere. Outside, three more cornets, another euphonium, the tuba and the big drum remained on unsullied ground. With practiced ease the dozen players stayed in touch with each other, at arm's length for some, shoulder to shoulder for others, in a kind of semi-circle. Inside the pub pints were distributed. Outside bottles of lemonade and non-alcoholic Cydrax were passed hand-to-hand. Loud cheers were heard. Customers inside waved cheerfully at bandsmen outside, who, despite a wet, cold and dark night, waved back with equal enthusiasm. Everyone wished everyone else a merry Christmas.

And "Once In Royal David's City" never sounded better.

The band's fund-raising collection box came round, and Mary put in a pound. "That can come out of the housekeeping," she told Derek.

"You're not going to say 'I told you so'?"

"I'm a kind person. I pity the unbeliever."

"From now on," Derek told her, "I'll believe anything you tell me.

Away from the pub the village streets were dark, even romantic, and the couple walked hand-in-hand towards home.

"Just think." Derek waved expansively at the rows of cottages. "All those kids, trying to get to sleep, waiting for Father Christmas. Kids are what it's all about, really, you know."

"You're drunk," Mary told him. "And don't worry, there'll be plenty of kids around tomorrow, at Mum's."

"Yes. I know. But..."

And this was a moment when either of them might have raised the subject of their own situation with regard to children. But he wasn't quite that drunk. And Mary wasn't quite that sober. The matter of their own children, notional though they were, could be left for a more appropriate time.

And as he fell asleep that night, Derek's mind's eye saw no children. Instead it conjured up an image of the tall girl in the cloak, the girl with the mane of dark curls, the girl with the long thin face, and the flagon. The Beatnik Girl...

CHAPTER FOUR

Some five miles from where Village Police Constable Derek Martin and the deputy head of English at the local Grammar School, Mrs Mary Martin, stumbled their beery way to bed, a small boy was wide awake. His name was Terry. Terry was not waiting for Father Christmas. For one thing, he was nine, and therefore didn't believe in Father Christmas. And for another, no Father Christmas was about to bring him anything in the morning. Or any time, come to that. He could expect nothing except bullying. Nothing except pain, humiliation, despair. And something he couldn't name, something too horrible for a name.

Terry clutched the thin ex-army blanket around his shoulders, buried his face in his prickly pillow, and waited.

There were fourteen beds in the dormitory where Terry lay. In term time all would be occupied. Occupied, that is, by the children of parents far away in the wide world, serving their country or their employers, and therefore feeling justified in packing their offspring off to English boarding schools, getting them conveniently out of the way. In the school's Christmas break the luckiest boys found sanctuary with relatives living in Britain. But a handful remained at school. The handful included Terry

That evening, despite it being Christmas Eve, Terry was sent to bed alone in the dormitory because at nine years old he was the youngest, and his bedtime was eight o'clock. The others were older – most of them thirteen and fourteen. An age when boys, surging with early testosterone, can seem devoid of the qualities of respect, tolerance, empathy and acceptance. Qualities which they replace with a kind of selfish cruelty.

In due course the other boys came to bed. Not that they actually went to bed. Instead they treated themselves to half an hour of fun and games. Fun and games with Terry.

It was no fun for Terry, of course. Some of it wasn't too bad. Being tossed in a blanket, for instance. That was bearable, when you got used to it. Except when they pulled away the blanket while you were in mid-air.

Thunderclap was much worse. The other boys had invented the game of Thunderclap. It consisted of placing the smallest boy – Terry, of course – under a bed. Then the players of Thunderclap formed into two teams, each team sitting in a row on either side of the bed with their backs to each other. The teams would take it in turn to kick back under the bed with their slipper-clad heels.

The winning team was the first to make Terry cry.

When he stopped crying, and a winner was declared, they'd have a re-match.

That night the boys eventually tired of Thunderclap, and they'd drifted off to their beds, to masturbate like all teenage boys, and to fall into a sticky sleep.

Snivelling under that itchy blanket, Terry quietly prayed that his torture was over for the night. But he feared it wasn't. At least twice, perhaps three times a week, there was worse horror to come. And on this night, on this bitter Christmas Eve, it came.

It came initially in the shape of Mrs. Jeeves, wife of the headmaster, Raymond Jeeves. Mrs Jeeves was a squat rotund figure with rosy cheeks who always wore a floral housecoat and masqueraded as Matron of Havenhill School. "She's a mother to the little boys," Headmaster Raymond Jeeves would tell prospective parents. She wasn't.

At this time of night she was a grim messenger. A co-conspirator. An enabler.

"Wake up, Terry. The Headmaster wants to see you in his study. No, leave your dressing gown. It's not cold."

Terry was already awake of course. And it was cold. He followed Mrs Jeeves around the first-floor corridor, and down the wide staircase. In the hall she abandoned him. He knew where to go. He shivered, but not from the cold. His legs trembled. He felt sick.

The headmaster's study, warmed by a three-bar electric fire, had a distinct smell to it. Tobacco, furniture polish, and something else Terry couldn't identify. It was a rich, self-indulgent smell. To Terry it meant authority. Power. And something he had no name for.

Jeeves himself was an impressive figure. He was tall, with thin black hair which he brushed straight back from his forehead. He had a pair of startlingly blue eyes, a veined, slightly hooked nose, long ears and well-shaved jowls surrounding a small wet mouth. He was broad shouldered, with a build that must have been impressive when young, but had now broadened and swollen into a less impressive middle-age spread. The result was, his expensive made-to-measure suit appeared to have been expensively made-to-measure for someone else. Around his shoulders there hung a scholastic gown which he rarely took off.

His mood, as Terry stood in the doorway and shook, was convivial. It was the voice of an uncle, trying too hard.

"Ah, young Terry. Come in, lad. Close the door. Come and join me. Eh?"

The man rose from behind his wide leather-topped desk, from where he had been writing, or possibly pretending to write, and moved to sit in an expansive and elegant green leather buttoned chair.

"Come on lad. You're not in trouble. Come sit on my knee."

Terry came. He knew from past experience that if he didn't, he would be dragged.

"There. Comfy? That's better, isn't it."

What followed had been puzzling when it first happened. Now Terry tried not to think about it. He shut his eyes and endured it. There was quite a bit of fumbling, of unbuttoning, poking, squeezing, and then there would be some rubbing and some moaning, Terry could smell the man's dinner on his breath, and then, before very long, there would be some louder moaning, and some deep sighs.

This finished abruptly. A final sigh, before Terry would be pushed roughly to the floor. A short silence. And then the voice of the eager uncle was replaced by something quite different.

"You dirty little boy!" There was the rattle of a desk draw being jerked open. Terry knew what the headmaster was reaching for. "Take down your pyjama trousers and bend over!"

Terry didn't need to take down his pyjamas. They were already around his ankles.

That night he made sure he slept on his front. It was less painful. And if his sheets were blood stained, he'd be in trouble in the morning. On Christmas Day.

* * *

Derek woke on Boxing Day with, as he expected, that old familiar seedy feeling. It had been a Christmas Day to remember, or perhaps to forget. A lunch of outstanding variety, including about six different types of vegetables, the glorious products of Mary's father's Devonian skill in not only growing the things, but also preserving them in big bottles; an afternoon of playing cops and robbers on a full stomach with what seemed like half-a-dozen eight-year-olds; an evening spent sipping 12-year-old Scotch with her father and other enthusiasts. His head hurt.

His Boxing Day mood wasn't helped when two things happened, one after the other.

First, bloody Joshua rang. Derek trod carefully down the stairs to answer the phone in his pyjamas.

"They've had another bugger!"

"Who's had?"

"Them bloody beatniks. They've thieved another of me chickens."

"What's her bloody name then?"

"How should I know what a bloody hen's called? You mazed or something?" He used the local term for crazy.

"I'll make a report," he told Joshua. And he would. The loss of one chicken was an incident. But if two go, one after the other, it might be, he giggled to himself, an indication of fowl play. He didn't pass on the pun to Joshua. He'd try it on Mary later. But as he put the phone down, he remembered the advice of an elderly Sergeant, given to him when he was a cadet at the Exeter HQ. – "Always put in a report. No matter how silly. Cover your arse. You never know."

He stood by the telephone for a few moments, shivering in his cotton nightwear. So Joshua again blamed the Beatniks, the group of apparently strange people who had suddenly appeared and settled into the ruins of the Fursdon chapel. Derek thought about them. Specifically, he thought about the tall girl, from Christmas Eve. Who was she? What was she? A gypsy? A wanderer? A witch?

He should investigate, he told himself. He should take a run out there, see the girl, talk to her. Get closer.

But then a combination of marital cowardice and post-Christmas lethargy persuaded him that it might be prudent to let sleeping dogs lie. The odd-ball group would probably move on soon, he speculated. Like travellers do. Then they could be some other poor bloody village copper's problem. And he could stop thinking about the girl.

His head still hurt.

Halfway back up the stairs, and heading for another warm snuggle underneath the blankets, he heard the front door letter box click. Laboriously he turned and went to the front door.

"Post? On Boxing Day?" The query came from Mary, who now emerged from the kitchen, holding two cups of tea and heading for the stairs. She wore her baby doll pyjamas – his inspired Christmas gift.

"Dunno." he told her.

There was a small white envelope on the floor, where there ought to have been a doormat, and would be if they ever got the house organised. Derek grabbed it, then followed Mary back up the stairs and back into a still warm bed.

He sipped his tea and examined the envelope. It was simply addressed: 'The Constable, North Tawe.' No stamp, but in the top left-hand corner there was an outline of a Christian cross.

"Look at that," he told Mary. "Could be from the vicar."

"Never. He'd call you Derek, for a start. Open it, clot."

Derek deliberately swallowed two mouthfuls of tea, to demonstrate his patience, then ripped the thing open. It contained a single sheet of paper. The message was written in a rounded and emphatic hand, in blue ink.

"'I have a matter to discuss with you. When your other duties permit, find me at the chapel or the Manse.'" he read. There was no signature.

He showed the note to Mary. "Not signed," he protested. "How am I expected to know...?"

"That'll be Simpson," she told him.

"Who he?"

"Oh, you know him. The Chapel chap. Non-conformist minister. You must have come across him. He's God's deputy for West Devon. Fills in for the Almighty when he needs a break. He's a big bloke, stands very upright, almost looks as if he might fall over backwards. Which some of us sometimes wish he would."

"Wow! You don't like him very much, do you!"

"Well. It's his holier-than-thou pose that gets me. I suppose he is holier than me, but... Anyway, you'll see him around. When he takes his goats for a walk."

Derek felt the conversation was getting unreal. "When he does what?"

"He keeps goats, then leads them down the lanes so they eat off the hedges. Not a bad idea, when you think about it. I'm surprised you haven't seen him and his goats. I won't say he's popular, but he's well known."

"Well, unless he's forgotten to get a dog licence or is participating in the slaughter of the first born... I mean, if he's that religious, he's not going to be doing too much wrong, is he?" He threw the note from the bed to the dressing table. "I'll have to pop round and see him some time, I suppose. I just don't like being ordered about like that."

"So not today then." Mary finished her tea and settled down under the eiderdown.

"Not today." He joined her there. His headache had fled.

"So what are you going to do today then?"

"You're about to find out, baby doll."

It was hardly his fault, Derek told himself a couple of days later, that the note from the minister somehow found its way underneath the copy of Hemingway's For Whom The Bell Tolls, which Mary had obtained from the mobile library, and had insisted that he read. But, out of sight, out of mind. He forgot about it.

Instead, in the inevitable lull between Christmas and New Year, he made a decision: he would take a couple of days of his annual leave. It had been a busy year, he reasoned. There had been the dire affair of the drug users and the poor dead girl under the nettles. And then the clash with the people-traffickers, the imprisoned Poles and the grim moments in the burning cowshed...all quite enough, he assured himself, for one inexperienced copper to cope with. He would now take the rest he deserved, and he duly claimed a couple of days' off duty.

"Off duty" in Mary's vocabulary, he now discovered, meant doing something about the garden. The creation of a small vegetable patch was one of the somethings that wanted doing, she suggested, putting a spade literally into his hands. One hour later she was tutting over his blistered palms and ladling out the TCP. Another problem solved, he thought, as he winced at the sting of the stuff, and reluctantly accepted her instruction to leave it for now.

Doing nothing for two days, he thought, might make time drag. But instead his idle hours seemed to whizz past, and with surprising speed. New Year's Eve was on the near horizon. He had been anticipating another cheerful evening in the pub, to see in 1953. Instead he was called back from his miniscule leave and required for duty on the Okehampton streets. The little town's Police Sergeant, Sergeant Welbeloved, explained to him over the phone that normally the place hardly stirred on December 31st. But this year, by happenstance, a Scottish regiment had taken over the army training camp high above them on Dartmoor. The result had been a New Year's Eve of fun, fights and good-natured helmet-snatching, and he'd finally ridden home, exhausted, at four in the morning, stinking of the whisky that had been poured over his head by the friendliest rioters in the world.

And next morning, when he un-gummed his eyelids to greet an unusually bright if frosty winter's dawn, he was on duty again.

It was January the First, the annual and traditional day, for as long as anyone could remember, of the North Tawe New Year's Day Fox Hunt Meet. And, as the representative of law and order, he was expected to attend in his official capacity. Personally Derek wasn't too sure where he sat on the issue of fox hunting, but he was wise enough to keep his mouth shut on the subject. In a West Devon village any opposition to the hunt would be close to heresy. The North Tawe New Year's Day Hunt Meet was a major event in the life of the village, rivalling the summer church fete and Bonfire Night in popularity, and far out-performing the August Women's Institute coach outing to Bude. So the local policeman was duty-bound to show his doubtful face.

He'd missed the event last year, being away on a course. Now Mary explained to him over the breakfast table that anyone who was anyone in the village would be there, and as he was a special 'anyone' his presence was most definitely expected. After a couple of cups of Camp coffee, he came round to her way of thinking, and went upstairs to struggle into his uniform.

And, as so often when obliged to attend some rather intimidating occasion, when he and Mary arrived in the village square, he was unexpectedly glad he'd come. The whole affair was quite something to see, something to remember, even in a sense something to celebrate. Somehow the best of remote West Devon country life seemed to be on show.

Trying to establish some sort of structure to what was happening in the square, Derek decided he could divide the meet and its attendants into three groups, each of which being clearly identifiable. Forming an outer ring to the event, in twos, threes and fours around the edge of the square, were ordinary villagers, just there to watch. Derek knew almost all of them by sight, and began exchanging nods and words with several of them. At one stage he glimpsed a tall figure at the far side of the square, and the sight rang a bell. It was a man, maybe six-and-a-half feet tall, standing very straight, almost leaning backwards. He remembered Mary's vivid description of the chapel minister. Damn! He'd forgotten the man's note demanding his presence. Better do something, go over, he thought, introduce himself, apologise. But when he looked again the figure had gone. Probably not the minister, he thought. A strict preacher at a hunt meet? Didn't seem likely.

Otherwise the greetings with those on foot were fairly brief, because while the watchers seemed pleased enough to see him, their interest was focussed on the next identifiable group.

These were the riders, the mounted followers, the horsemen and horsewomen who came from the farms and estates, the riding schools and the pony clubs, most of which were situated within a handful of miles of the village, but sometimes emanated from much further afield, judging by the line of horseboxes stretching up the nearby streets. The riders and the horses were a class act, Derek decided. Apart from some nervous youngsters on rather solid little ponies, most of them looked as if they had just trotted off the pages of Country Life magazine. And they were dressed to kill – and for the kill as well – in sleek riding gear that shone in the weak sunlight. They made quite a contrast to the usual standard of sartorial presentation in villages like North Tawe, where fashion trends usually approached "scruffy" from the wrong direction.

Derek had half expected the men to wear shiny top hats and red coats, and said so to Mary.

"Of course they don't" she told him with mock indignation. "Top hats went out years ago, and only the hunt master and his whips wear the coats. And for heaven's sake, it's pink. Hunting pink! Not red." She giggled. "God, I can't take you anywhere, can I!"

At that point she didn't take him anywhere, because she saw a friend of hers, and abandoned Derek to his terminological confusion. Which meant, of course, that he now had the freedom to gaze lasciviously at the women riders, without fear of wifely denunciation. God, was there anything sexier, he asked himself, than a woman in tight jodhpurs, straddling her mount, rising in her stirrups? And often swearing fluently at horse or spectator? Or perhaps there was. Because two of the women riders were riding side-saddle. Wearing long black skirts flowing over the tops of their riding boots, with one leg in a stirrup and the other hooked over a leather support on the same side of their horse, they were less blatant sexually than their sisters in jodhpurs, but somehow their elegant pose emphasised their femininity. Derek found himself staring a little too fixedly at one of these women, who caught his eye in return, and frowned. Derek at once jerked himself out of his voyeuristic mode, and assumed the role of the officious policeman, shifting his gaze to one of general observance, and starting to stroll around the square. He felt a little flushed.

More horses and riders turned up. The buzz from the crowd grew louder. There was a distinctly earthy, rustic, almost rancid atmosphere to the occasion – not surprising, he noted, as he stepped over streams of horse urine and avoided clumps of freshly deposited rosebush manure.

He now moved until he had a clear view of the third and central section of the assemblage – the Master, his two whippers-in, and of course the hounds. The three men were of course in red - whoops, sorry, *pink* - coats, plus black riding helmets, and all three were frowning with professional authority. The two "whips" as they were known, were both younger men, and their concern was obviously the control of the twenty or more hounds milling about in a kind of canine mob between them. Both of the men had voices like mechanical saws, and rasped commands like firecrackers at the odd hound that ventured too far from the pack. What astonished Derek was that, firstly, the whips seemed to know each dog by name, even though they were all the same breed of foxhound and to Derek's eyes looked identical to each other; secondly any errant hound responded immediately to his name and obeyed the command. It was a remarkable example of man and animal partnership, and he realised he was watching a demonstration of a genuine rural skill. No, more than that, an almost uncanny country talent. What's more he was on hand to witness it. Unlike the case of that old nuisance Joshua and his nominated hens. But a thought struck him. If the huntsmen knew the individual names of their numerous pack, perhaps Joshua actually knew the names of... No, don't be ridiculous. Of course he didn't. He couldn't.

It was about now that Derek became aware that the hunt meet had an affinity with alcohol. Booze was flowing like the River Tawe. At nine-thirty in the morning, too. Neither of the whips was drinking. But the Master clearly was. He was a heavy-set man with a face that alternated between purple and red – and this was certainly red, not pink. There was a glass in his hand, and he wasn't happy. He glared down from his huge grey mount.

"You! You, girl!" he shouted gruffly.

The girl in question was Sandy, teenage daughter of John, the landlord. She had a tray in her hand, and was clearly helping out with drink distribution. Anxiously skirting both hounds and horses, she responded to the man.

"Call this a bloody whisky?" the Master asked her. "Take it away, and get me a proper one. A double, girl!"

Sandy grabbed his glass, and disappeared through the crowd and into the pub, re-emerging almost at once with a larger measure. The Master received it without a word and swallowed half in one gulp. No money changed hands. Sandy retreated, and Derek intercepted her as she headed for the bar.

"That wasn't very nice of him," he said sympathetically.

"Silly old sod." She gave him a twisted grin. After a rocky start Sandy had come to like and trust Derek. "Bugger thinks he's God."

"Yes," Derek agreed. "I suppose he is God for today, at least. Well, let's hope God doesn't crash over a fence and break his thick neck, eh?"

Sandy giggled. Then, "Oh sod. there's Neville."

Derek looked where she looked. Entering the square was a group of lads on cycles, and one of them was Neville Parsons.

"That Neville, he's sweet on you, you know," Derek told her.

"Silly bugger." There was a reluctant affection in her voice. She hesitated, said "Look, tell him..." then changed her mind, and ran back to the Dragon, passing her father as he emerged with more drinks.

It was hours before official pub opening time, but there was certainly a lot of booze being sunk. And cash changing hands. Probably – no, certainly – the licensing laws were being trampled on. But Derek wasn't about to interfere. Village policemen must know when to act and when to keep quiet – something which, if he didn't know by now, he never would. He stepped back a little and surveyed the square. There was something grandly traditional and splendid about the colourful and highly energised scene. It spoke of rural history, continuity. Scenes like this must have occurred here in West Devon for hundreds of years. It was a coming-together, a gathering, and a moment of harmony and peace.

And then, suddenly, it wasn't.

A burst of angry shouting, a small forest of waving arms, the sound of a row getting out of hand. When he thought about it later Derek was pleased to recall that his first instinct was to move towards the trouble, not away from it; a reaction that his probationary training had drummed into him. He pushed his way through people, even past some skittering horses, to find himself confronted by a near-violent quarrel that showed signs of getting worse.

On one side of the confusion were a group of five people, who Derek immediately realised must be the Beatniks, the group that had apparently moved into the abandoned chapel, the oddballs he had heard about on Christmas Eve. There were at least two males, each bearded, and dressed in a variety of unconventional clothes. One wore what looked to be ill-matched military items, another a monk's robe complete with a cowl pulled over his head. Two women – girls, really, he decided – were equally flamboyant, in bright colours and floor-length skirts, and each of them wore their hair long and uncombed. But the most outstanding member of the tribe, as he had begun to think of the group, was the tall girl he had glimpsed all too briefly in the pub. She stood head and shoulders amongst the others, and while they were jumping and shouting slogans, she gazed calmly at the crowd, wearing the same long elegant robe and hood that she had worn in the Dragon, and an expression of defiance on her thin brown and fascinating face.

All the beatniks held home-made placards which, it was easy to guess even if there was no time to read them, were denouncing fox hunting. The tall girl's slogan was the biggest and most legible of the lot, and it read "A Curse on all Fox Killers!" She held it high, making sure it could be read by the growing crowd of spectators. A 'curse'? Derek wondered briefly. Perhaps she thought she was a witch.

The group with which they were clashing consisted of perhaps only four active participants. Derek vaguely recognised two local lads, and was pleased to see that Neville wasn't one of them, but the noisiest and most belligerent of the group was a man who was a stranger to him. He was about 40, dressed in highly polished shoes, long socks and jodhpurs, a bright yellow waistcoat and a black jacket. He carried a riding crop in his hand, but something said he wasn't an actual rider. No horse, and no riding hat - an ersatz huntsman perhaps, all mouth-and-jodhpurs, with an irritating air of self-importance. He was confronting the protesters with the antagonism and contempt of a local squire clearing walkers off his front lawn.

There was a lot of noise, the Beatniks chanting their slogans, and their opposition shouting back. "Bugger off!" seemed to be the popular response, in which some members of the general crowd – but, Derek noted, not all – joined in.

And now, as Derek took in the scene, the man in the yellow waistcoat seemed to jump forward and grapple with one of the male beatniks, reaching to grab the other man's placard. He failed to get it, and was pushed off. Furious, he raised his riding crop and struck at the man, who ducked underneath the blow, and the stiff stick just swished harmlessly over his head. The placard clattered to the ground. Undeterred, Yellow Waistcoat moved in, raising the crop high to strike again.

"Stop that!"

Afterwards, Derek would again be pleased with himself, this time specifically with, as he recalled it, the force of his voice. It was full, loud and commanding. Parade-ground stuff. And it worked. All action ceased, at least momentarily, and every head turned towards him.

He didn't waste that moment. He stepped rapidly between Yellow Waistcoat and his intended victim, pushing the former back.

"Put it down!" he told Yellow Waistcoat, his voice still as hard as he could make it, but not so loud. Without time to think about it, he sensed instinctively that a good shout might work as an instant shock, but only once. Shouting soon lost its power to influence anything. Now

It was time to add a quieter degree of reason and subtlety to the steel.

The man still held his riding crop high in the air. "No listen. They can't come here, trying to..." he began to complain.

Derek cut him short. "Put it down. Now. Or you will be arrested for assault."

Yellow Waistcoat lowered his arm. He was red in the face and breathing furiously through his nose. He wanted to say more, but Derek didn't give him the chance.

"I said down," he insisted. "Put it on the ground. Drop it!"

The man hesitated for a moment, then dropped the riding crop

"Now step back." The man complied, turning to his supporters, shrugging to indicate that he had no choice.

"You ought to arrest him." This from one of the beatniks behind him. It was a deep tone, almost harsh, and, turning, Derek assumed it emanated from one of the men. But the speaker was, as he realised at once and which later, he told himself he should have expected, the tall girl.

"Do your duty, Mr. Policeman." Her voice was clear, her accent from the Home Counties. She sounded both well-off and well-educated. "That was assault. With a weapon. We all saw it. Arrest the man!" There was an irony, too, in the voice, as if she knew the action she demanded would not take place. In any case, her spirited response produced some cat-calls from the spectators.

Derek turned and faced her. "He missed, didn't he?"

"But he tried to hit Harry. That's still assault," she insisted.

"And so is disturbing the peace," Derek told her. "Of which you and your friends, including Harry, are clearly guilty."

There were a few cries of "Bugger off!" from the more vocal if less imaginative members of the crowd. Derek turned to face them, his expression as grim as he could make it, and the cries diminished. One or two of the crowd began to drift away. Even yellow waistcoat seemed to subside, and was contenting himself with muttering to his associates

Derek turned back to the beatniks, pushed a couple of them to one side, until he was face to face with the tall girl.

"Listen." he kept his voice low. "Are you the leader of this lot?"

"We don't have a leader. We are a commune. All are equal." She told him.

"Okay. Then I have just elected you leader. De facto, if you like. And..." he glanced by at the others, "I don't think they're going to argue, do you?"

The girl sighed. "Say what you have to say, then."

Derek took a deep breath. "Then listen. It's over. You've done what you came for. You've had your demonstration. You've made your point. I think it would be best if you left."

"You can't make us." She sounded a little less sure of herself now.

"No. Well. Actually I could, if there were more of me. But as it is, I'm on my own. So I'm asking you instead."

He was quite close to her now, looking directly into her pair of intense dark eyes. And he smiled. She didn't return the smile, but perhaps she saw it and recognised it for what it was, a genuine attempt to reach an understanding, a solution.

Abruptly she turned away. "We're going home," she told the rest of the group. They didn't argue, and started to move away.

Then the tall girl turned back, as if on an impulse. "You want to know about us, don't you," she said quietly. "Why don't you come and see me? I'm sure you know where."

Her eyes flashed, and Derek felt his stomach lurch. His reply, a feeble "Yes." went unheard. He stood and watched as the group shambled down the side street, to where, he could see, they had left their transport – a pony and trap. The tall girl led the way, and took the reins of the pony. He watched as she swung her slim figure up onto the driving bench.

They might be all equal, he thought to himself. But one of them is more equal than the others. Something, a quotation, he'd read it in one of the books Mary kept shoving in his direction.

And now, taking him by surprise, there came behind him the evocative wail of the Master's hunting horn. It was a signal, Derek thought wryly, that the man had had enough whisky, at least for now. It was also the signal for an immediate and loud clattering of hooves, for a chorus of excited yelping from the hounds and harsh commands from the whips, for the revving of engines of motorbikes and cars, and soon the whole caboodle, including walkers and cyclists and even infants in push-chairs, began moving out of the square, some to head for home, but many to follow the horses. The hunt was on. And Derek, who had earlier been caught up in the pageantry of the whole meet, was now thoroughly glad to see the back of it.

"Wow! My hero!"

It was Mary, joining him out of nowhere, and looking up at him with bright eyes.

"Oh – you saw all that, did you?"

"Most of it. And I was very impressed. You did brilliant."

He looked at her sideways, raising an eyebrow, but she shook her head.

"No, I'm not being sarcastic. I saw it all. Couldn't hear what you said, but you obviously nipped it in the bud. It could have been nasty. Thanks to you, it wasn't."

She's right, Derek thought to himself. Thanks to me, it wasn't. But it was good to hear someone else say so.

CHAPTER FIVE

Some North Tawe residents referred to the home of the Reverend Donald Simpson as "The Manse" but most didn't bother, however much the Minister instructed them so to do. Even his deacons thought of it as Number 1, North Road. This was its official postal address, and a slightly redundant one, North Road being only a short lane off the main thoroughfare, and Number 1 being its only residential property.

If you passed by the Manse, you would think it a typical West Devon dwelling – a slate roof and a rather blank whitewashed frontage, with only one small window facing the road. But you'd push your way through the garden gate, come round to the west side of the building, you'd find yourself looking at a much more cottagey home with a small porch, all set in a pretty if not very well-maintained garden, leading to a neglected orchard, and on to the further couple of acres where grazed the Minister's two majestic goats. When he felt the rare need to make a joke, usually only to avoid a point he didn't want making, the Rev. Simpson would quote Mathew Twenty-Five, verses thirty-one to forty-six, and say that by avoiding keeping sheep he also avoided the task of separating them from the goats, a challenge which he found difficult enough amongst his human North Tawe congregation. It was a convoluted joke, and not even funny, and would often be met by blank faces and puzzled silences. But it suited Simpson. His personality was convoluted. And he wasn't funny.

The Reverend Simpson's chapel stood about a hundred yards away back up towards but still on the outskirts of the village. It was a grey and solid-looking 19th century construction, stone and brick built but faced with concrete, which in places was beginning to fall away, exposing Victorian brickwork. It stood side-on to the street, and you entered it by a short path leading to the porch which protruded half-way along the length of the building.

Looking at it as unemotionally as he could, the Minister himself would privately admit that his House of God was possibly the ugliest building in the village, even when compared to the handful of post-War council houses. But every Sunday its pews were fully occupied, and the sound of joyful Wesleyan hymns and heartfelt yet modest prayers rang through the local streets. The Reverend Simpson made sure of that.

Police Constable Derek Martin, technically C of E, and actually not very much of anything when it came to religion, entered the chapel with some hesitation, even though, on a weekday morning, it proved to be empty. He only just remembered to remove his helmet. It was, he realised, the first time ever to find himself in a non-conformist establishment, and the interior came as something of a surprise. He'd expected to find himself in a poor man's version of a village church. Instead, after passing through a rather blank vestibule, he found himself in a large room of rows of highly polished pews, a glisteningly clean tiled floor, and an atmosphere of quiet yet determined solemnity. A large cross dominated the scene but there was no altar. Instead the general congregation would sit or stand - but not kneel of course, kneeling was for Anglicans and Catholics, not stalwart chapel folk – facing a bank of more gleaming seating, and accommodating what must be, he reasoned, the minister, his deacons, and a choir. One of these seats was centre stage, as it were, larger than the others, slightly raised, and with broad polished arms. That, he assumed must be reserved for the minister, Simpson himself, apparently serving to emphasise his importance. Behind Derek, as he came in, a set of steps led up to a first-floor gallery containing more benches and serving no doubt as a useful overflow space when needed.

The effect of these general seating arrangements contrasted with a typical Church of England set-up, as he knew it. Not that his knowledge of church interiors was at all extensive, far from it. But in a C. of E. church, he felt worship was directed from the congregation towards the high altar. The vicar sat sideways, and only confronted his flock when obliged to do so. In this chapel, however, the congregation would sit under the constant beady eye of the minister. Any who giggled, or picked their nose, or fell asleep, would be spotted instantly. Perhaps this arrangement, Derek speculated, fostered a sense of community, as worshippers faced each other, equals before God. But, once again, one of them, the one in the special chair, was undoubtedly more equal than the others.

Derek shook himself mentally. He was getting fanciful. He wasn't here to muse on contrasting religious ceremonies and rituals. He was here, as requested, to answer the call from the Reverend Simpson.

It was Mary who had spurred him into action. She had found the Minister's peremptory note which had hidden itself under Derek's unread improving book. When she produced it at breakfast one morning, Derek was actually relieved. Because the note, only partly forgotten, had become a niggle. He had sort-of remembered it when he had glimpsed what might have been the Minister across the crowded square at the hunt meet. But then he'd pushed the thought to the back of his mind. Where it niggled. Only faintly. But a niggle it definitely was.

Niggles. In the world of Constable Martin niggles were a fact of life, and a driving force within it. They couldn't be ignored for long, not even minor niggles like the note. Derek's niggles, irritating twitches in the brain, drove him on to get involved, to court trouble, to solve problems, to achieve solutions. They were his talisman, his conscience and his ambition, all rolled into one force. It had been a niggle that had driven him on to confront the drug abusers who killed their victim, even though he himself had been under suspension at the time. It had been a niggle that made him follow up insubstantial clues that led him to the blazing barns of the people-traffickers. Derek couldn't ignore a niggle for long. He hated them, and at the same time he needed them. They frequently led to trouble but equally often to a sense of achievement and self-worth.

Now Mary had produced the note – indeed, waved it between his nose and his Puffed Wheat – that particular niggle faded in strength. That was to be expected. It was an uncomplicated situation. Normally, while he might know what event, however trivial, was causing the niggle, he would follow it up like a terrier after a rat, never knowing what the end of his chase would be. But this time, this simple demand that he go to meet a minister of religion. How could that lead to trouble? To any kind of challenge?

Nonetheless he re-read the note carefully. The man sounded impatient. He'd have to remember to apologise with sincerity.

"I'm so late. I'll have to grovel." He told Mary.

"You better pop round there today," she told him.

"Yeah. Where will I find him? In the chapel?"

"Try it first. But he's more likely at home. You know where the Manse is?"

"Yes. North Road. All on its own, right?"

"Well he's probably there. Unless he's taking his goats for a walk."

"Unless he's doing what?"

"I told you. He takes his goats for a walk sometimes."

"I thought you were kidding. In fact you probably are." Derek pointed an accusing finger at his wife. "You're at it again, aren't you! Making fun of the credulous townie! I'm not falling for that one. No-one takes goats for a walk. No way."

Mary shrugged. "Please yourself. You better hurry up, anyway. Before he complains to Okehampton."

"Right."

"I mean the last thing you want is old Welbeloved on your case again, right?" She was referring to the Sergeant at the Okehampton headquarters, who liked nothing better than to bring his full 17 stone down on the naïve necks of his junior constables.

"You're right," Derek agreed. "Another ear-bashing from Welbeloved is the last thing I need right now."

He was nearly out of the door when the phone in the hallway rang. It was Sergeant Welbeloved.

But it wasn't an ear-bashing, quite the reverse.

"Got a special duty for you, young Martin." The Sergeant sounded almost jovial.

"Oh, really?"

"Really. They asked me who was the brightest and smartest young lad under my command, and I said you."

"Oh, thanks. Um. Who asked?"

"Doesn't matter. You know Colonel Critchley, don't you? Bit of a pal of yours, isn't he?"

"Well, he is a friend, yes."

"Right. Be at his place, South Reed farm, nine o'clock tomorrow morning. Got it?"

"Well, yes, but..."

"And listen, Constable Martin. Are you wearing an official police shirt at the moment?"

"What?"

"I said..." a distinct hint of his usual irascibility now edged into the Sergeant's voice. "Are you, at this precise moment, wearing a police issue shirt?"

"Well, yes."

"Good. Tonight, don't stick it in the wash. Bring it with you tomorrow. Separate."

"What? Why on earth?"

"Oh, for heaven's sake, Constable!" This was the usual Welbeloved, back at full bossiness. "Stop asking damn fool questions, and do what you're told. Nine o'clock tomorrow! And I'll be there, too, so don't be late."

Derek put the phone down. Mary raised an eyebrow. "What did he want this time?" she asked.

"Apparently, he wants the shirt off my back."

CHAPTER SIX

The Reverend Simpson was not in the chapel – not in the vestibule, not in the main place of worship, not even in the small side-room which featured two upright chairs, some cupboards and a chest, and a cross on the wall.

Well of course he wasn't in the chapel, Derek told himself. On a Tuesday at ten in the morning? Of course not. Yet he was pleased he'd taken the time to take a look inside. The cleanliness of the place, the formal solemnity it evoked - that, perhaps, was West Country nonconformist worship. Quite a contrast to the village Anglican church, where cracked floor tiles, last week's drooping flowers, and the vicar's habit of telling funny but rather intellectual jokes gave the place an almost rackety atmosphere. He wondered which place of worship the Lord himself would prefer. Which would resemble heaven? Would he one day find out? Would he even get that far?

The Minister's house, the Manse, was only a few minutes away, and that gave Derek little time to consider the fate of his immortal soul, before he moved on to wonder why on earth Simpson wanted to see him, what he might want him to do. Security guard at the annual flower-and-veg show? Arrest the organist?

It appeared that the minister might be at home. An ancient but well-polished Austin 7 stood just inside the wide front gage. But a vigorous knock on the Manse door produced no result. Neither did a peep into a large field shed, or a wander through the bare and, at this time of year, rather depressing orchard.

Derek shrugged, both physically and mentally. He'd made the effort. The man wasn't there. Probably off spreading the word of the Lord amongst the heathen of the village. Or amongst the few who still attend the Church of England services. Whichever was more numerous. He grinned to himself and walked back up the lane to the road.

Something made him stop, turn, and look down the road leading out of the village. Fifty yards away a figure was approaching. No, make that three figures were approaching. One man and two goats. The goats were making rather jerky progress as they constantly stopped to bury their noses in the luxurious weeds and scrubs, spikes and thorns of the typically Devonian hedge that lined the tarmac, tearing off great mouthfuls of greenery and chomping on it with apparent relish. The man leading them was, judging from Mary's description of him, undoubtedly the Reverend Simpson – a tall impressively built man, very upright, though whether that was his natural stance or whether one forced on him by his lively companions pulling on the chains attached to their collars, it was difficult to tell. Simpson might have an imposing figure, but he was dressed like a typical local farmer – wellingtons, corduroys, and an ancient mackintosh buttoned up to the neck against the weather. On his head was an equally aged flat cap.

The threesome drew to a halt a couple of yards from where Derek waited. Simpson looked grimly down at Derek, apparently summing him up.

"You take your time," he grunted, in way of a greeting. "I assume you are our local bobby."

"Yes, Sir, sorry for the delay but..."

"Take off your helmet." It was a command.

"What?"

"Take off your helmet. You do speak English, I hope. Take... it... off!"

Derek could think of no sensible reply. He took off his helmet.

"Yes. You're him. They told me you had a head like that."

Derek put his helmet back on. At primary school he had been signalled out as "that little boy with the red head." At senior school, at least in the first year, he'd been chased round the playground by a gang shouting "Get the ginger!" Now he was an adult, and while some yobs might shout "Oi! Copper Nob!" at him, and consider themselves witty, few adults had the bad manners to refer to the admittedly bright colour of his hair. But Simpson had proved to be one of them.

"Follow me!" It was another command. Derek narrowly avoided being trampled by the bigger of the two goats, as the threesome swept past him to turn down the lane to the Manse. Derek followed. He was tempted to turn on his heel and go home, thinking that whatever bothered this man could wait until he developed some respect for the law. But he resisted the thought. As the old Sergeant had told him, "You never know."

While he waited in the Manse garden, watching as Simpson efficiently fastened the goat chains to what were obviously permanent stakes, he consoled himself with the thought that he had just witnessed one of the sights of North Tawe he had thought to be fictional: The Reverend Mathew Simpson actually taking his goats for a walk!

When the Minister returned, Derek decided that the man had been sufficiently rude to obviate any need for further apologies about not responding sooner. Instead he simply asked briskly: "So what can I do for you, Mr. Simpson?"

"I like to take my goats for a daily walk," Simpson said. "The hedges provide them with a healthy diet." He gave Derek a suspicious sideways look. "Some people find that strange. Do you?"

"Not at all. Sounds very sensible," Derek told him, forcing himself to be diplomatic. "Is that why you wanted to see me? To see you, doing that?"

"Don't be ridiculous. Of course not. No, the fact is, there's something I need to show you. Something about which I shall expect you to take action. As you see fit, of course."

He smiled grimly at Derek, leaning backwards and looking at him down a long nose. Derek couldn't help comparing the two village clerics – the vicar thin, stooping, vulnerable, Simpson solid, big, upright. They'd told him at Sunday School that God made Man in his own image. Sort that one out, he told himself.

"Come on inside," Simpson jerked his head. "I must change." He seemed to think that some explanation was in order. "Can't be seen in public like this." He looked down at his muddy boots, his spattered mac. "Then if you don't mind, we'll take a short walk. Not far. Shan't need the car. No petrol anyway. We'll walk and then... well, you'll see why you're here."

* * *

Terry was going. He was running away.

It was the only answer, the only thing to do. He was going to run. He wasn't staying. Not in this dreadful place. With these dreadful people. People who kept hurting him. The Headmaster, the things he did. The caning. No. No more. He was off. He was going to run. Where? Anywhere. Anywhere was better than here. He was going. Tonight.

He was scared, he admitted to himself. After all, he was just a nine-year-old boy. But then he remembered he was nearly ten. That felt better. And Terry had a plan.

The Christmas holiday was over. The Boarding School, beloved old Havenhill as Headmaster Jeeves referred to it in the school brochure, was groaning back into life. Those lucky boys – the sons of the ex-pats who had somewhere to go in Britain – were now returning, resentful, depressed, to their dormitories. They were hard-done-by, they felt. So they needed someone to take it out on. That someone was, of course, Terry.

That first evening's bullying had been well up to standard. A brief bout of Thunderclap had been succeeded by a great new game which one of the returning boys had discovered during the holiday, and now introduced to his mates. It was called The Gauntlet. It had an elegant simplicity to it. Each big boy armed himself with a damp towel. They then stood in rows along each side of the corridor that ran down the middle of the room, between the beds. A small boy was then detailed to run naked down between the two lines, while each boy attempted to flick the towels at the runner. The small boy was, of course, Terry. He was first choice because he was the smallest. Each accurate flick stung like an angry wasp. Theoretically points were scored for a successful flick. However amid the general hilarity the scoring system tended to break down, and eventually to be ignored.

Certainly Terry was in no position to keep count.

But Terry had a plan. And now, this night, when the lads grew weary, and took to their beds to indulge in their own private amusement, Terry would put that plan into action. Yes, he reassured himself. He would go. He would go now. Tonight. As he lay in his sanctuary of a bed, later that night, in the distance he heard a lorry engine, the driver crashing through his gear box as the vehicle climbed some nearby Devonshire hill. He wondered where it was going. He wondered if he could go there. Go there, wherever it was, and be free. And safe. As snores began to resonate through the dormitory, Terry held his breath and waited. He had a plan.

He did not expect a summons to the Headmaster's study. The previous night he had endured a grim session at the man's hands. Things occurred that he didn't know could be done. The subsequent caning had been applied with equal intensity, and Terry's bottom still burned and bled from the punishment which Jeeves assured him he so richly deserved. However, experience told Terry that the session had been enough to satisfy the distinguished educator, for at least two days, possibly three.

So, when all around snored, Terry would, that very night, put his plan into action. It would be imperative that he not make a sound. If he was caught out of bed after lights out his punishment would be medieval.

One part of his plan was already in motion. Food. He'd need something to eat when he ran. That evening's supper had been cold and stale bread-and-butter pudding. Much had been abandoned in disgust by the boys as they left the dining hall. Terry, hanging back, had snaffled a large segment. It now lay in two halves, beneath his pillow, wrapped in toilet paper. It would have to do.

He would need clothes to run in. His day things were in one of a row of mini-wardrobes at the far end of the room. He dared not try to get them. And obviously he couldn't escape in his pyjamas. That would be silly. But at the foot of the stairs was a short corridor which led to the sports cloakroom. There all sports clothes were kept. And pairs of gym shoes. Could he get there without being apprehended? Yes, he could, and he would. His rugger kit was there, and it would have to do.

The kit was not exactly substantial, especially for a grim January night. It consisted of quite a thick rugby jersey and some rather flimsy shorts, which were far too big for a undersized nine-year-old. When he put them on, he had to tie a sort of knot in the waist band to tighten it, and the knot kept coming undone when he ran. He hated rugby. But tonight the shorts would serve another purpose. For some unknown reason they included large pockets at each hip. Pockets ideal for transporting chunks of solidified bread-and-butter pudding.

So tonight he would climb into that rugby kit, he would stuff the pockets with pudding, he would pull on a pair of plimsolls, and he'd go. He would run, holding his shorts up with one hand if he had to. He would run away.

* * *

Derek sat in the Revered Donald Simpson's living room, with his helmet perched rather ludicrously on the Minister's dining table. Upstairs he could hear clumping sounds, as the Minister changed into clothes in which it was suitable to appear amongst the throngs in the busy streets of North Tawe. As if! thought Derek.

He was bored. There was nothing to read except non-conformist tracts and a dusty copy of the Bible. Derek felt he knew how that book ended. He knew, he said to himself, whodunit! He smiled at the thought. It seemed rather daring to make a joke about the Holy Bible in the Minister's sitting-room, even if the joke remained unvoiced.

He got up and looked around the room. This, he thought, is about as ordinary as it could be. Faded linoleum on the floor. Drab furniture, but of good quality. Pre-war stuff, not the gimcrack utility rubbish that people kept offering Mary, and which she firmly if politely rejected. As a result the police house remained half-furnished, but what they had didn't offend the senses. Or, when you sat on it, your bottom.

The Minister's choice of art was equally inoffensive and tedious. Sea views. Some roses in a bowl. A ship on a placid sea. Boring.

And yet, Derek thought, this was the home of a man who took goats for a walk. Could he really be this tedious? This uninteresting?

A traditional Welsh dresser stood against one wall. Big, black, solid – and the more Derek looked at it, the more he liked it. It was, he decided, the one item he'd seen so far that he would happily send a van round in the morning to collect. The top half of the thing consisted of shelves, most of which were bare. The lower half was formed by a set of three drawers, and below them were three cupboards with swing doors. Very conventional in one sense. But somehow, for a piece of furniture, the thing had style.

Derek paused for a micro-second. Suddenly he wanted to open those cupboards, to know more about the man who walked with goats. There were still vague thumps and clumps above his head. He knew, or rather hoped, that in this creaky house he would hear different sounds when the Minister began to descend the stairs. His big frame would surely give sufficient warning.

What the hell! Go for it! Derek told himself.

Getting down on his knees, he cautiously turned the knob on one of the cupboard doors. It was a mistake. Under pressure from whatever had been shoved inside, the door swung open abruptly, and the contents spilled out onto the linoleum at Derek's knees. Dust clouded the air.

"Bloody..." Derek coughed quietly as the tiny specs caught at the back of his throat. Most of the emerging material consisted of papers and folders, but there was also a small box, maybe ten to twelve inches long, and a couple of inches deep. It was of painted wood, had a padded lid, and was fastened by a tiny metal hook. Lord knows what it was for. Perhaps, he thought, it was the sort of box that held jewellery or cosmetics on a woman's dressing table.

Above his head came the unmistakeable sound of a lavatory being flushed. Hastily he pushed the papers back inside the cupboard. But the box...there was still time...he flipped open the metal hook fastener and lifted the lid.

For a moment or two he didn't recognise what it was, even when he picked it up. Something metallic, heavy. But then he realised what he held in his hand, and simultaneously his fingers found a small lever and, as his grip tightened, he pressed it automatically. With a jerk that nearly tore the thing from his grip, a long narrow blade whipped out like a striking cobra.

The thing was a flick-knife.

Derek stared at it. Flick knives were Teddy Boy weapons. Gangland armoury. They were deadly. The threat of the knife as he held it, the danger that it represented, the sheer glistening nastiness that came with it - it was palpable.

Above his head he heard a footstep on a stair. Moving as fast as he dared, he folded the blade back into its handle. But, in putting it back, he saw that there was a scrap of newspaper, folded in the box. Not really knowing why – perhaps because it had been hidden away in the box with the knife - he pulled the paper out of the box, and shoved it in his uniform breast pocket. Then, after a quick fiddle with the tricky little catch, he pushed the box in on top of the other paperwork, closed the cupboard door carefully, and was back in his chair wearing a politely bored expression as the Minister re-entered the room.

"Right then." The Reverend Donald Simpson, pillar of the community, the man who walked with goats, rubbed his hands together and nodded at Derek.

"Right then," he said. "Shall we take that little walk?"

Derek rose and walked with him. Guilt made him swallow with embarrassment. He shouldn't have taken the cutting. It was theft, for God's sake. But now it was too late, far too late, to put it back.

And he wouldn't put it back, even if he could. An ancient newspaper cutting, hidden alongside a flick knife – there was a minor niggle to get on with.

CHAPTER SEVEN

The regular bus service between North Tawe and civilisation, otherwise known as Okehampton, was in the hands of Thorne's Tours, the village's own coach company.

That morning the ten o'clock departure of Thorne's Tours from the village square left at 10.17. A couple of villagers missed it because it was unreasonably early, when you consider that one normally didn't expect the 10.17 bus to leave until at least half past ten. What was the rush? they asked each other.

One person who didn't miss the bus was Sandy, the landlord's daughter. In her purse was a financial reward for helping her Dad out on Christmas Eve and Boxing Day. In her mind were a pair of jeans she'd seen a few days ago in the dress shop window. They would just about fit her, she judged. And they were pink.

One other individual deliberately missed the bus. Neville Parsons had ridden his bike into the village to pick up a haunch of venison from a local rabbit trapper with connections on Exmoor. Mrs. Parsons was planning a massive all-the-extended-family dinner. But as he arrived, the bus was leaving, and on it, glimpsed through a rather smeary window, was Sandy.

The bus was slow, and made occasional stops. Neville and his bike were fast. Legendarily so. The lad kept a safe 50 yards behind the vehicle all the way into Okehampton. Sometimes he had to slow down, to avoid coming too close. His bike was a single-gear brakeless and much battered thing, but Neville's legs were objects of wonder and veneration amongst local cyclists.

In Okehampton he stopped by the simple method of turning the bike abruptly sideways, lowering one foot, and allowing the thing to skid to a near-horizontal halt. He hid in a doorway until he saw Sandy set off on her shopping trip, then he persuaded Joseph, Thorne's Tours Senior Driver – indeed, Thorne's Tours' only driver, but Joseph liked the title - to let him put his bike in the vehicle's spacious luggage compartment.

Then he found his way to the recreation ground, sat on the roundabout, and went round and round, thinking about Sandy.

* * *

"Where are we going then?" Derek asked, quite reasonably, as he and the taciturn Reverend Simpson walked up the short length of North Road.

"To our burial ground, if you don't mind," the Minister told him curtly.

"Anything you say."

When they reached the main village street Derek automatically turned right, in the direction of the church and its graveyard. But Simpson stopped him.

"No, no." he said irritably. "This way."

They walked together out of the village for about a quarter of a mile, then turned from what was a narrow lane into one which was even more constricted. Then after a few more yards, the Minister stopped at a small wicker gate that was almost hidden by clumps of hawthorn. They went through the gate, and Derek found himself in a fenced enclosure, about twenty-five yards square. It was a tiny cemetery, well kept, and dotted with small tasteful gravestones.

"Many of our members prefer cremation these days. But some still choose to enjoy their rest here," Simpson's voice was reverently hushed.

"So, what have you brought me here to see?" Derek was beginning to wonder if he wasn't wasting an entire morning.

"These." Simpson walked over to the nearest stone, and pointed. "They renew them when it rains hard. Or if I remove them. See."

Attached to the top of the gravestone, possibly with some sort of gum, was a white card, the sort of plain item one buys in a stationer's. There was a message printed on the card.

Derek reached to take the card, then hesitated. "Mind if I...?"

"Go ahead," said the Minister. "There's one on every stone. Wretched things."

Derek pulled the card free – yes, it had been stuck on the stone – and looked at the writing. There were nine words, in an elegant type-face. He read them aloud.

"Remember Mary Trembles. Remember Susannah Edwards. Remember Temperance Lloyd." He turned to the Minister. "Temperance?"

"It is a name," came the reply. "Denoting abstinence. I'm sure you know what is meant by abstinence...don't you, Constable?" It was almost a sneer.

"Who are they? These names...are they people buried here?"

A shake of the head. "No. None of them. I've checked. No-one is lying here, in my garden of remembrance, under anything resembling these names. I have no idea who the women are."

"And do all the cards say the same? The same names?"

"Indeed they do."

Derek read the names again. "Well. Do you want to register a complaint? Vandalism, desecration of sanctified ground?"

"No, no, no. Littering! Littering of course! It's a disgrace. And I'd like to know who put the things there in the first place. Which is your job."

"Yes. I suppose so." Derek agreed.

"Your people must have some way of finding out. These names – perhaps they have criminal records. Find them, and then you can prosecute them."

"For what exactly?"

"I told you. Littering, for a start." The Minister was getting worked up, standing even straighter, even arched, and glaring at Derek. "Or committing a nuisance. The point is, this is a sanctified plot. Holy ground, if you like. That should mean something, even to the police."

"I'll look into it." Privately Derek thought it was not exactly a major offence, perhaps ranking in importance slightly below Joshua Voden's chicken theft. "Mind if I take this?" He held up the card.

"Help yourself." The Minister told him, and waved a hand at the gravestones. "I've got lots of the damn things., haven't I!".

CHAPTER EIGHT

Derek showed the card to two more people.

"Not a clue!" The vicar, the Rev. Hugh Shelley shook his head, his white hair flopping in the cold January breeze. Derek had waylaid him halfway across the village square, as he returned from the shop with the day's Times under his arm, concealing amongst its folds a copy of the Daily Mirror.

"No idea who the women are. But I've seen the cards before. They're all over the churchyard. Good quality card, this is," he added. "Professional job, I'd say. Must have cost a bit."

"Are they a problem?"

"Not really. Bit of litter. Better than confetti, let me tell you."

"All the same, I'm intrigued to find out what it's all about."

"Someone will know," the vicar told him. "And then we'll all know. And we can all remember, what were those names again? No, don't tell me." He gazed up at the grey sky. "Let's see. Mary, Susannah and Temperance." He gave Derek an artful smile. "See? The card asked me to remember them. And I've remembered them!"

* * *

Mary ran her eyes over the card as she swallowed her Puffed Wheat at breakfast the next morning.

"Nope. Never heard of any of them. Not much point in checking the school register either." Mary taught English at the local Grammar. "Common enough names, Lloyd, Edwards, but Trembles? I think that name would stand out."

"They'd be laughed at, right? In the playground."

"You know kids. Anyway. I think it's nice that someone's gone to all this effort to have someone remembered." She frowned. "Presuming, of course, that they're being remembered in a nice way. For something nice."

Derek took the card back from her, and studied it again. Mary glanced up at his face. "Oh dear," she said.

"What?"

"It's niggle time again, isn't it."

"Well..."

"Yesterday you had a minor niggle, about remembering to see Simpson. Now you've got another. Who are these women? Why should we remember them? You'll keep at it until you find out. Right?"

"Am I that transparent?"

"Yes."

"And that predictable?"

"Yes."

"That tedious?"

"Yes"

They grinned at each other across the kitchen table.

"Well, I'll have to leave it for today," Derek pointed out. "I've got to get up to the Colonel's place. Meet

Welbeloved. And deal with whatever stupidity the fat bugger has in mind this morning. "

"You better get going," Mary told him. "Oh – and don't forget your shirt from yesterday. Nice and sweaty."

She handed him a large brown paper bag. Derek opened it and sniffed.

"Christ, is that what I smell like?"

"Well, it's had time to cook overnight. But basically, that's you." And then with mock lubricity: "And it's so sexy!"

"Then I'll be home early tonight!"

* * *

Half an hour later Derek was humming down the long but smooth concrete drive that led to Colonel Critchley's farmhouse. He parked his motorbike in its usual place, hung his helmet on the handlebars, and noted that already in the yard - and with two wheels on the Colonel's front lawn - was the Okehampton police patrol car. Its presence, and the cack-handed parking, meant that Welbeloved had arrived before him. Damn.

"Morning, Derek!" Colonel Critchley came striding out of his front door, his excitable little collie Sally frisking at his heels. "Time for a coffee?"

"No time for coffee, Colonel!" This was Welbeloved, stumbling out in the Colonel's wake. "The constable's late. He can go without. Serve him right."

"I'm not la..." Derek began, but Welbeloved overwhelmed him.

"Did you bring your dirty shirt?"

Wordlessly Derek handed him the paper bag.

Welbeloved sniffed it. "Woooh!" he exhaled in an exaggerated fashion. "Smelly little sod, aren't you, constable. Now, where's that van with the unit? Ah, talk of the devil, here he comes. Right on time."

Ah, Derek noted to himself. The van is on time. I am late. Even though I got here first. God bless Sergeant Welbeloved.

He didn't recognise the actual van and concluded that it must emanate from either Exeter or Plymouth. As it drove into the yard, he noted that it had a wide rear door, replacing a normal boot, plus a grilled window. The Okehampton force had nothing like it. The Sergeant moved forward importantly, waving to the van driver and indicating a place to park, which the driver, to his considerable credit as far as Derek was concerned, completely ignored, and parked tidily and appropriately instead.

Derek turned to his friend. "Colonel – what's all this about?"

"You haven't been told?" The Colonel looked concerned. "I assumed you'd volunteered for this. Welbeloved gave me to understand..."

"That's Welbeloved, well on form. Go on then. What is it?"

Before the Colonel could answer there was a shout from the fat Sergeant. "Better get that dog of yours inside, Colonel. Could get nasty."

"By God yes!" The Colonel turned, and ushered Sally rapidly into the safety of the house.

Derek, feeling that things were suddenly leaving him behind, turned back to the van. The driver was now opening the back door, then swinging back some kind of grill, and with yelps of delight two enormous dogs leaped out.

Derek automatically stepped back. Large dogs were not his favourite animals. During the War an Alsatian, driven mad by the bombing, had taken an ultimately harmless but painful bite of his forearm. Welbeloved might have had a similar experience at one time, judging by the way he was suddenly to be found on the other side of the van.

It came as a relief to see that each dog was held by a slim chain to the interior of the van. The relief was only momentarily, because the driver now reached in and unfastened the chains. Happily, he kept a firm grip on both chains as the dogs leaped about enjoying their restricted freedom.

Christ, Derek said to himself. First, it's goats on a lead. Now, dirty great... Then aloud to the dog handler:

"Hi. I'm Derek Martin.".

"John Langdon," said the handler. "Heard about you. Good things. I would shake hands but..." he gestured towards the dogs as he kept a tight grip on the chains.

"And what do you call these then.?" Derek asked him.

"This is Dagwood, the boy, the big one. And his sister, Blondie. After the cartoon, you know."

"And they are what? Wolves? "

Langdon laughed. "They're bloodhounds, mate. Best trackers in the world. We're introducing them down here in Devon. You know, got to do something after that cock-up with Rubber Bones."

"Rubber Bones" was the nickname of the criminal Harold Webb, a man of extraordinary athleticism, who had successfully escaped from the allegedly escape proof prison on Dartmoor through a narrow drain, and had subsequently evaded a massive police cordon around the moor and slipped away to London to see his girlfriend.

"It wasn't a cock-up," Welbeloved protested, coming closer now the dogs began to calm down. "We were unfortunate. I should know, I helped organise the operation."

Dog handler Langdon, the Colonel, now back with them without Sally, and Derek all allowed their mutual silence to serve as a comment.

"So. Anyway." Welbeloved covered his awkwardness with bluster. "All right. You ready for this, young Constable Martin?"

"Ready for what?"

The Colonel looked from the Sergeant to Derek, and back to the Sergeant. "You mean, you really have no idea why you're... Sergeant! You didn't tell him about this, about what he's meant to do?"

"Oh, don't you worry, he's a good 'un, young Derek is. He'll do it, no bother."

Derek felt a sort of weary scepticism come over him. "Do what?"

"Look, laddie." This was Welbeloved demonstrating his rather greasy charm. "It's quite simple. It's an official training exercise. You go off for an amble in the countryside, then after a bit we give the doggies a sniff of that shirt of yours, and see if they can track you down. Okay?"

Derek looked at him, then at the dogs slavering on their chains, their tongues protruding, their teeth gleaming, their loose lips dripping... then back to Welbeloved. He couldn't stop the words. "You can go fuck yourself."

"Constable!" Welbeloved would have swelled to twice his normal size, were that conceivable. "That's gross insubordination to a senior..."

"Sergeant!" The Colonel's military tones silenced Welbeloved. "I have to tell you that if you made such a proposition to me, my language would be even stronger."

Welbeloved hesitated, and Derek got a belated grip on his tongue. "I apologise for my language, Sergeant. But do you seriously think that I'm going to let myself be chased down by those animals? Find another sucker. Better still, Sergeant. You do it."

"Now look here, Constable." Welbeloved rallied. "This is serious police work. You should be proud to do it."

"And get eaten alive when they get me? Jesus!"

"Don't be ridiculous. They will be on their chains. There'll be two of us, and we won't let them go. We will control them."

Derek looked at Langton. "Will you?"

"Well, I will," the handler cast a doubtful look at Welbeloved. "But I can only handle one at a time, once they're on a scent."

"I'll take the other one, of course I will," Welbeloved blustered. "I'm quite capable." Then: "Hey, where are you going?"

"Home," Derek told him over his shoulder as he walked towards his motorbike. And he would have gone, too, he told himself later, serious police work or no serious police work. But the Colonel's interruption stopped him.

"Hang on, Derek," the Colonel said. "We have more visitors, apparently."

The others looked up to see a sleek grey Jaguar saloon coming carefully down the lane. It pulled to a halt in the middle of the yard, and a uniformed police driver sprang out of his door, and ran round to open the front passenger door. From it emerged a tall figure, also in uniform, but one smarter, better cut, and decorated with several rows of military medal ribbons. Derek knew him immediately. It was the Chief Constable. Sir Arthur Beer. The biggest of the Devon and Exeter Police Force bigwigs had arrived.

The driver now opened on of the rear passenger doors, and from it emerged a figure who Derek had only seen in official photographs. It was the legendary Detective Chief Superintendent Paul Anderson, a small, dark and enigmatic figure, known for his steely determination, his forensic approach to crime, his extreme contempt for his subordinates, and his inability to solve anything more complicated than a case of shoplifting at Woolworths. Anderson was feared throughout the West Country force, not for his detection statistics, which were supposed to be confidential because they were so appalling, but certainly for his cutting sarcasm and his ability to reduce his subordinates to incoherent rage. Now the man showed his contempt for the current proceedings by turning his back on everyone else and gazing stolidly at the Colonel's tool shed door.

There was one other passenger in the big Jag. It was Derek's Okehampton boss, Inspector Reed, who had to open his own door, and who got out carefully, stumbling slightly on the uneven ground, and smiling obsequiously in the presence of those he considered superior beings.

"George!" The Chief Constable raised an arm in greeting, then strode over to shake hands with Colonel Critchley. "Sorry to drop in unannounced."

"You're welcome any day, Arthur. You know that," the Colonel told him. "And... um...so are they, of course, "and he waved a general hand at the detective and the Inspector.

"Just wanted to check that this is happening," Beer said. "Hope it's going to work. Especially after that bollocking I got over Rubber Bones. So. Who've we got here?" His glance swept around at the others, his eyes narrowing.

"Good morning, Sir," the Sergeant began. "I'm..."

"Yes, I know you, Welbeloved." The tone was not curt, but not that friendly either. "And you, of course, Langdon. Keep a firm grip on those puppies of yours, won't you."

The handler grinned and nodded.

"So..." The Chief's gaze zeroed in on Derek. "This must be the splendid young man who's volunteered to help us today."

"Sir, I haven't actually..." Derek began, but again the Chief swept on.

"Good for you, young man. You understand, we had to find a member of the force to do this for us. Couldn't use a civilian. I mean, if something went terribly wrong. But it won't, will it, Sergeant?"

"No Sir!" Welbeloved's reply was that of a soldier on parade to his senior officer.

"And of course you're just the chap we need. Martin, isn't it? Yes, Constable Martin. Been hearing a lot about you recently. Excellent work. That bunch of drug users and the poor dead girl. And then there were those thugs doing the people smuggling. I tell you this, young man. You've made an excellent start in the force. You could go a long way. Chief Constable's baton in your knapsack, eh?"

"Sir." It was Derek's turn to sound like a squaddie.

"Well, I won't keep you. I'm sure you're anxious for the hunt to start, eh? Goodbye – and good luck!"

The Chief Constable stuck out a hand for Derek to shake, then strode briskly back to his car, where his driver was already holding the door open for him.

"Got a meeting in Barnstaple," he shouted over his shoulder to the Colonel. "Bloody people, keep asking for more money. I ask you!"

Then he was in the car, and his driver had the Jag purring like a spoiled kitten. The Inspector and the Detective Superintendent, neither of whom had said a word throughout the visit, disappeared into the rear seats with surprising alacrity, before the driver demonstrated his skill, and the car seemed to turn on a sixpence, then swept off up the track, with a small shower of the Colonel's mud flicking up from its rear wheels.

Welbeloved smiled grimly at Derek. "Right," he said. "If you can find somewhere to stick your Chief Constable's baton, we'll start."

* * *

Mary finished making the bed, not an easy task because Derek, always an unruly sleeper, had kicked so hard in the middle of a dream – he claimed it had been about being forced to eat a pasty, an item of West Devon fare that he notoriously found repugnant, but she didn't believe it – that in his un-waking struggle he had managed, incredibly, to tie the bottom sheet into a tight knot with his feet. It took her ten minutes to untangle the thing, and when she finished the sheet was as creased and wrinkled as a prune. But, she decided, if she tucked it in at the foot of the bed, it wouldn't be noticeable.

That job done, and the bathroom and kitchen already sorted, Mary faced the rest of the day. School was still out, not back until next week when the spring term would begin, but there was some admin work to do. She'd do it later in the morning, on the kitchen table.

Meanwhile, almost without intending to, she wandered into the spare bedroom. It was a nice room, she thought. It would catch the morning sun, and look out over what might one day be a pleasant garden if

Derek ever recovered from his allegedly almost terminal blisters and picked up the spade again.

The spare room was, of course, bare. No furniture yet. Only a couple of suitcases, left over from when they moved in, and containing, if memory served, some few unwanted or unnecessary or utterly hideous wedding presents.

They'd have to do something about the floor. At present half was covered with old linoleum and the remainder left as bare boards. A fitted carpet – that would be terrific. She had heard about fitted carpets from colleagues at school, but knew no-one in the village who had one. What a treat it would be!

There were two alcoves in the room, created by the boarded-in chimney breast. Mary considered the one nearest the window. It would be just the right size for a cot. And the playpen could go in the centre of the room, and...

Stop it! She told herself. She had her job. Promotion was possibly imminent. They needed the money. Yes, one day, cots, baby clothes, rattles, prams. But not now. Not yet.

Mary firmly closed the spare room door and went downstairs to work on the spring timetable.

* * *

Despite Welbeloved's enthusiastic urgings there was a short hiatus in the Colonel's farmyard. Derek looked at the Colonel, the Colonel looked at the handler, and the handler looked at the Sergeant, and the Sergeant looked at all of them with a superior smile.

Derek broke the silence. "When do I start then?"

"Soon as you like, soon as you like." The Sergeant spluttered with a combination of relief and impatience, with even a touch of gratitude thrown in. "You start from here, of course. Run around a few fields and woods and such, and we'll probably track you down in no time."

"You'll give me a start, I suppose."

"Of course. Ten minutes, all right?"

The Colonel put in: "I think perhaps fifteen, Sergeant?"

"Right," the handler, Langdon, spoke before Welbeloved could. "We'll give Dagwood and Blondie a sniff of your shirt in just 15 minutes.

The Colonel's much-admired new Landrover stood in an open-fronted shed at the far end of the yard, and he now made a move towards it.

"I must leave you too," he explained. "Meeting of the Egg Marketing Board." And then, with a remarkable mimic of the Chief Constable's voice, "Bloody people keep asking for more money. I ask you."

As he watched the Colonel's vehicle disappear up the lane, Derek felt a pang of loneliness. Everyone on his side, he felt, was leaving. But then he caught a wink from Langdon, and felt better.

"We'll keep a tight grip," the handler told him.

"You do that. See you later then. Hopefully in one piece. Not in chunks."

There was a farm lane leading out of the yard, giving access to the fields, and Derek made his way down it at a dog-trot. He felt foolish trying to run. His police boots were far too clumpy, his handcuffs jangled at his belt, his truncheon in its special pocket banged against his thigh, and the heavy serge uniform didn't help at all. Thank heaven he'd left his helmet on his bike. If he'd known what he was in for he'd have broken out some of his old sportswear and a pair of gym shoes. If Welbeloved had only told him what was entailed...but then, if he'd known in advance that he was going to be chased around the countryside by two slavering hounds, he wouldn't be there. He'd be in Acapulco. Or anywhere except here. All too late now.

Three hundred yards down the lane he came to a closed farm gate. Typical of the Colonel's approach to agriculture, it was a modern steel construction. Derek took it in his stride, getting one foot on the second bar up, then vaulting over the top, to land heavily but safely in the thick mud on the other side. He pictured Welbeloved trying the same trick, and grinned. Then he pictured Welbeloved trying to open the gate, with a slavering bloodhound pulling him in every direction. And then he pictured Blondie slipping easily through the bars of the gate, and hauling Welbeloved slap against the bars, totally stuck, spread-eagled, marooned by dog power.

He was tempted to hide behind a hedge and see which of these scenarios played out, but no, duty called, and he jogged on.

Now he went down the side of a grass meadow, keeping to the left, then along the bottom hedge, past a huge rabbit warren – he wondered if this would distract the police dogs, but doubted it – and then through a gap and into a small spinney. He pushed on. There was no path to follow and brambles and hawthorn and young elder whipped at his face as he trampled through them. They stung, but then it would be the same for his pursuers. He wondered if they'd set off after him yet. Perhaps they were already close to catching him.

He burst through the last of the spinney, jumped over some half-concealed old barbed wire fencing, and found himself in a long narrow meadow, which seemed hardly used. Clumps of rushes grew at random across it. Another similar meadow followed, before he decided to change direction. Realising that the ground now sloped upwards quite steeply to his right, he decided to aim for height. Perhaps he would be able to find a spot sufficiently high to enable him to see how close Langdon, Welbeloved and the bloodhounds were getting.

He negotiated another gate, and found himself in a broad field of winter wheat, with the lines of small green shoots struggling through the soil in their search for spring. He knew better than to run across the crop, and instead stuck to the left-hand hedge, climbing steadily across and upwards until, quite out of breath, he reached the top of the field. A few steps to his right took him to another gate, where he stopped for a breather.

Looking back down the field, he realised he had achieved his objective. He now had a clear view of his route, of most of the way he'd come, and he searched anxiously along it, seeking his chasers. But there was no sign. Where on earth? He made himself look again, this time methodically. But there was no-one in sight. No-one had followed, not man or beast. No trees were disturbed. No bushes trembled. Not a soul, human or canine, moved.

So what had happened? Where were they?

Derek could only conclude that the whole thing had been an abject failure. Which was very possible. After all, it was Welbeloved who was in charge of it.

Or maybe it was the dogs. Dagwood and Blondie. Perhaps they were acting like their comic namesakes: Dagwood being a twit and Blondie too self-regarding to run around after a smelly old shirt, or the smelly old person who'd worn it.

Or perhaps, thinking it was dinner time, they had turned on Welbeloved and were biting juicy chunks out of his big fat...

Stop being silly, Constable Martin, he told himself. He was on his own, no sign of anyone else, and this meant he had time for a bit of a peaceful think, about his latest niggle, or rather, when he counted them up, about all four of his current niggles. They had been hovering at the back of his mind, even when he'd been absorbing the news that he was to be the human target for two ravenous bloodhounds. He briefly reviewed them.

First, someone was stealing chickens. Joshua Voden might fancy himself as a rural prankster, but Derek believed him when he claimed at least one fowl had gone missing, probably two. But who in the village would think of committing such a mean un neighbourly crime? North Tawe wasn't like that. He'd put in a report, of course. Always cover your...

What else was he niggling about? Well, and there could be a connection with his first niggle here, the Beatniks. Odd place for a bunch of tramps and drop-outs to end up. A sleepy West Devon village. Miles from the sea. What were they up to?

And then, third niggle, there were those cards. The mysterious attachments to gravestones in the village's two cemeteries. Mary Trembles. Susannah Edwards. Temperance Lloyd. Why should we remember them? Who wants us to remember them? Who needs us to remember them?

And finally there was what he thought of as the Big Niggle. What was a flick-knife doing in a cupboard in the home of the apparently most upright man in the village, the chapel minister, the Reverend Simpson? And not forgetting the newspaper cutting, concealed with it. He touched his breast pocket. The rustle told him the piece of newsprint was still there. But this wouldn't be a good moment to produce it and read it, not with a keen drizzle-bearing wind sweeping across the fields.

He looked back down at the way he'd come. Still no sign of pursuit. The whole exercise was clearly a failure. Time to call it a day. Where was he, anyway?

Derek turned and climbed a couple of rungs of the gate, an ancient wooden one, this time, with rusty hinges. And, looking out, he realised that he'd ended up remarkably close to North Tawe. There it was, his village, squatting, as it were, on the next hill. He could see the path of the Tawe itself; he was nearly home. He might as well go home, he decided. Home was now much closer than the Colonel's place. He'd get Mary to run him out later to reclaim the motorbike. And his sweaty shirt.

He put his weight on the next rung of the gate, but took it off as the wood began to give way under him. Better open this one, he decided, and had dismounted and was reaching for the rusty catch when...

Something stopped him. A noise, very faint. A voice? A yelp?

He looked back, focussed on his route, and there they were. Far away, but yes, it was them. His pursuers. Well, at least one of them. Screwing up his eyes, he recognised the handler, Langdon, emerging from the spinney with its whiplash bushes and brambles. In front of him Dagwood, the big male beast, was straining against his chain, but the handler had brought him to a halt in the field with all the rushes, and was turning and waiting.

After a long pause the reason for the snail-like progress of the dog team became obvious. Welbeloved burst out of the spinney, not by his own volition but by the desperate strength of Blondie, determined not to be left behind. Welbeloved had clearly had enough even though he'd barely begun the chase. He was staggering, comically exhausted, both by the speed, slow though it must be, of the chase, and by the efforts he was making to restrain Blondie. He came to a halt by Langdon and the other dog, and, like marionettes the two distant figures began pointing, waving, and gesticulating. Eventually they stopped their argument, and Blondie and Dagwood got back on the trail Derek had left.

Welbeloved started to follow... and fell over. If he had fallen over one of the clumps of rushes that dotted the field, it would have been understandable. But no, Welbeloved simply fell over his own feet.

Then things happened fast. For a moment or two Blondie actually dragged the large body mass of the Sergeant several feet across the grass. Derek guessed that Welbeloved must have wrapped the chain around his wrist to get a better grip on the urgent dog. Not a wise decision. The metal must be cutting into the man's arm as the dog struggled forward. He imagined both Sergeant and Blondie yelping. But then, probably to Welbeloved's intense relief, the chain tore free from the Sergeant's hand.

Blondie took off like a rocket, the loose chain dragging behind her. She crossed the first field in no time, and was soon halfway across the next. Derek stopped grinning. Suddenly there was nothing funny going on. Blondie was running free. Blondie was on his trail. Blondie was coming for him.

CHAPTER NINE

Derek shoulder-charged the ancient wooden gate, which gave way before and under him. He sprinted forward, realising as he did so that the new field sloped steeply away, that he was running downhill in the direction of North Tawe, his feet pounding in loose soil and odd patches of water between the furrows. He ran on, he ran for his life, and he knew it was a race he would lose. He ran as fast as he had ever run, and he knew it wasn't fast enough. No-one can outrun a bloodhound. On the scent, they ran faster than Derby winners. Blondie would catch him, and there would be no-one to hold the bitch back. The thing would be on him, its jaws working, its claws scrabbling, it would be at his throat, and he would be lost.

He was stumbling towards the bottom of the field now. Ahead, over another barrier, was the river, and before that a pleasant stretch of river bank, where he and Mary had once taken a picnic, back in the summer. It was a place of small bushes, rushes, tall grasses, almost a shady sanctuary. If he could make that, then the river was just a few strides away, and then, perhaps, there might still be a chance.

He paused and risked a glance back over his shoulder. It was a mistake. He caught a glimpse of the brown leaping shape back on the crest of the field. Bonnie must have followed his trail with lightning accuracy. Now she was charging down towards him, howling in triumph as she came, and he ran again, and Oh Christ! He tripped, sprawling forward, smashing his face into the soil, thumping the air out of his lungs. Him and Welbeloved, he thought in the briefest of moments. Both fallers. Both losers.

But something, fear, panic, despair, got him back on his feet. He was at the bottom of the field now. In front of him was a small hedge, gorse or something, only a few feet high and clinging to a similar-sized wooden fence, which was falling apart from age and neglect. Beyond that, a few yards of rough flat ground, then the river, and then, by God, houses! The village. The lower end of North Tawe! Which meant people, help, sanctuary. If he could just...

But he couldn't. Not a chance. As he jumped over the hedge and fence, he heard Blondie behind him, heard her harsh panting, heard her give a yelp of triumph. She'd done it. She'd caught the quarry. She'd hunted him down. She had proved her worth to the Devon and Exeter Police Force. And now, totally out of control, she could go in for the kill.

But for some reason the dog hesitated at the fence Derek had just vaulted, looking for an opening perhaps, and with renewed effort born of terror, he ran for the patch of shrubs and greenery along the so-pleasant river bank where they'd picnicked in the July sunshine...only this was January. A winter's rain and snow had already fallen. This was no longer a pleasant place, no longer a sanctuary. It was a bog. A riverside marsh.

Plunging into it, Derek's left foot disappeared from under him, his leg sinking up to his knee in God knew what, and throwing him forward on his face into a small patch of bramble. He flailed his arms, scrabbled with his other leg, but it was hopeless. He couldn't move. He was stuck. He was finished.

Blondie had decided to leap the fence. Derek actually heard the impact of her paws on the earth as she landed safely behind him. He held his breath, closed his eyes, tried, for Mary's sake, for his own sake, to be brave. And waited.

And waited. Nothing happened. And yet Blondie was there. He could hear her panting. He could smell her. She was close, but she wasn't attacking him. She wasn't trying to chew on his jugular, or scratch his eyes out with her claws, or bite off any of his protrusions.

No, she was snuffling at something. Licking it, perhaps? Swallowing?

Derek opened his eyes and looked to his right. There was Blondie. She was eating something with relish. A chunk of it dropped from her mouth. Astonishingly, unbelievably, it looked like bread and butter pudding. But then, as he raised his head and looked more carefully, Derek saw that on the other side of the animal, huddled up against Blondie, was a small white human figure, It was a child. Scantily clad. Dead? No. For as Derek listened, he heard another sound along with Blondie's munching. It was the sobbing of a small lost soul.

And as he watched, he saw a thin white arm reach up, curl around a huge hairy neck, and pull the great dog's head down and in. Blondie's tail wagged like an electric fan.

* * *

It took another seven minutes for John Langdon, the handler, to reach them, which was pretty creditable when you thought about it. Afterwards, replaying things in his mind, Derek reckoned that while the chasing dog would have followed the scent of the shirt and skirted around the crop in the big field, the man must have sprinted right up across the winter wheat. And good for him.

In the meantime Derek struggled to free his trapped leg, and failed, and gave up. Frankly he felt he deserved a rest. He had tried to talk to the child, but the only communication that was going on, there on the boggy river bank, was between child and dog. And even if the child had responded to Derek's polite enquiries: "Hello" and "What's your name then?" His replies would have been muffled by a great floppy bloodhound ear, and a mobile tongue relishing the last crumbs of bread-and-butter pudding.

Langdon proved himself both a thoughtful and a practical man. He left Derek alone with his leg stuck in the bog, and attended at once to the child. He half enticed, half tugged the child, who proved to be a boy, out of his little shelter of bushes and onto a firm patch of turf. This proved more difficult than first envisaged, because the boy refused to relinquish his grip on Blondie, and Blondie had no intention of deserting his new friend either. Langdon took his uniform jacket off, and managed to wrap most of it around the boy, who still shivered and sobbed almost violently. He talked quietly to the lad, but got no response. And it seemed sensible not to harass him further, to let him recover in his own good time. But John sat beside him, and the three of them, man, boy and bloodhound, seemed to find a little peace together.

"You're stuck, are you?" John finally got round to asking Derek.

"Of course I'm... I mean you can see I'm bloody... Yes, John, yes, my leg is stuck."

"Welbeloved will pull you out."

"You think?"

"If he ever gets here, that is."

"Listen." Derek had to know. "I don't understand. How come Blondie went all friendly with the boy, and left me alone?"

"What else would she do? He had the grub. She was hungry. She's always hungry."

"Well I was her quarry, wasn't I? She caught me, why didn't she attack me? Kill me?"

"Why on earth would she do that?"

"Well, I thought that was what bloodhounds do. What she'd do."

"Nah." There was the sneer of the expert in Langdon's tone of voice. "Who told you that?"

"I thought you did."

"Good God no. Not Dagwood and Blondie. Soft as butter, these two. I brought them up from pups, you see. They love to chase, that's natural. But they wouldn't hurt a fly."

"Not even whatsisname, Dagwood?"

Langdon shook his head, and half-laughed at the ridiculous idea. Derek, still lying half face down on the ground, thought about his run down the hill, remembering his panic, his desperation, his glimpse into the approaching threat. A horrible assault at best, death at the worst. Death from the teeth of a ravenous wild animal. He shivered. He was about to tell Langdon about it, about how scared he had been, but then stopped himself. No-one had seen his panic, his mad rush, no-one knew of his despair. If he confessed it the story would race around every police force in the West of England, how cocky young Constable Martin had run for his life from a harmless dog. Silly bugger. Twit.

He'd already said enough. He decided to shut up. It never happened. Finish.

He looked for Dagwood, The male dog seemed to have realised that the hunt was over, and was now sitting peacefully, occasionally glancing at his sister, and possibly looking askance at the way she was developing a cuddly relationship with the unknown boy. "Typical female!" Derek interpreted Dagwood's thoughts. "Over-sentimental, that's bitches for you. Not like us dog dogs."

Welbeloved discovered them after another five minutes, which for such a grossly fat and unfit man, was another creditable performance. He was purple, but again to his credit, he wasted no time in excuses or recriminations, but, after a couple of brief questions, instead put both hands under Derek's armpits, and with a strength so far unsuspected and a burst of energy totally out of character, hauled him out of the boggy ground.

He even helped him stand and brush off some of the mud.

"So!" Welbeloved clearly decided that he would take charge. "Who's the boy?"

"He won't say," Langdon said. "I've asked him. He hasn't said a word yet. I think he's in shock."

Welbeloved accepted this diagnosis. "We'll have to find out who he is, what he's doing out in this weather. Looks like he was here all night, if you ask me. But first we need to get him somewhere warm. Quick."

"My place," Derek told him. And when the Sergeant seemed to hesitate, "It's just up the road, for chrissake!"

"All right, keep your hair on, laddie. So. Let's get him to his feet." Langdon and Derek slowly helped the boy up from the ground. And as the lad straightened two things happened.

Langdon's jacket fell away from the slim shoulders. And the boy's shorts, which proved once again that they were much too big for him, slipped down over his knees, to his ankles. Naturally, the boy stooped to retrieve them.

Welbeloved saw it first. "Oh bugger!" he gasped.

The other two looked where he was looking.

Langdon said: "Shit!"

Derek said: "Jesus!"

CHAPTER TEN

"Sergeant Welbeloved, if you don't get out of my house now, that is this minute, this second, I am going to clobber you with this!"

"This" was a rolling pin, the traditional weapon of the outraged housewife, and one that Mary might, if she'd thought about it, have been ashamed of wielding, for reasons of incipient feminism and for its association with battling wives in Punch cartoons and the adventures of Denis the Menace. But the thing was to hand, lying on the work surface of her kitchen, she'd grabbed it from sheer frustration and need, and it was working for her.

Welbeloved backed off with all the speed he could muster, accidentally bumping his bulky frame against the kitchen door and then into the wall of the narrow entrance hall, in the process bringing a framed photo of Derek in his police cadet uniform crashing from its hook.

"Mary. Mrs Martin. Please! Listen." the fat man babbled. It was a futile appeal.

"Out! Out!"

The Sergeant turned and fled, with all the grace of an oil tanker making a U-turn on the Serpentine. He burst through the front door and came to a shuddering halt on the front path. He turned and found four figures staring at him with some apprehension – The Colonel, Langdon the dog handler, Dagwood looking as mournful as a bloodhound can, and Derek himself, who had sensed that Mary was winding herself up to full pitch, and had wisely stepped out of firing range. It was drizzling again, and the atmosphere was gloomy and cold. But anything was better than getting in Mary's way right now.

She came to the door. Welbeloved quailed, backing further down the short path. Derek, the Colonel and Langdon stepped back too, feeling like unwilling spectators at a Spanish bullfight, watching the matador about to dispatch his – or rather, her - beefy opponent.

"Now you listen to me, Sergeant Welbeloved," she began. Mary's arms were, Derek thought, in the pose known as "akimbo". Her hands were on her hips, her elbows tending to poke forward, and the symbolic rolling pin was still in evidence, sticking out of her right fist like a pistol half-out of its holster. She spoke. And everyone within hearing distance knew they better listen.

"Listen to me. That boy is going nowhere. He is staying here. With me. You are not hauling him off to your police station, which is a concrete dump smelling of wee. You are not shoving him into some grim children's home, where he'll be bullied by the evil little hooligans currently resident there. And you are not taking him to that officious hell they call a hospital, where he'll be left sitting on a hard chair until some adolescent straight out of medical school can poke him around as if he's a window dummy. No, you're not taking him anywhere. He's staying here with me." And then, as an afterthought, to Langdon, "And so's your blessed dog. The boy loves it."

You had to hand it to Welbeloved, Derek thought. Out-gunned, on the ropes, teetering on the brink of defeat, he didn't give up.

"Mrs Martin, please. This is an official matter. Enquiries must be made. The authorities will be anxious to find out who the boy is, what he was doing when he was found, where..."

"Sergeant!" Her voice was a stinging whiplash, thought Derek. Christ, what had he married? "The boy is wounded. He has been physically harmed. Beaten. Recently, and on previous occasions. Our local nurse, Jean Chalker, a state registered nurse, who is with him now, tells me he has been traumatised. Do you know what that means, Welbeloved? Do you? Traumatised?"

Welbeloved didn't, but he could guess. He made one last plaintive attempt.

"But my inspector will..." he began, but Mary cut across him.

"As to that, Welbeloved, I have just finished speaking to your inspector on the telephone."

That was a lie, Derek registered silently. He knew perfectly well that Mary hadn't been near the telephone, ever since that moment when she had opened the door to find Derek, looking filthy and exhausted, holding an apparently unconscious and equally filthy young boy in his arms. But Welbeloved believed her.

"Oh," he said blankly

Mary went on: "He told me quite definitely that I should take care of the boy for the meantime, and, and here I quote the Inspector verbatim, tell that fat buffoon to leave you to it!"

Derek wondered if this whopper of a fib would rebound on him and Mary eventually. Then he thought it wouldn't. And then he thought he didn't care if it did.

He himself had made one phone call, to their nurse friend Jean. But for Mary, the boy had become the entire focus of her attention. Derek thought he would remember her response to the situation, this out-of-the-blue confrontation, for as long as he lived; the way she had simply opened her arms, lifted the boy, held him close, and hurried into the kitchen, putting him down with infinite care on a padded chair close to the Rayburn, which was, as ever in January, burning with a healing warmth. Blondie padded after the pair of them, and lay down placidly where the boy could touch her head when he needed to.

Then Mary, grabbing a tea-towel from somewhere, knelt and began wiping the worst of the mud and tears and saliva and snot from the boy's face, while whispering to him, a cascade of soothing words which she interspersed with curt instructions to Derek.

"There now, that's better. What a nice-looking lad you are under all that mud, goodness me. Derek! Milk. Are you thirsty, my love? Yes? Here we are then. There, nice and fresh. Derek! Big towel. Now then you, young Sir, d'you want to tell me what your name is? Don't worry, you can tell me, I won't tell anyone. Well, all right, it doesn't matter. Ah, here's a nice towel, I think we'll wrap you up in this, eh? Derek, run the bath! Now let's get these wet things off you, shall we? No, don't worry, I'm a nurse, well nearly, I'll look after you. Here we go, just slip these off. My, they're a bit big for you. Oh!

Derek, half-way up the stairs, heard her muffled exclamation, and knew she had discovered the cruel criss-cross welts on the boy's buttocks, some faded, some still raw and livid. The injuries that had so stunned himself, Welbeloved and John Langdon. He entered the kitchen, and Mary looked up at him silently, her face a mask of self-control. Then she renewed her monologue.

"Well we have been in the wars, haven't we! Never mind, I think a nice warm bath is the ticket now, don't you? Come on then. And yes, doggie can come too. And after the bath we must get you some breakfast. Puffed Wheat? Do you like Puffed Wheat? Have you ever had Puffed Wheat? No? Oh, it's ever so nice."

The nurse, Jean, arrived at that moment, and with professional efficiency she kept any silly questions until later. The four of them, Mary, Jean, Blondie and the boy, made an awkward unit climbing the narrow stairs, but they made it to the top and into the bathroom, closing the door behind them.

Derek felt a little spare. He waited for a while to see if Mary had any future demands to make, perhaps a dog biscuit, or a suit of armour, or peace in the Middle East. But there was nothing except muffled female chatter coming out of the bathroom. He felt he should be doing some investigating, but nothing could be done until the boy spoke, and so far, he'd shown no sign of uttering a word. Not that he'd get one in when Mary was at full spate. Derek smiled to himself at his own silliness, and decided to get a breath of fresh air.

On his front doorstep he learned that Welbeloved had flagged down a local jobbing builder and assured him that he wouldn't be reported for lack of road tax if he gave himself and Langdon a lift to the Colonel's farm. Once there, Langdon had reclaimed his dog van, the Sergeant had reclaimed his badly parked police car, and the Colonel – his meeting with the egg marketing board had been cancelled due to food poisoning. "Bad eggs" he explained - had happily loaded Derek's motorbike into his land rover, not forgetting the helmet. And his sweaty shirt. Then all three vehicles returned to North Tawe for a grand reunion, effectively cluttering up Derek's village street.

Then came the confrontation between Mary and Welbeloved, leaving the former flushed with triumph and the latter flushed with humiliation. On the grounds that no-one should suffer such public ignominy without solace and restitution, the Colonel exercised his regimental skill at man management.

"Now, Sergeant," he said with a degree of formality, "I think you are making the right decision, in leaving the lad in Mrs Martin's very capable hands. And I shall say so to Inspector Reed when I see him at Rotary tomorrow. Indeed, I shall commend you on your handling of this whole unfortunate business."

The Sergeant's demeanour, which had been one of defeated hang-dog, changed in an instance and booted itself up to approaching his usual stance of over-efficient jobsworth.

"Thank you, Colonel." He sketched a slovenly police salute. "And you, Langdon, looks like you're going to be a dog short for a while."

"I'll come back in a few days for her," Langdon told him politely. "The lad's welcome to her for now."

And then, after more goodbyes, self-congratulations, and cheerful waves, three different vehicles roared off down the village street, and Derek was left alone on his doorstep. He took a deep breath and went back inside.

Mary stood at the foot of the stairs, her arms folded aggressively, her face set.

"And don't think you can come in here with any more of your police official bloody nonsense. That boy, he needs proper looking after, and I'm the one to do it, so you take your rules and duties and stuff 'em. Like I told bloody Welbeloved!"

"Yes," Derek said. "You were wonderful. I was never more proud of you."

Mary tried to say something, but then her face twisted, and she burst into sobs. Derek went to her, held her, and let her cry. Typically, her tears didn't last for long, but her body still shook silently. Derek led her into the kitchen, and rather awkwardly they sat down at the table, close to each other.

"Who did that to him?" she pleaded. "Who could have done that to him? How could anybody?"

"We'll find out. How is he?" Derek asked.

Her reply was a disjointed babble, but it made sense. "I put him in our bed. He's asleep. His poor bottom. I suppose he's going to get petroleum jelly all over the sheets, but you should see him. The dog won't leave him, and he won't let it. It's on the rug, and he's got one hand down to touch it. What's it called, anyway?"

"It's a she. Called Blondie. Guess what her brother is called."

"Dagwood?"

"You're an English teacher, and you read comics! Tut, tut."

They laughed together now.

"Sorry for all the weepies," Mary said, her voice steady now. "Got to be practical. I was thinking. We've got an old camp bed at home. I'll get Dad to bring it over. We can keep him here, can't we?"

"I'm sure. For a bit, perhaps. At least until we find out who he is. Where he comes from."

"And who did it to him!" Mary looked sideways at him. "Must be his father, I suppose, or even his mother. But how could anyone do that to a child? All right, you hear about child cruelty in grim places, big towns, but not here. Not..." she waved her arm vaguely. "Not here... Not..."

Derek knew what she meant by "here". Here amongst these gentle fields, with their rushes and their cowpats and their tediously bleating sheep, here along these narrow lanes where grass grows down the middle. Here amongst the little whitewashed cottages, here in the valleys, the coombes, and the little trout rivers of West Devon. Not this cruelty. Not here.

"Have you asked him anything about it yet?" Derek asked.

"He's still not talking. We'll see when he wakes up. Meanwhile, listen. There's nothing you can do here. I'll make some coffee, then you go off and do some work. Make yourself busy. Chase up one of your current crop of niggles. Your beatniks, for instance."

"They're not my beatniks," he protested.

"Ha! But you fancy their leader, don't you. That girl."

"Ah-ah." Derek shook his head. "I've got a rule. Never go with a girl who's taller than you. Why not? Because she'll only look down on you."

Mary groaned.

Later, after coffee and when Derek had got himself organised, and Mary had checked on the boy who was still fast asleep, she came to the door with him.

"I lied about one thing." she confessed.

"Yeah?"

"He did speak. Earlier. Just the one word. I asked him his name, and he told me."

He waited.

"It's Terry." And her eyes shone with unshed tears.

CHAPTER ELEVEN

At first, as he chugged the three miles out from the village, to the crossroads known locally as Fursdon, Derek was asking himself why he was checking out the beatniks. Did he have a good reason to bother them? Apart from the incident at the Hunt Meet, which was something and nothing even if it was a little unusual, there had been no more complaints about them.

But then he remembered he did have good reasons to investigate the newcomers. There had been the apparent theft of Joshua Voden's chicken. Joshua claimed it was the beatniks. Trivial, yes. Unprovable, certainly. But nonetheless, he might as well make a formal enquiry. Ask a few questions.

Another good reason – those cards, the ones placed on the graves and the tombstones. The cards urging the reader to remember, what were their names? Temperance was one, but the others escaped him. However, it was perhaps the sort of thing a beatnik might do, wasn't it? To make a protest, start a movement. But was it a crime? Hardly. Littering, this sort of littering, was harmless, wasn't it? Whatever The Reverend Self-Righteous Simpson might claim. All the same, he could ask about it.

It was no good. He knew these so-called reasons were nothing but flimsy excuses. An urge to be honest with himself took over. He was going out to the ruined chapel, to the new home of the beatniks, because the tall girl had told him to. And he wanted to see her again.

Fursdon came in sight. Not that there was anything much to see. It was one of those lonely little road junctions one can come across in West Devon. Once it had been a minor centre, perhaps a hamlet. A hundred years ago there would have been a small cluster of cottages here, and more out in the fields where farm labourers virtually lived on the job. Perhaps there might even have been some kind of store – shop would be too formal a word – and perhaps even a forge. And, after a passing visit by John Wesley and his brother, with just a few words, but words of fabulous inspiration, a grand new chapel would have been built. And on a Sunday its pews would be packed and the sound of hearty unaccompanied hymns would have drifted down the then un-metalled lanes of Fursdon.

Not now. Now there was little left of the former cottages. One such dwelling was a ruin overgrown with ivy and bushes until it was just a lump on the side of the road. An equally festooned lean-to shed was still attached to it. Other dwellings had completely disappeared. And the chapel itself? It was the last building still standing alone and not obscured by the local undergrowth, but if it was standing, it was definitely on its last legs. Its four walls still remained, amid a small cluster of graves, but the slate roofing was in a state of near collapse, and the front entry porch was crumbling. No-one knew or cared how much the place had deteriorated inside. Anyone who could remember it in its glory, perhaps in the early years of the century, had long gone. No-one now alive could describe the Sundays when the ground floor pews were filled, when the gallery high up at the back was full, and when late coming worshippers were obliged to sit on the wooden gallery staircase.

So what had happened to the congregation, which had once sung Wesley's words so lustily? The older members had suffered from natural wastage. Most of the young men had died in Flanders. The word 'most' here is not an exaggeration. The death rate per head for Devonian sons-of-the-soil in the First World War exceeded all other districts of the country, even those of the much-vaunted Dewsbury Pals and the like. With them gone, other young men came from the cities seeking the young and lonely country girls and taking them off to urban bliss. Or a fate worse than death. The 1919 flu took the chapel minister, and a couple more. And, almost without anyone noticing, Fursdon became a ghost village. Only spirits worshipped in the chapel. Today, even hardened and cynical farmers, who still ran the four or five major farms in the vicinity, preferred not to walk past the ruined chapel on dark windy nights. So for most of the time Fursdon chapel stood alone and deserted.

But not anymore.

Life had returned to the moribund building. From 200 yards away Derek could see wood-smoke pouring in a steady stream through one of the holes in the roof tiles. A small horse was grazing in the overgrown graveyard, and a cart stood nearby – this he knew from the hunt meet to be the beatniks' means of transport. And there was something else. A small car, a well-polished Austin Seven, stood at the entrance to the chapel yard. And he knew the car too. It was the means of travel for the notable chapel minister of North Tawe. The man who took goats for a walk. The man with the hidden flick knife. The Reverend Donald Simpson.

Derek let his motorcycle putter up to park just behind the Austin, wondering what on earth was the man doing there. He switched off his engine and at once heard a cacophony of noise. Someone was playing a record, jazz perhaps, and was attempting to play along with the music on a saxophone. Meanwhile there were voices raised in anger, two people could be heard having an increasingly irate argument, and after a moment he realised it was Simpson and the tall girl.

Derek sighed. If he'd thought about it, he might have seen this coming. He put the bike on its stand and reluctantly went to interfere. The two combatants stood facing each other at the chapel porch, and for once the cliché was valid: they were going at it hammer and tongs.

* * *

In Okehampton Neville's plan was working. Sandy was in his sights. Now was the time for courage. Now or never.

It was going-home time. With his bike safely stowed in the bowels of the coach, he hid in a doorway and watched. And sure enough, and in plenty of time, there came Sandy, swinging along the broad Okehampton main street, a carrier bag in her hand, a satisfied smile on her sweet face.

The coach was almost due to leave. He waited until Sandy was safely aboard, then leapt on himself. She had taken a window seat and, bless his luck, the seat beside her was vacant.

He nerved himself, then slid casually in beside her, blandly looking the other way, before turning and acting as genuinely surprised as he could.

"Hey! Sandy! Good grief! Fancy meeting you here."

Sandy supressed a giggle, and said: "Yes, just fancy." And then "Where's the bike?"

"Oh. I didn't. I mean... in the storage place. Underneath. I just didn't fancy the long ride home."

"It would be quicker by bike. Well. It was on the way in. You had to wait for us then, didn't you!"

A shiver of embarrassment ran through Neville's body. "You saw me?"

"Of course. And honestly, Nev. Waiting three hours in Okehampton, just to get a ride back with me. How did you pass the time? Go to the park? Sit on the swings?"

Neville felt his face and neck turning pink. His head drooped and he looked at his shoes. "On the roundabout." he managed.

"You're a fool, Neville Parsons. What are you?"

"A fool." Something dared him to look back up at her. And he saw that she was smiling. Not laughing. Smiling.

They sat quietly while the coach wound its way out of the town and headed for home. Sandy put her carrier bag by her feet and let her left-hand rest on her lap. Neville looked at it, and wanted to hold it, but he didn't dare. So, after a mile or two, Sandy took his hand and held it firmly.

A little later the coach passed the Fursdon crossroads with its abandoned chapel. A car, and a motorcycle were both parked up, and a uniformed policeman and some others were visible outside the chapel. But neither Sandy nor Neville noticed them. Passion for each other obscured their view.

* * *

Derek's impression of Simpson had so far been of a solid if rather severe man, but certainly one always under strict self-control. Not now he wasn't. Instead, as he stood at the semi-ruined entrance to what had once been a modest chapel porch, he was a towering figure of rage and condemnation. He seemed to be standing even taller than ever, looking as if at any moment he might actually topple over backwards, as Mary had put it. His face was flushed, and his right hand was raised high, his forefinger point heavenwards. Moses, Derek thought. Moses parting the Red Sea. Or was it Abraham and the Dead Sea? One of the two. Mary would know. Simpson too would know, of course, but this clearly wasn't an appropriate time to ask him about events in the Bible. Not when a somewhat biblical row was happening, right there in front of the abandoned chapel.

Standing astride the entrance to the building was the girl who apparently led the off-beat tribe, and Derek caught his breath as he saw her. She looked magnificent. The robe with its hood had gone, and now a great shock of her hair – it had looked black in the pub's dim lighting, but now he saw it had a copper sheen, a more subtle colour than his own ginger crop, sprang up in tangled coils that had seen neither brush nor comb in the last twenty-four hours. She wore what might have been a schoolgirl's white blouse, too tight for her, and similarly tight men's trousers with cut-off legs reaching just below her knees. Her figure was faultless. The sight of her, Derek decided, would make the coldest, most self-controlled and stolid policeman want to whimper to himself.

Derek whimpered to himself.

The way the woman stood reminded him immediately of Mary's stance at the door of their home that morning, when she was facing Welbeloved and telling whopping lies with a hard but very straight face. Mary had looked sexy too, he remembered, even in a pinny and a shirt-waister. But this one. Oh boy. He swallowed hard, then walked forward to get involved, to mediate, to treat both sides of the confrontation with equal fairness, ignoring the fact that one of the parties involved was far more attractive than the other. Like a good policeman should. Especially like a good married policeman should.

It was clear that an angry confrontation between Minister and Head Beatnik had been on-going for some time, and any reasoned argument had now disintegrated into a series of rather alarming epithets.

"Blasphemer," Simpson bellowed.

"Bigot!" the girl shot back.

"Anti-Christ!"

"Fanatic!"

"Witch!"

It'll be stone-throwing next, Derek thought, as he shoved himself into the firing line between the two.

"All right, all right," he found himself saying, trying to adopt a lighter tone. "If the bigot and the witch will just calm down, let's try and sort this out, shall we?"

Both the bigot and the witch spoke at once. The girl said with heavy irony: "Oh, good it's Mr. Policeman. On the side of the establishment, as ever."

The Minister said: "Thank heaven you're here, Constable. You can help me throw these people out. Out of this house of God!"

"Nobody's throwing anybody anywhere," Derek said calmly to Simpson, and to the girl: "And I'm not on anybody's side, either. Mr. Simpson, I know you of course. But," turning to the girl, "Can you tell me your name please?"

"My name is Aphrodite Wondergirl," the girl announced.

"And your real name?"

"That is my real name. "

"No it isn't," Derek replied patiently.

"My real name is what I say my real name is," she shot back.

"Okay." Derek fished out his notebook and pencil, and wrote in it. "Is that 'Aphrodite' with one or two 'd's?" he asked innocently.

"Just the one." The girl seemed for a moment to suppress a giggle.

"Now then. Minister." He turned back to Simpson, who still appeared top-heavy with fury. "Let's start with you. Can you tell me why you are here today?"

"Obvious, isn't it," came the reply. "This is a chapel. It is a sacred building. It stands on sacred soil. These people are devil-worshippers, they insult the Lord, they transgress the laws of civilised Christianity, they foul the very air we breathe."

"Yes, all right, Mr Simpson, I take the point." But Simpson wasn't finished.

"And anyway. This is a chapel, and as such it belongs to me and to my congregation. It is a holy building. And these people are trespassing."

"Mr. Simpson, please. You've been heard. Now, Miss, err, Wondergirl, is Mr. Simpson is correct in what he says?"

She snorted. "We may not be Christians. Who wants to belong to a cult of hypocrites that has killed millions down the years? But we're not devil worshippers. Oh, young Harry, who travels with us, he occasionally scares himself silly with a Ouija Board. But basically, we believe that God can be found in nature. In trees. In flowers, in grass, in the very..."

"Yes, thank you." Good grief, Derek thought. Another windbag. "Let's leave the matter of individual beliefs aside for a moment. Mr Simpson makes the point that this property belongs to the non-conformist community, and that you are indeed trespassing illegally."

"Mr. Simpson doesn't know his law. Mr Simpson doesn't know his arse from his elbow, come to that." She turned back to the Minister. "Listen, numbskull. It's only trespassing if you cause damage. It would be difficult to damage this place any more than the elements – or that God of yours - have already. If anything, we've improved it. At least the door shuts properly."

She turned, and opened the closed door behind her, then slammed it home with a satisfying crunch.

"You couldn't do that two weeks ago," she told him.

"Nonetheless," Derek broke in, "the question of ownership is something which..."

"There's no question of ownership, man!" Simpson snapped. "No question who owns the place, not for one moment. I own it. Or rather my church owns it. It's a chapel. Our chapel."

"And haven't you looked after it! Such care, such loving concern," the girl sneered.

To make her point, there was a sudden gust of wind, the kind that portends a sharp shower, and two ancient slates rattled. All three of them automatically ducked.

"Let me tell you what I think," said the girl, who had ducked less fearfully than the men. "I think this is an abandoned building. I think we have as much right to be here as anyone. But if Mr, whatever, can go home and produce proof that he and his fellow Jesus-lovers own the place, then we will agree to move on. Can you produce proof of ownership, Mr. Holy-Joe?"

Derek turned to Simpson. "Could you do that, Minister?"

Derek half-hoped he could. If the girl meant what she said, then, given proof that the building was chapel-owned, the beatniks would move on, and the whole silly business would disappear. Of course that would mean no more contact with the girl, but...

"Certainly. I'm sure." Simpson didn't sound either certain or sure. "But..." he paused, then seemed to make up his mind. "We shall see. Meanwhile I have other duties to see to. Constable, I'd like a word in private, please."

Derek caught another ironic sneer from the girl, before turning and following Simpson out to his car. The chapel door crunched home once again behind him. And the promised rain began.

Simpson waited for him at the door of his car.

"Constable, I'm disappointed in you," he began.

"I'm sorry to hear that, Sir." Derek kept his voice on a low level.

"You're taking her side, aren't you! Of course you are. Any decent policeman would have had that sacrilegious mob out of there on the spot. But not you. You're weak. You're a coward."

"No Sir." Derek began, but the Minister had more to say.

"And I know exactly what's going on here. It's that woman, isn't it. That tart. Wearing those men's clothes, the perverted... and shoving her great big dugs at you... Oh yes. I saw that all right. Now..."

He moved closer, reached down from his imposing height, and grasped Derek's uniform lapel, leaning back in his typical pose, glaring into Derek's face.

"I know what you were thinking. You were thinking, I'll get in with her if I get rid of that boring old preacher.

Yes, I know what people like you think of someone like me. Tedious old fool, right? But you're wrong."

Derek gritted his teeth against the man's onion breath. "Sir, take your hands off me. Now."

The Minister ignored him. "I'm no push-over. I'm tougher than you can imagine. I'm not a weakling, I don't give in on these matters, especially when..."

He paused for breath, or perhaps he realised he might be saying too much. Derek suddenly remembered the flick knife. And the newspaper cutting, which he had stuffed into his uniform breast pocket, and was still there, if the rain hadn't turned it into sodden scraps.

"Yes!" The Minister resumed. "You cross me, sonny, and believe me, you will regret... Ow!"

Derek had lifted his right hand and brought the edge of it smashing down on Simpson's wrist where he had gripped his lapel. He knew it must have hurt the man. It certainly hurt his hand.

"I told you to take your hands off me," he said grimly. "Try that again and I will arrest you for assaulting an officer of the law."

The man glared at him. "You're no officer of the law. You're a jumped-up little popinjay."

"Popinjay?" That's a new one, Derek thought.

At this point Simpson seemed to remember that his wrist hurt. "You'll be sorry for that," he muttered, rubbing it, then turned and climbed, rapidly for a man of his size, into the small car. Derek watched him roar off in the direction of North Tawe. He breathed out noisily with relief and gratitude. Christ, that had been bad, that had been awful. Something that shouldn't have happened. He felt confused. Was this the upright man who took his goats for a walk, and enjoyed the respect, if not the love, of the village? Or was it the overbearing bully who threatened others and kept a flick knife hidden in a drawer?

He shook his head, and a spray of rain flicked out from his helmet in a sparkling arc. The shower was ending. He pulled himself together. He hadn't come to the ruined chapel to referee a bust-up between a beatnik and a priest. He'd come here to start solving a couple of niggles.

He walked back to the chapel, and knocked firmly on the door.

CHAPTER TWELVE

Five minutes later he was still knocking on the door, and his knuckles were beginning to hurt. This was ridiculous. He could hear the beatniks inside, hear them talking, laughing – presumably about him. But this was a police enquiry. He wasn't going to give up. Professionally speaking he couldn't. And personally. That girl...

He bent, found a loose stone, and used that on the door. It made a sharp insistent crack. Something surely the girl, Wonder-thing or whatever she called herself, couldn't ignore.

She didn't. She opened the door.

"Persistent little bugger, aren't you!" She said brightly.

"I'm on police business. I am making enquiries. And you, young woman, are guilty of an offence already."

"What offence?"

"Wasting police time. Now, I have some questions to ask. May I please come in?"

She made a show of stepping to one side reluctantly, holding the door so that he had to duck under her arm to get in. He caught a hint of some dusky, subtle, almost earthy perfume, very different from the flowery kind that Mary favoured. Once in, he straightened up and looked around.

His first thought was that given the state of the exterior, the chapel inside was in surprisingly good condition, and tidier than he had expected. Some farmer had once clearly used it as somewhere to store items he had now forgotten about. Derek noted a broken pitchfork, an ancient galvanised tub, a half-used pack of binder twine, and a couple of buckets, all now stacked neatly against one wall. Glancing behind him he saw that up on the back wall was a gallery, similar to that in Simpson's chapel, and also reached by a flight of steps. Unlike its fellow in North Tawe, this gallery looked highly precarious, with some of its supports having come away, or been wrenched, from the side walls. He thought it could fall at any moment, and he noticed that the current chapel occupants had kept well clear of it.

The main room was smoky, and he felt his eyes water, but blinking the moisture away, he saw that the beatniks had got a small fire going in one corner, using one of the abandoned buckets with holes in it, standing on a couple of bricks, as a brazier. They had tried, less successfully, to manufacture a kind of chimney, using bent sheets of rusty galvanised iron – something in plentiful supply on and around Devon farmland – and hoping presumably to guide most of the smoke up to a particular hole in the slate roof. It had been that smoke, of course, that Derek had seen as he approached the chapel. A couple of the few remaining pews in the building were grouped around the brazier, together with some sleeping bags. Recent nights must have been bitterly cold, a price to pay, Derek thought, for the freedom of life on the open road.

Apart from the girl – Derek found he couldn't think of her as Aphrodite, or even Miss Wondergirl - there were four others present, two girls and two men. Derek nodded to them.

"Hello," he said in what he hoped was a comradely tone. They looked back at him but said nothing. Their contempt for his presence and his uniform, was palpable.

"I better introduce you, now you're here," the girl said. "Girls and boys, this gentleman in the helmet is... Oh dear. I don't know your name."

"Derek." he said rather weakly. He should have said "Police Constable Martin," but it was too late now.

The others seemed unmoved, then one of the men raised a hand in a mock Roman salute, and said: "Hail Derek!"

The girl continued with the introductions: "This," she indicated one of the young men who had hair over his ears and a guitar his lap and a saxophone by his side "is Phillip. He's our musician. And the lady by his side," she indicated a remarkably pretty little girl of about 17, with long ringlets cascading down over an old paisley dress "is Sammy, she's his girlfriend and his singer."

"Hello." Derek tried again. No response except for a chord on the guitar. At least, he thought, it was in tune.

"Now over here..." the tall girl indicated with a sweep of her hand, "This is Jennifer. She's our doctor."

The girl, dark and intelligent – well, at least she wore glasses – looked up from the corner of the floor, where she sat surrounded by jars, small bottles, and various bits of greenery. "I'm the apothecary," she corrected, in a distinctly upper-class accent. "Herbalist, if you prefer. Or homeopath. Whatever. How can I help you today,

Constable Derek? I have a cure for everything. As you see."

Derek, caught off guard, mumbled: "Sorry, there's nothing wrong with me."

"I doubt that, somehow", said Jennifer. "Can I suggest a dose of this?" She held up a small bottle with a tiny cork in its neck. "It would do your wife a power of good. Make her very happy."

Derek pulled a face. "You expect my wife to drink that?" he asked.

"Oh no. She doesn't drink it. You do. Then you will make her very happy. All night."

A burst of laughter from the others told Derek he was being teased again. Good God, as if the local yokels weren't enough. He felt himself blushing.

"You've gone pink, Constable," said the tall girl. And the others laughed again.

"And who's that?" Derek, anxious to move things on, pointed at the second of the men, a squat and furtive-looking chap of about twenty-five, crouched over something in an enamel basin. Derek remembered him as the lad who had clashed with Yellow Waistcoat at the hunt meet.

"That's Mad Harry. He's our provider, if you like. He gets things for us."

"Things?" Derek queried. "What things?"

"These things!" said the man Harry, and held up the contents of his basin. It proved to be a half-dismembered rabbit.

"I wish you'd do that outside," said the tall girl, with an unexpected glimpse of domesticity.

"Too bloody cold outside," came the reply.

There was a moment, then the man got up and began to collect up some kit, heading for the door.

"So this lot, they do what you tell them, do they?" asked Derek.

"They do what I need them to do. Of course they do." She adopted a histrionic style. "Why? Because I cast a spell on them. I am their guru! Like your holy man said, I'm a witch!" She pulled a mock-devilish face.

"Sure you are." Derek tried to re-take charge of the conversation. "And Mad Harry, you say he gets you things. Like rabbits?"

"Yes, he does."

"And chickens?"

There was a brief but perceptible hiatus. Harry stopped at the door. The girl called Sammy coughed, and tried to smother the sound. The tall girl's expression didn't change, but the other four looked as guilty as poachers caught in the beam of the gamekeeper's torch.

"Chickens?" Derek asked again. "You see, there's a man called Joshua Voden, got a small place in the village. He says you've been nicking his chickens."

Nobody said anything, but he could sense the tall girl struggling with conflicting emotions. Then, abruptly, over her shoulder, she said: "Harry! You said they were run-over!" The boy didn't reply, just looked at the ground.

"So what were you doing with other people's chickens," Derek asked. "Casting the entrails?"

"We ate them!" the girl said tersely.

"Even the entrails," Harry contributed.

"Don't admit to anything, Lucy!" the dark girl, Jennifer, said sharply.

"Oh it's Lucy, is it?" Derek exclaimed, with a certain feeling of triumph. "Not Aphrodite. But Lucy. Lucy, Jennifer, Sammy, Phillip and Mad Harry. Quite a crew, aren't you. I think our local magistrates would describe you as thieves and vagabonds. Well? What have you got to say for yourselves?"

Lucy sighed. "Would you like a cup of tea, Constable?" she asked.

* * *

For the fourth time in ten minutes, Mary slipped silently up the stairs and into the main bedroom. The boy, Terry, was still asleep, and the dog Blondie was nearly so, opening just one eye at her and grunting peacefully.

She stepped quietly to the bedside, and looked down at Terry, wondering yet again who he was, and why he bore the scars of severe punishment. It wasn't hard to guess the reason he'd been found collapsed and unconscious in the marshland. He'd been escaping from something, from somewhere, she was sure. But what?

Well, no doubt Welbeloved was making enquiries. And no doubt the boy would be reported missing. And no doubt at all that in due course she would be told to hand him over, presumably to those from whom he had run.

"Over my dead body," she murmured aloud.

Terry stirred, his face emerging from being part-hidden between pillow and blanket. Instinctively she reached down and stroked his hair.

It wasn't that he was the most attractive of children, she thought pensively. He wasn't the perfect pretty bubble-blowing soap advertisement type of child. Mousy hair, a snub nose, even his ears stuck out a little. And his mouth, open now and dribbling slightly, showed uneven and protruding teeth. And that didn't matter. What he looked like was irrelevant, it didn't come into it. He was a child in desperate need. Which was why he was there, in her home, in her bed.

She stroked his hair again, and his eyes opened to look up at her.

"Hello Terry," she said.

"Hello Mummy," he said.

* * *

The tea was strong and good. Derek found a place on one of the pews near the fire and sipped it thirstily. He felt better now. A truce seemed to have been agreed. And one of his niggles was over. The fate of Joshua's chickens had been revealed.

Lucy came to squat down on the floor at his feet. She produced an every-day housewife's purse.

"So how much do we owe for, Joshua, was it? anyway, his chickens?"

"How many were there?"

Lucy looked at Mad Harry, who seemed to have abandoned his rabbit-skinning. The boy held up two gore-stained fingers.

"Ten bob should do it," Derek said, thinking if it wasn't enough, it would serve the old boy right for all his nonsense in the chicken shed about knowing the things by name.

The girl dug in the purse. There were, he saw with some surprise, quite a few one-pound and five-pound notes in it. He accepted a rather crinkly ten-shilling note, and pushed it into his breast pocket. As he did so, he felt his fingers contacting the cutting that he had taken from the Minister's home. That niggle flared in his mind. After today's fracas with Simpson he told himself he needed to read it, as soon as possible. It might tell him a lot more about the overbearing man. But not now. He watched as Lucy snapped the purse shut.

"You're not exactly short of cash, are you!" he told her.

"None of your business." She said it with a smile.

"It might be. And it explains something else."

"What?"

"The cards in the graveyards. Expensive print job. That has to be you, doesn't it? Couldn't be anyone else. I was thinking you couldn't afford printing of that class, but now..."

Lucy nodded. "It's us."

"I thought it must be. Certainly couldn't be someone local. They're a nice lot in North Tawe, you know. Even the hunters. But something like those cards - not their style."

"More likely it was that bunch of weirdos, as they undoubtedly call us, camped down in the old chapel. That was your deduction, was it, officer?"

"It was. And by the way, you're known by the local civilians as the Beatniks."

"Hear that, you lot?" She called to the others. "We're the Beatniks."

The others gave a minor cheer.

Derek felt he was on a roll, and it was a chance to tackle another niggle. "So tell me about the cards," He insisted. "What's it all about?"

"We just want you to remember those women. Which I hope you can."

"Do you indeed? Let's see. Temperance." He paused. Lucy looked at him sardonically. "Hang on. Temperance." and then, in a rush, the names came tumbling out. "Temperance Lloyd. Susannah Edwards. Mary Trembles."

"Good boy!" Lucy clapped him briefly. "You remember them. It's a start."

"Bully for me. But what have they got to do with North Tawe?" he asked.

"It's more like what have they got to do with Devon. In fact the whole of the west country. We've been spreading them around ever since we got down this way. Even in Exeter. You'd think the local papers would have picked up the story, but..."

"Local papers - they're more interested in the fat stock prices, and who's dead," Derek told her. "So. Who are Temperance and her other ladies?"

Lucy shot a look at him, and now, not for the first time, Derek felt intuitively that she was interested in him, even liked him. He felt suddenly nervous, but at the same time, incredibly pleased.

"I think I'll leave you to find that out for yourself.," she said. "You will find out, you know. I can tell. I can foresee the future." She pulled another fantastic face. "Remember what Holy Joe called me, just now? I'm a witch! I dance in the dawning light. I howl at the moon. I commune with the spirits, with the elves and the fairies."

Derek laughed hesitantly. "Fairies, eh?"

"Don't you believe in fairies? You should. There are fairies at the bottom of your garden, you know."

"I don't think there are, you know."

"How do you know? Have you looked for them? Have you gone down to the bottom of your garden and called for them? Left them little gifts? Have you listened carefully? Have you heard them singing their fairy songs?"

"Well no. Course I haven't."

"Then truth is, you don't know whether they do or don't exist. Right?" Her big eyes bored into him and seemed to glow with a kind of inner heat.

Derek floundered. His insides lurched again. He could think of nothing to say. Some of the others saw his discomfort, and giggled to themselves.

He sipped his tea, and decided to drag the conversation back to practicalities.

"Leaving aside all that sort of thing. One other thing I would like to know," he said. "How do you lot make ends meet? I know there's the dole but..."

"They don't give the dole to people like us," the girl sneered. "You must know that. Give national assistance to a scruffy lot like us? Drop-outs? Satanists? No chance. No, we earn our living. We put on a show for people."

"What sort of show?"

"Phillip plays. Sammy sings. I do my thing. Harry takes the hat around. We did well in Exeter, in the Cathedral Close. But the Christians got stroppy, so we thought we'd give Okehampton a try, but the weather's so bad, and no-one's got the time, all too busy doing things to the soil with their poisons..."

"Hang on a minute," Derek interjected. "Your thing? What's your thing? Summoning up the devil?"

"Close. I'm a knife-thrower."

"A what?"

"Knife-thrower. You know. Get someone out of the audience, stand them up against a bit of board and chuck knives at them. It's called, if you want to get technical, the Art of Impalement. Though the idea is not actually to impale anyone. Just come close."

Christ, he wasn't being kidded again, was he? "And you do that? Seriously?"

"Mmm. My Dad had an act, back in the twenties. Taught me."

Derek said without thinking: "Now that I'd like to see!"

"Why don't you show him, Lucy?" the girl Sam urged her. The other three joined in. "Yeah, show him your stuff, Lucy. Go on. Let him see."

"All right." Lucy grinned, perhaps a little maliciously. "Why not? Fix it up, Harry."

The boy Harry hauled a large board of about seven feet by four from a corner of the chapel. He propped it up against a space on the wall. Then, from the same corner, he pulled out a flat box of highly polished wood, and handed it to Lucy.

Lucy looked into Derek's eyes, watching his reaction as she opened the box. The contents glittered, even in the dull light of the chapel interior. Knives. Two, a matching pair, with carved wooden handles and wide blades, each about twelve to fifteen inches long.

More knives in boxes, he thought, remembering Simpson's flick knife.

But this was different. The more he looked at the girl's knives, the more they impressed him. The blades were flawless, at least at an amateur first glance, and the handles had gold threads running through the woodwork.

"They were my father's knives," she told him, and there was respect and pride in her voice.

"Your father?"

"Antonio – The Fiend Of The Flashing Blade."

"Antonio? You're Italian then?"

"No." She gave a rueful smile. "He was Tony from Northampton. But..."

Derek wanted to handle one of the knives, but decided it would be bad manners, and possibly unwise in other respects. Instead he said: "They look sharp."

"They have to be. Got to stick in the board. Or wherever they land. Come on."

She was on her feet, the knives held together in one hand. The other caught Derek's arm and lifted him up.

"Okay. Stand over there," she ordered.

"Over where?"

"Against the board, silly!"

"What? Me? No way. Thanks very much but..."

"You're not scared, surely. A big bold policeman like you. And one with flaming red hair. Redheads are ready for anything, aren't they?" There was challenge in her voice. Then, making it a compelling command: "Stand against the board, man!"

Derek stood against the board, his back to it. First, they make dogs chase me, he told himself. Now they want to throw knives at me. And it's not even tea-time. He almost giggled. Why was he doing it? Was he hypnotised? Something in the tea? That girl Jennifer and her potions? Or was it just the way Lucy looked at him? He could easily chicken out. He could walk away. But he didn't.

The girl took up a position some eight or ten feet away. One knife remained in her left hand, gripped by the handle. The other she held in her right hand by the tip of the shining blade. Her legs were braced, her head high, she looked magnificent.

"Whatever you do, don't move."

Derek didn't move. Not a muscle twitched. It is questionable whether he could have moved. His legs, his arms, felt gripped, as if with a bad cramp. He tried to say something, but nothing came.

Lucy's arm swung up and back, then forward. The blade hissed through the smoky chapel air.

CHAPTER THIRTEEN

On his ride back to the village Derek debated with himself whether to tell Mary about the beatniks. She'd want to know, of course. She'd be suspicious, too, especially if he went on too much about Lucy. Which, if he wasn't careful, he might do. The woman, he no longer thought of her as a girl, was unforgettable. He'd never known anyone so emotionally powerful, so sure of herself, so sensually appealing.

She'd come to the porch of the chapel when he'd finally decided to leave, and she stopped him with an arm on his sleeve.

"Derek, I should thank you for not chucking us out," she'd told him, without smiling.

"Well, I can't guarantee you can stay. That Simpson, he's respected around here. He could complain to the Okehampton station. Probably will. Get a court order or something."

"I hope not." Lucy's voice wavered for a moment. She sighed with apparent exhaustion. "God, I hope not. Lord knows where we'd find somewhere else. It's too cold for sleeping in haystacks or barns... at least here we can have a fire. I don't know. This lot tend to rely on me, you see. But sometimes I feel quite desperate. "

So there's another side to Lucy, he thought. A vulnerable, even a guilty side. A gentler side, certainly. For a moment he thought the girl was near tears, then she seemed to rein back, to get tough again.

"Why did that bloody preacher have to interfere?" she suddenly demanded. "People like that, trying to get rid of us, kill us off. There's always one, you know. Or more than one. Wherever we go. They seem to hate us. Want to kill us. Just because we're different. I tell you, give me half a chance, I could kill them. Honestly, I could!"

Derek was a little shocked by her sudden aggression, and was relieved when she went on: "Anyway, thanks for... well, not taking his side. You're a nice man, Derek. For a policeman, a very nice man. You can always come here, you know. You know where I live, don't you? For the moment, anyway. And that's how life should be, don't you think. For the moment?"

She smiled and then she did something he had never seen done before. She kissed the tips of the two fingers on her right hand, then reached and pressed them against his lips.

Then she ducked back inside, and Derek went rather uncertainly to his motorbike.

* * *

He didn't go straight home. Instead he stopped off at the untidy homestead of Joshua Voden.

"They'll deny it if I try to bring a charge," he told Joshua as they sheltered in the doorway of the man's chicken shed. "And there's no evidence. But I reckon they did nick a couple of your birds.

"Told you, didn't I!"

"Yes. But there's no proof, nothing I can take to court. But I told them they owed you something for the birds. How much would you say they're worth?"

Joshua shrugged. "Coupla bob, maybe. Each, mind you."

"Then you're in profit." Derek fished the ten-shilling note from his breast pocket, and handed it over. Joshua stared at the note with ill-concealed glee, then looked at Derek slyly.

"I reckon they may have taken a couple more, you know."

Derek glanced at the milling flock of chicken. "No they haven't," he said.

"How do you know?"

"I just counted them. Like you do. They're all there. Even Esmerelda."

At last, he thought with grim satisfaction. At last he'd got one over the local yokel. Hurrah for me!

* * *

"It looks like it's coming straight at you. Like an arrow. It flashes out of her hand, and for a moment you think it's going to stick in your head. And then at the last possible moment it seems to swerve away and goes thwack just past your ear. Honest, I thought I was a goner. And then she says 'stay quite still' again, and the other one comes straight at you before going thwack again just past the other ear. Bloody amazing. Bloody terrifying!"

"Bloody silly, too." Mary snapped. She had listened with what was obviously growing impatience as Derek related what he had undergone that afternoon, but he was regretting it now as he realised his wife wasn't impressed.

"What do you think you're doing, getting involved with people like that?" she asked with considerable asperity.

"They're quite normal, really, you know. Quite ordinary. You'd like them."

"Normal? A chicken thief? A busker? A knife thrower? And some girl making quack medicine?"

Derek suddenly decided he needed to change out of his uniform, and escaped upstairs. He used the empty spare room, as Terry slept on in their main bedroom. Taking his jacket off, his hand touched the clipping he had lifted from the Minister's house. The niggle over that flared up. He must read it properly, try to make something of it. He was ever more inclined to believe that there was indeed something to make of it.

Downstairs, over tea and scones, he managed to steer the conversation away from the subject of Lucy, and instead now related the whole saga of the afternoon. Mary had grimaced when he mentioned his confrontation with Simpson.

"I'm not sure about that man," she admitted. "Not cos he's chapel and I'm church, but he stands so tall and proud, so sure of himself. Still, he's right, that old ruin is still a chapel. Possibly consecrated ground. And you wouldn't want a bunch of weirdos moving into a place that belonged to you, now, would you?"

"They're not that weird."

Derek found himself trying to find positive things to say about the tribe, finishing by describing Jennifer and her herbalist activities. "Quack medicine," as Mary had described it.

Then she added: "I hope she didn't give any of her potions to you."

Derek hesitated. Tell the truth, he told himself. The whole truth. And nothing but the truth.

"Well, she insisted," he confessed. "When I was going. She said I should have this. It seemed rude to refuse, so..."

He produced the girl's small bottle of liquid.

"And what's supposed to be for, then?" Mary demanded.

"Oh, you know, general good health." Watch it, he warned himself silently. Better not tell the whole truth.

"No, tell me. Specifically. What does it do? What happens? Does it make mushrooms grow out of the top of your head? What?"

Oh all right, she better have the whole truth. "No, it, well, it's supposed to make me last longer. I mean, be more of a man, you know."

"In bed?" Two loaded words. Loaded with Lord knew what.

"Well. Yes."

"And you were going to try it, were you?"

"No, no, of course not." Derek didn't even convince himself. Let alone Mary.

She snatched the bottle from his hand, stood up, marched the two steps to the kitchen sink, uncorked the flask, and poured the contents away.

Derek waited. When she was sure she'd got all the contents out, she dumped the bottle in the rubbish bin, then came and sat down facing him again.

Derek felt himself blushing. Mary reached across the table and took both of his hands in hers. Then she leaned forward and looked into his eyes intently. He blushed some more.

"You. Don't. Need. It!" she said, drawing each word out with heavy emphasis.

Then she grinned, and he grinned, and they had a very good moment together.

There was a noise above their heads. Two bare feet?

"Terry!" And Mary had gone in a flurry, and Derek heard her footsteps tripping up the bare wooden stairs like the tapping of a side drum. They needed a stair carpet, he remembered. One day...

* * *

Christmas and New Year were a bonus season for the North Tawe village pub, the Green Dragon. Apart from the major celebratory evenings there were plenty of visitors seeking bucolic weekends with country relatives and friends, and then there were those lucky enough to have the time off work, and all this meant some busy lunchtime sessions.

But there was a sad cloud hanging over the pub. John the landlord's wife, Cathy lay upstairs, suffering from an ever more aggressive cancer of the lung. Once she had played a full part of the running of the place, taking a cheerful turn behind the bar, and even baking miniature pasties in the kitchen range, which sold for 10 pence each, and you had to be quick to get your change across the bar before the supply ran out. But that had been then, in long-lost summery days. Now, Cathy would never bake another pasty or stand behind a beer pump again. Three months ago her husband had learned the meaning of the word 'metastasis' and he and his daughter knew they would lose her, probably early in the New Year.

Daughter Sandy did what she could, learning to prepare family meals, helping keep the place tidy, but everyone agreed that it was a lot to ask of a teenage girl. John meanwhile determined to make his wife's last days as comfortable, and even diverting, as possible. An informal rota of local wives popped in to sit with her, talk village gossip, perhaps read to her. Becoming more imaginative, John installed one of the first television sets in the village in a corner of the bedroom, and its flickering blue screen helped Cathy pass the long evenings. Expensive, of course, but without being asked the darts team and some prominently placed collection boxes took care of that. Looking further afield, John read in the Daily Express about the new reel-to-reel portable tape-recorders that were just coming on the market. A sympathetic bank manager helped him buy one, and the couple took turns recording little messages to each other on it. Then John set it on the counter of the bar, and regular customers left their own beery messages of good will, which he would play back to her in the morning, the two of them rocking with laughter. It all helped. A little.

Then John had another idea. One of his regulars, an ageing professional rabbit-trapper known to everyone as Old Gerry, had a reputation, mostly self-promoted, as a folk singer. Indeed, he had sung some of his collection of old Devon melodies at the occasional village hall concert, and there was no doubting the authenticity of his material, even if the church organist on the hall piano found it a struggle to keep up with the actual tune. John decided to capture Gerry's songs on tape, partly for posterity, but mostly because he knew Cathy would find them fun.

And that was exactly what he was doing, on this quiet Monday morning with just a couple of customers plus Gerry himself in the bar. Gerry was just warming up by rehearsing one of his favourites – a grim little ditty about blackbirds, which went something like this...

"Here come a blackbird through the window...

"Here come a blackbird through the door.

"Here come a blackbird through the window

"Hey diddle dee dum day."

Not that inspiring, John thought, but it was a start. Armed with a free pint – essential for vocal lubrication, of course – the old man crouched over the little machine. John's finger was poised over the 'record' button, he snapped it down, and like a true trouper, Gerry began.

But he only got as far as the second blackbird when the recording came to an abrupt half because the blasted telephone rang.

The phone in the Green Dragon was situated not in the bar, but in the hall, further back towards the newly-constructed 'Gents'. (A new 'Ladies' had not been provided or even considered by an old-fashioned brewery when they fitted the place out. Females in need were directed up the stairs to the household bathroom.) So when the phone rang, John had to apologise to Old Gerry, who grumbled, even now beginning to exhibit the temperament of a Johnnie Ray. Meanwhile the phone kept ringing and John had to head off down the hall to answer the thing.

* * *

In the red telephone kiosk on the North Tawe village square Neville waited breathlessly, the receiver jammed up against his ear, and his heart pounding. When the muffled ringing stopped, and John's voice came on the line, Neville, a youth who considered himself well up with the complexities of modern technology, stupidly pressed button 'B' instead of 'A'. His four pennies rattled into the change compartment and the line went dead.

"Bugger," said Neville.

"Someone playing silly buggers," John told daughter Sandy, who had joined him in a rush.

"Oh." Sandy looked guilty.

John nodded. "You were expecting the Brain of Britain, I suppose."

"He'll probably try again," Sandy half-confessed.

"You sure about our Nev?" John asked. He tried hard not to interfere with his daughter's love life, but Neville Parsons, of all people...

"He's very good hearted," Sandy protested. "He means well."

"Uh-huh. Those are the ones to watch out for." John wandered back up to the bar, whistling lightly. He felt rather pleased with himself for that last remark.

Sandy waited. She waited for five minutes. She was about to give up when the phone rang again.

"Hello. Nev?"

In the phone box Neville jabbed furiously at Button A, hurting his thumb in the process.

"Oh fuck," he said.

"What?" Sandy said.

"Oh. Sorry, sorry, sorry, hurt me thumb on the thing, sorry." A pause then, as rehearsed a hundred times. "Can I speak to Sandy please.?"

"Sandy speaking, for heaven's..."

"Oh hi, Sandy. This is...err... "For a fraction of a millisecond Neville forgot his own name. "This is Neville."

"Hello Nev. Was that you just now?"

"Yeah. Pressed the wrong button, didn't I!"

"Clot." It is impossible to say precisely how Sandy managed to convey affection in that one word, but she did. "So. What do you want? As if I didn't know..."

"Yes, well. I was wondering when we might get together. You know. Like we said." As indeed they had said, on that bus ride back to the village, when a certain mutual attraction had rapidly become scorching desire on both sides, and Neville had nearly forgotten to collect the haunch of venison his mother was waiting for.

"Well, when?" Sandy asked.

"Any time. You say."

"And where? I mean, I was thinking about it. Where can we get any privacy? Can't come here, it's a bloody pub. Can't go to yours, too far away and anyway I'm not biking out there, I'm not like you."

"Well..." At least she'd been thinking about it.

"And I'm not walking round the streets and hiding in doorways. Not in this weather."

"No, course not, but... if I can think of somewhere. Somewhere safe. I mean, I really want to see you again, Sandy. And quick."

"Me too, Nev. I want to see you too."

The warmth in her voice made Neville's heart swell with hope.

"Find us somewhere then," she told him. "And ring me, soon as you do."

Neville put the receiver back on its stand, pushed open the kiosk door, and stood, gazing around the square. There had to be somewhere.

Jesus, there was. He was almost looking at it. It was just down the road. Bloody hell! Just round the corner, down the little road...and it would do!

He was back in the phone box, dialling frantically. Then slamming the receiver back again. Pennies! He needed four more pennies. Out on the village square and a quick sprint across to the grocery store. A Penguin, and could he have four pennies in the change? Please? Out again, another dash, and... oh effing hell and damnation, now there was someone else in the call box. And it was a woman. It had to be a woman, didn't it! They talk, they talk too much, women do. Well some of them do. Not

Neville's Mum, she only talked when she had something to say. And Sandy, she said nice things. Naughty things... But most women, it's all chat, chat, chat, about nothing, too. Dammit. Dammit to hell.

Neville paced up and down, passing the box each time, peering in, making sure the woman, who he vaguely recognised but not enough to know her name, was actually speaking, and not just holding the receiver and nodding off to sleep where she stood. Neville longed to jerk the door open and demand to know how long the woman was going to be with her pointless chattering, and did she know he had an urgent call to make... but he didn't. He knew that if he did, such scandalous behaviour would spread through the village with the speed of the Black Death, it would be another sin to lay at the door of the Parsons family, none of them's no good, that's what would be said, and his father would find out and there'd be hell to pay. All the same, he could just open the door gently, and enquire. Couldn't he?

He didn't have to. Abruptly the caller put the phone back on its cradle and turned to exit. In turning she had become a little confused, and began pushing madly at the side of the box that didn't open. Neville swooped. He gallantly opened the door, and almost bowed the lady out into the open air.

"Thank you, young Neville," she told him.

"My pleasure, Missus," he replied.

She began to say something about the weather, a comment that she had just made several times during her phone call to her sister, but her rescuer wasn't there to hear it. She turned to see that he was already back inside the phone box, pumping pennies into the slot, waiting motionless, then banging Button A as if he loathed the sight of it.

"Hello Sandy? Just to tell you, I got an idea! A place! Somewhere we can be alone. I got to check it out, and I'll get back to you, but I reckon it could be just the ticket!"

CHAPTER FOURTEEN

Terry sat at one end of the kitchen table, perched on a mercifully soft cushion, eating Puffed Wheat. Blondie lay on a rug which Mary had spread in a corner by the door, and chewed on a cartoon-sized beef bone. Mary stood at the stove in her apron, stirring some milk in the milk saucepan.

Derek sat and marvelled.

"These two are going to eat us out of house and home," he remarked casually.

"The butcher heard about Terry and Blondie. He brought round the bone for free. And some sausages."

"For us?"

"For Terry. He likes sausages, he told me. He's going to have sausages for supper. With chips. Aren't you, Terry?"

The boy nodded, his mouth full of cereal.

"Cocoa, Terry?"

More enthusiastic nodding.

"He likes cocoa too," Mary said, snatching the milk saucepan away from the heat just before it boiled over.

"You two have had quite a conversation, haven't you."

"Just chatting. You know. That reminds me, can you slip across to the shop, and get him a toothbrush a bit later? He says he'll get into trouble if he doesn't brush his teeth. Number One Punishment, apparently." She pulled a face at Derek which said 'something wrong here.'

Derek turned to the boy. "Don't worry, Terry. You won't get into trouble here. Sometimes I forget to brush my teeth, and I don't get into trouble."

"Oh yes he does," Mary said, in a roguishly mock-severe voice, and she and Derek laughed. Terry looked from one to the other, and managed a smile.

The door knocker echoed through the house.

"Who's that now?" Mary shrugged off her apron and disappeared.

Terry made a noise, something between a groan and a sigh, and, clearly scared, he went to get up from his chair.

Derek quickly reached across and laid a gentle hand on the boy's arm.

"It's okay, Terry," he told him. "No-one's going to hurt you. I know you've been hurt, but that's in the past now. I promise you; I won't let it happen again. You're safe now."

The boy nodded, half-convinced. Then he said: "You won't send me back?"

"Never." Send him back to what? Derek wondered. And if it came to that, would he be able to stop it? He was promising something he had no right to promise. But you have to say these things. You have to tell kids lies. Don't you?

There was a burst of laughter from the door, Mary with an explosion of both surprise and pleasure. Then a loud man's voice said something, in an unusual accent, and then the two voices were talking and laughing together. Derek and Terry exchanged glances. Derek grinned reassuringly. Whoever was at the door didn't sound very threatening.

Then there were footsteps in the hall, and Mary was saying "No, don't be silly, come on in. Come on..."

And then, in something of a flurry, and contrasting with her normal calm and collected manner, Mary was back in the kitchen, physically leading by the arm a tall and rather apologetic-looking man in his mid-twenties.

"Look who's here!" Mary exclaimed.

"Yes, look who's here..." Derek said rather dryly. "In fact – who *is* here?" He smiled to take any sting out of his words.

"It's Matt! You remember Matt. Oh no, wait a minute. Of course, he'd gone by the time we met. Matt and I were at college together. Doing the Dip. Ed. Sorry, I should introduce you properly. Matt, this is my husband, Derek. Derek, this is Matthew Mark."

Derek rose from his chair, and the two men shook hands. The hand Derek shook was dry and firm, and the man met his eye steadily, even warmly. Matt loomed large in the small kitchen. He wore a stylish suit in a gentle beige colour, and his brown sweater and dark gold tie were in excellent taste, even Derek, despite his doubtful fashion sense, could recognise that. What's more, the man generated a sense of good will, of friendliness. It was difficult not to like him, even at first meeting.

"Call me Matt," he told Derek. "Good to meet you, mate. You know, we always wondered who our Mary would bestow her favours on. She wouldn't have any of us. We all tried, but," he grinned confidentially and gave a knowingly comic groan, "she just wanted to be friends."

"I know what you mean," Derek said, warming even more to the man.

"We used to tease you, didn't we," Mary remembered. "Because of your accent."

"Yes, what is that accent?" Derek queried.

"Accent?" said Matt, with mock indignation. "What accent? No, I speak proper, mate. The Queen's English. At least I think she is. Ha! No. No, truth is, mate, I lived in Australia, till I was sixteen. You ever heard of Australia? God's country, they call it. And he's welcome to it."

"And now you're another teacher, are you?" Derek asked.

"Sorry, no. Teaching's not for me. Too difficult. Hard sums, and all that. No, I'm in child welfare. Part of Devon social services. Which is why I'm here." He turned to focus on Terry, who had stayed motionless in his chair, a spoonful of Puffed Wheat halfway on the journey to his mouth. "To say hello to this young man. Hello. My name's Matt. Matt, like what you wipe your boots on. What's your name then?"

"Terry." the boy said, then smiled at Matt.

Derek felt a slight twinge of jealousy. The boy clearly liked this big chattering man. But then, he liked him too.

"He likes you," he told the tall Australian.

"And I like him," Matt said. "Which is how it should be."

"Careful. He's still very traumatised," Mary told him.

"Of course he is. I'm not here to ask him a whole lot of questions. Just to make contact, to see he's all right. Which, judging from the amount of Puffed Wheat he can get on one spoon, he is."

Then he dropped the avuncular manner, and quietly asked Mary: "I understand he's been damaged, is that right?"

"Viciously," Derek put in.

Matt sighed. "Bastards. In that case, I really should take a look. For the record."

"Oh please, Matt. No," Mary protested. "For heaven's sake. How would you feel if you were a little boy and everyone kept looking at your bottom?"

"You've got a point," Matt said. "Problem is, marks fade. Children heal so quickly, and then there's no evidence. I know. Let's ask the man himself." He turned to Terry, but before he could ask him anything Terry said: "Okay. Don't mind."

"But upstairs," Mary said, taking Terry's hand. "And I'll get you that cocoa after." And then, to the suddenly stirring Blondie, "all right, doggie, you can come too."

Left alone, Derek remembered something. He fished in his breast pocket, and produced the piece of folded newsprint, purloined from the Reverend Simpson's drawer, and now getting ever-more crumpled and creased. It proved, with a quick glance, to be a cutting from some religious newspaper, the title of which had been missed when the cutting was made. The date was there – May 4,1927. And the headline read: "Plymouth Gangster Thompson 'Washed in the Blood of the Lamb'."

Before he could read more, Derek heard footsteps on the stairs, with a combination of dog and boy clearly leading the way, and he put the cutting back safely in his pocket. He'd look at it again. Soon. When he had a minute.

Dog, boy, Matt and "Mummy" clattered back into the kitchen, and she began the business of cocoa-making all over again. But Matt stood at the kitchen door, caught Derek's eye and with a subtle head movement indicated that he wanted a private word. He followed Derek into the front room that served as the police office, shutting the door behind him. Then Matt turned, standing in the middle of the room, tall, upright, a picture of outrage, condemnation, and fury. The cosy, chatty nice man of the kitchen had been replaced by someone somewhat different.

"I trust you'll get the bastard who did that," he said grimly.

"We will," Derek said. "He shouldn't be hard to find, once we establish exactly who Terry is."

"Get him. Lock him up. Then birch the bastard." Matt was almost incoherent. Then he pulled himself together. "How can they do that?" he demanded. "How can an adult do that to a child? Such cruelty. Bastards. You know who they are, don't you? They're always the ones who look holier than thou, the stuck-up ones, the ones who butter wouldn't melt in their... "He changed tack again, becoming earnest and enquiring. "What will he get?" "He asked. "The culprit? What punishment?"

Derek sucked his teeth. "It's a tricky area, you know. There's no law against a parent smacking their kid. Or caning them, for that matter. Of course there's a law against cruelty to children, but, well, you said yourself. Scars fade. Statements can be challenged. Kids are frightened to speak up. Cases fail. I know it's hard, but..."

"You know what they have in Australia?" Matt interrupted. Once again he was spitting with rage. "Vigilantes. When they can't get the law to act, the people get together and serve out their own justice."

"And a lot of innocent people get lynched?" Derek suggested dryly.

"Yeah, yeah." Matt took a deep shuddering breath. "Listen, I'm sorry. I shouldn't go off on one like that. I know – God, I should know, should be used to it, the job I'm doing. But then I've only been at it a short time. Before they made me Child Welfare Officer, I was on domestics. Adults. They get beaten up, too, but, when it's kids, it's so much worse."

"Of course it is. But you have to stay calm. You can't get emotionally involved. Difficult, I know." Derek felt another wave of affection for the big awkward character, who seemed to wear his heart on his sleeve.

"Well." Matt managed an apologetic grin, and seemed to come down about two inches in height as he did so. "Again, sorry I blew my top."

Derek was about to say something equally pacific, when the telephone rang, and he went to answer it.

"North Tawe police. Yes. Oh. Yes. He's right here, I'll pass you over."

He called Matt into the hall. Matt took over the receiver, fumbling a notebook and pencil from his sports jacket pocket as he did so. Derek left him to it, and returned to the kitchen.

"So how are we all getting along in here?" he asked. "Finished our cocoa?"

Terry looked up from his mug with a grin. His top lip was chocolate-coloured.

"We've nearly finished," Mary said. "Then we're going to have a game of football in the garden, before it gets dark."

"Yes," Terry said, with a more definite tone than he had previously shown. "You and me and Matt and Mummy."

"Then Mummy's going in goal," Mary told him.

Derek put gentle arms around her. "You do sound like a Mummy, you know. Must be a natural."

Then for almost the first time the boy spoke up without being asked a question. "I know she's not my real mummy," he told Derek. "But I like to call her that. If it's all right. I do have a real mummy, but..." his voice tailed off.

"Would you like to tell us about your real mummy," Derek asked, quietly but firmly.

"She's very pretty. But sometimes she's a bit funny. She lives in London."

"Uh-huh. And what about Daddy?"

The boy grinned for a moment. "He's nice. He lives in Hong Kong." Then, with a typical mood change: "I don't see him much." He got up, clearly feeling he'd said enough. "Can't we play football?"

"Oh right, yes, course we can." Then to Mary: "Hang on, we haven't got a football."

"We have, haven't we, Terry!" Like a magician pulling a rabbit out of a hat, Mary pulled a full-size leather ball from beneath the kitchen table. "Dad brought it round earlier. Borrowed it from the club."

"Right!" Derek took the ball, and handed it to Terry. "Football it is. All of us. Including, I suspect, Blondie."

The dog looked up eagerly on hearing her name.

"And Matt," Terry said. "He can play."

"No he can't." Matt had appeared, framed in the kitchen door. "'Fraid not. Sorry, got to go. Duty calls."

"Oh shame," Mary cried. "And I never even offered you a cup of tea. Can't you stay for supper?"

"No. That was my office. Bit of an emergency. Apparently, you've got a group of beatniks or travellers, camped out in an old chapel. Place called..." he consulted the notebook in his hand. "Fursdon?"

Mary and Derek exchanged glances. "Yes, we know about them," Mary said.

"Well, apparently they've got a couple of toddlers with them, half-starved, filthy, you know the sort of thing."

Mary began: "But surely..." but Derek cut her off. "Matt," he said seriously, "I was just up there this afternoon. There are no children there, I promise you. Five adults, beatnik types, yes. But no kids. Who on earth said there was?"

"Some informant. On the phone. Anonymous of course. Someone with an axe to grind. Still, I've got to check it out. Better get there before it's too dark. But I'll see you soon. That's a promise." He grinned. "Or maybe a threat!"

Derek saw him off at the door. He cut quite a figure, he thought, in his stylish clothes, as he jumped into a smart little MG. Derek watched jealously as it roared up the road. Then he, Terry and Blondie played football. Mary cooked sausages and, rather nervously in a pot of boiling lard, chips. Terry and Blondie won the football game. Terry ate a mountain of chips. But Derek's mind wasn't on football or chips. "Someone with an axe to grind." He couldn't get a worrying picture out of his mind. A picture of the Reverend Donald Simpson wielding a huge axe.

CHAPTER FIFTEEN

"I checked it out, and it's perfectly safe, honest it is."

"You sure, Nev? Think how dreadful it would be if someone, you know, caught us at it. I mean, my dad would go bananas!"

"They won't. Promise." Neville found Sandy's voice thrilling on the phone, especially when she half-whispered to avoid being overheard.

"Yes, but all the same..."

"Listen. I been checking it out. There's never anyone there in the mornings, not on a week day. I promise you. Place is deserted. And no-one will see us go in, cos there's only that big wall opposite, no windows. And you go in round the side, through that porch. It's just the ticket, honest."

"But isn't it a bit sinful? You know, to... in a chapel?"

"Well." Neville was almost stuck for an answer on that one, then had an inspiration, and took a chance: "Sinful anywhere we go, isn't it?"

It worked. Sandy snorted with laughter. "But won't it be locked up, though?"

"No. They never lock up churches and that. That's why the poor box keeps getting robbed."

"By your lot, eh? The Parsons clan?"

"You don't think I'd stoop that low, do you?"

"I didn't mean you. I know you wouldn't. It's just..."

"Our reputation. I'm used to that." Neville's family had possibly deserved a certain reputation during the war, when they served as a conduit between townspeople who lacked eggs, butter, poultry and game, and countrymen who had an excess of all those goodies. And once acquired, a reputation is not easily lost, not in the small villages and hamlets of West Devon.

But Sandy's thoughts had moved on. "Yes, but what about the floor? I don't fancy lying on them cold tiles or whatever. Especially with your great frame on..."

She didn't finish. Perhaps it was just as well, because Neville had a sudden vision of himself lying on top of Sandy, and standing up in a cold, draughty and smelly phone box is no place for such a riot of imagination.

He found his voice: "No worries there, sweetheart. I had a scout around in there earlier, and they got these long cushions, like the ones that go on benches. They don't put them on the pews, I reckon they like the poor buggers to suffer during old Simpson's sermons. Anyway they got them stacked away, in this little side room. I reckon we nip in there, put three or four of these together, and it'll be like a double bed. Almost."

There was a short silence at Sandy's end. Then she said: "Oh Nev. I can't wait."

"Me neither. So. Listen. How about tomorrow?"

"Oh I can't. I'm off tomorrow, this course I'm on."

"What's that?"

"Well it's about nursing. They want me to do three days at the hospital in Exeter. See if I'm up to being a nurse. I've got to stay over. Sort of like an introduction to it."

"Three days?" It felt like an eternity. Or three years, at the least.

"I'll be back Thursday. Call me then. We'll fix it up."

"Okay." And then, tentatively, for the first time, "I love you, Sandy."

"You better!" A giggle, then, "Oh me too. Course I do."

"And I think you'll be a bloody marvellous nurse."

"Night, night." The line clicked off.

Neville's body blazed. He stepped out into the Square, and the sweat froze on his body.

"Sandy loves you," he told himself. "You lucky, lucky sod."

* * *

Sergeant Welbeloved rang Derek late that afternoon.

"Well Constable. How's that boy?"

"He's fine, Sergeant. So's Blondie."

"Never mind the bloody dog. Not our problem. Look, I've held off making a big fuss about this lad, putting out big enquiries and that, out of respect to your good lady. Told Child Welfare, of course, you'll hear from them, but other than that I've left things to her until now."

"She appreciates that, Sergeant. And I think she is the best person for the job at the moment. And she knows where he's come from, too."

"Oh, he told her, did he?"

"No. But you remember that top he was wearing? It was a rugby shirt. Mary recognised it. It's from a place called Havenhill School, they played the Grammar at rugger a couple of months ago. It's this side of Oke. No name tag, but she recognised the colours."

"Bloody hell. She's hot stuff, your Mary, isn't she! Should have been a Police Sergeant! Ha ha!" He laughed at the absurdity of the idea.

Someone should have been a Police Sergeant, Derek thought to himself, but didn't say so. Instead, "According to her, Havenhill is a private school, and pretty pricey."

"Yeah. I know it. Near Meldon Quarry. Back up into the moor a bit."

"Apparently, it's a bit special. Takes in boys with parents overseas, mainly. Government helps with the fees. And they also pay for the odd member of the awkward squad, lads who have worn out the state system. Strict discipline, apparently."

"Good thing too, if you ask me."

I didn't and I won't, Derek thought.

"Another thing," the Sergeant went on. "There's been some complaints. About a gang of beatniks near you, a wild bunch, living in a consecrated building." the Sergeant spoke slowly, clearly reading from a report, "Something about sacrilege, devil worship."

"I've looked into it, Sarge," Derek told him. "They're in that ruined chapel at the crossing they call Fursdon. Place is a wreck, no-one wants it. And that's nonsense about devil worship. They're just a bunch of youngsters, they're harmless, no problem, and they reckon they'll be moving on soon."

"They haven't summoned up the devil, then?" The man was only half joking.

"No. Mind you, if they get down to Cornwall, they might have more luck."

Welbeloved laughed. Jokes about darkest Cornwall always went down well. "All the same, glad to see the back of them. Don't want that sort around here."

"Matter of interest, Sarge, how many complaints have you had about them?"

The Sergeant hesitated, clearly reading from the incident book. Then: "Well, just the one, it seems. Anonymous, too."

The Reverend Donald Simpson? Grinding his axe?

"Well, duty calls." The Sergeant was, thankfully, ending the call. Probably time for his first visit to the bakery for a cream bun.

"Right-oh, Sarge."

"And you better check out that school of yours. See if they're missing one small boy. I'd send someone from here, seeing where it is, but we're a bit tied up at the mo. Let me know how you do."

Derek put the phone down. Typical bloody Welbeloved, he thought. One moment shocked by the sight of the boy's ill treatment, the next too busy to do anything about it. Well, he could. And he'd do it by doing what they were always telling him he shouldn't do – he'd do it on his own.

* * *

Half an hour later Derek and Mary knew more of the reasons why a small boy would run away from a decent school like Havenhill. But not quite all of them.

As a local teacher, Mary, of course, already knew more about the school than Derek. But even she only had a vague impression of it. It was housed mainly in a stern stone-built Victorian mansion, only a couple of miles out of Okehampton, but on the other rather inaccessible side of the Meldon Quarry. The quarry was a significant institution in West Devon, with a long and noisy history of extracting limestone and granite from the earth.

He was struck by another thought. If Terry came from that school – and that was still not confirmed - then the boy had run like a junior Zatopek. Some six miles, over some fairly wild Devon countryside. And presumably in the middle of the night. No wonder he'd been so... what was the word again? Traumatised. Good word to remember, that one.

Over tea he related the gist of what Welbeloved had told him to Mary. "It's boarders only, about 100 or so, a bit spartan they say. It's got one of these strict old-fashioned headmasters, the sort that believes in a healthy mind in a healthy body. Which translates to cold showers, long runs, and no talking after lights out."

"And what do you call it? Corporal punishment as well?"

"Yes, probably."

"But surely not a flaying like someone's given Terry."

Mary pulled a rueful face. "If you ask me, the real problem with schools like this is, they give senior boys, prefects, the right to beat the small ones. The sort of thing that leads directly to, well, cruelty. Abuse, anyway."

"Poor little sods." Derek thought of the regime in his own day-school, where no master would beat a boy for fear of being beaten himself outside the school gates.

Not a healthy situation either, but at least no boy went home with blood running down his legs.

Mary, deep in thought, made an awkward change of topic. "What did you think of our new friend Matt then?"

"I like him," he said frankly. "Bit of a character, but..."

"Bit of a lunatic, too," she said more soberly. "He goes over the top a bit, every now and then." She paused, but Derek sensed she had something else to say. She did. "Fact is, he had a real go at me, once. Out of the blue. Suddenly I was the love of his life, he couldn't live without me. Going to kill himself if I didn't go out with him."

"Bloody hell!"

"Exactly. Then suddenly, nothing. All back to normal. Weird."

* * *

Now in a morning brighter than most of the previous week, Derek stumbled down to the kitchen, and found Mary was making toast under the grill and their small guest, wrapped in one of Mary's spare dressing gowns and with a face bright and shining from a warm bath rather than a cold shower, was eating it by the slice.

"No puffed wheat today?" he asked him.

Terry's mouth was too full to answer, but Mary did: "We've run out. Surprisingly. I'll get some more from the shop. But Terry likes toast too. Especially toast with butter. Which is a new experience for him, apparently. The school gives it to them plain."

"Toast with butter, eh, Terry?" Derek said, as he sat down.

The boy nodded with obvious enthusiasm.

"It's good with dripping, too," Derek told him. The boy's face creased with enquiry. "You never had dripping toast?" Derek asked. The boy shook his head.

"You haven't lived." Derek turned to Mary. "Dripping toast for dinner, please Mummy."

"If I can find some. John's usually got some. Women give it to him, since poor Cathy was..." Then, quietly, "and don't call me Mummy. He's not going to be here for ever."

Terry heard. "Have I got to go back?" Suddenly he was about to cry.

"Terry." Derek put his hand on the lad's shoulder. "You're never going anywhere where someone can hurt you again. I promised you that, didn't I? And I keep my promises." There I go again, he thought. Making promises I can't keep.

"And I'll make sure he does." Mary dumped three more slices of toast on the table, then sat down, with Terry sitting at the end of the table, and she and Derek on either side. "But, love, we really have to have a little talk. About what made you run away from school. It's Havenhill, that's your school, isn't it?"

Terry nodded.

"You're very young to go there, aren't you? I thought it was for bigger boys."

"I'm the youngest," Terry told her, with almost a hint of pride.

"Terry," Derek asked him, "Do the bigger boys? Do they bully you?"

A long pause, then "A bit."

"You can tell us. What do they do?"

"Thunderclap."

"Thunderclap?" Mary asked. "What's Thunderclap?"

"Where they kick you. Under your bed."

"Good grief." Mary turned her head away for a moment, then said to Derek: "You ever hear of Thunderclap?"

"Not called that," he said. "But I can imagine the sort of thing. What else did they do, Terry?"

The boy was gaining in confidence. "They make me do the gauntlet. They have wet towels. I have to run. With nothing on. It hurts."

"I bet it does, old son." Derek smiled, hopefully consolingly, and Terry achieved a small smile in return.

"But that didn't make those sore marks, on your bottom, did it?"

"No." The boy shook his head decisively.

"But someone did," Mary persisted. "I'd say someone made you bend over and then they hit you with a sort of stick. Am I right?"

Terry nodded, his face down again.

"Who did it, love? One of the boys?"

Terry shook his head.

"Then who? You must tell us, Terry."

The boy spoke barely above a whisper: "I'm not supposed to say."

"But you can, Terry. Really. You can tell us. We won't tell anyone, I promise." Mary glanced at Derek. They both knew she was lying. Another lie to join the others. But surely...

The boy gave a sigh which seemed to be mixed with a shudder. "The boss." he said, this time in a very quiet whisper.

"The boss?"

"That's what the boys call him."

"Do you mean the headmaster?"

The boy nodded. "You have to say 'Sir' to his face. But when he's not there, we call him the boss."

"And he did he beat you? With a cane, yes?"

Terry nodded again. Derek gave Mary a look that said "At last we're getting somewhere." Then turned back to Terry.

"Okay, Terry. You're a brave lad for telling us. But why? What made him do it? Had you done something wrong?" He felt stupid asking the question. As if anything a nine-year-old boy could do would deserve such punishment.

"I'd been very naughty!" Terry exclaimed rather suddenly. "Very, very naughty. He told me. Every time. Very naughty indeed!" His face was turning red, his mouth working spasmodically.

Despite a warning look from Mary, Derek persisted. "Doing what, Terry? What did you do?"

Terry managed one world. "He..." and then his composure abandoned him. He half-rose from his chair, his hands to his face, sobbing uncontrollably, wracked with distress and despair.

Mary moved. She swept the boy up in her arms and hugged him.

"Enough!" she declared. "Enough. No more silly questions. Come on you, we're going to get you dressed in the new clothes people have given us, and then we're going to go for a lovely walk around the village. Here we go."

Half carrying him, half walking him, she manoeuvred the sobbing boy out of the kitchen, with Blondie following on, apparently indicating with his drooping head and drooling tongue that she was all too aware of her friend's distress.

Derek sat very still at the kitchen table. What the hell was this? What the bloody hell was this? Bloody hell, he was bloody well going to find out.

CHAPTER SIXTEEN

Sandy rang the North Tawe Square call box from her Exeter hostel at exactly eleven o'clock the next day, when there was a mid-morning break in the course she was attending. She's promised Neville she would do so but warned that the call might not get through if someone was in the box making a call at the same time.

Neville nullified this possibility by occupying the box from half past ten, standing with one hand on the cradle rest and the other holding the receiver to his ear, and pretending to talk. Sometimes he actually said things, including a list of the names of the Plymouth Argyle first team squad for the last five years, and sometimes he just pretended to speak, opening and shutting his mouth, looking, he feared rightly, like a rather anxious goldfish.

During the whole half-hour of pretence no-one else wanted to make a call from the box. No-one even approached the box. But Neville was making sure.

He was so engrossed in the pretence that when the phone rang, right on eleven o'clock, he dropped the receiver, and had to grope for it wildly as it swung on its lead and became entangled around his knees. As he struggled to haul the thing up, he could hear Sandy's voice calling.

"Nev? Neville? Can you hear me? Neville!"

"I'm here, it's me, hang on." Neville managed to get the receiver to head height, and began gabbling before he realised that he had it the wrong way round and was speaking into the ear-piece. He used both hands to get it the right way round, and even then, the cord seemed to be twisted round his neck. But at least he could talk.

"Sorry about that. I dropped the phone."

"Twerp!" But Sandy said it with a giggle. "I don't know what I see in you."

"Neither do I," Neville said quite truthfully.

"Anyway. Listen."

"Everything all right? We still okay for Thursday?" As he spoke Neville realised, he was sounding too eager. Too amateur. Too virginal. Shit.

"Sorry, no. Got bad news I'm afraid."

I knew it, Neville said to himself. I bloody knew it. She's changed her mind. Bloody women. Then, aloud, into the phone, keeping the tremor out of his voice only just, "Oh. Well. Another time then. You still getting back Thursday?"

"Yes, but not till late. So, can we make it Friday?"

"Of course, of course." Neville felt like the condemned man who had knelt at the block to await the axe, only to be told by the executioner that the King had changed his mind, and would he like a cigarette instead? It meant waiting another long twenty-four hours, but that was nothing when he remembered his worst fear, that Sandy would say she really had changed her mind. But she hadn't. And the mild disappointment at the day's delay was washed away on a tide of affection and admiration for this wonderful girl who for some reason didn't think him a hapless idiot.

"So. Friday. Definite." She sounded definite, too. "You be in the chapel by eleven-ish, yeh? Be sure no-one sees you go in. I'll get there the same time. Okay?"

"Yes, yes."

"And don't be late."

"No, no."

It was unbelievable. She was actually taking charge. Making sure that... it... would actually happen.

"I got to go now. Kiss, kiss." And she put the phone down before he could return the kiss.

Neville opened the door of the kiosk. Cold air hit him in the face. A middle-aged woman – possibly the same one who'd been making a call before – pushed past him, and he held the door open for her.

"Woof!" the woman exclaimed, as she stepped inside. "It's like an oven in here. Neville Parsons, what have you been talking about?!"

* * *

Matt rang Derek the next morning. Derek was pleased to hear from him. He found that, after his initial slightly wary reaction to meeting a man from Mary's past, he actually liked the chap. Yes, he might be a bit of a lunatic. But Matt's emotional outburst about the cruelty sometimes inflicted on children had, in its semi-hysterical way, been admirable. Matt wasn't afraid to show his deeper feelings. Perhaps his upbringing in Australia had rubbed off on him. The Australians Derek had met – admittedly few – had always impressed him by their straight-forward open manner, the way they spoke about how they felt, with no inhibitions. Not like young British men, amongst whom Derek numbered himself, repressed types who held back from expressing their emotions in case they made fools of themselves. He felt that he too should have stormed with outrage at what had been done to Terry. He should have let rip, let it all out, like Matt had done. And he would.

"Well mate, how's young Terry? Still eating you out of house and home?" Matt's voice was as confident, even ebullient, as ever. Derek had a vivid mental picture of him, standing tall as ever, even bending backwards, as he spoke. Rather like the Reverend Simpson, he realised. But that was the only similarity. Matt was warm, not stony cold. Cheerful, not a harbinger of woe and damnation.

"He's fine. Slept like a log, like kids do. And he no longer needs a cushion."

"Like I told you, scars fade. And then where are you with your evidence? Up shit creek without a paddle."

Unless, Derek said to himself, you've taken a picture. A photograph. Which Mary had done, using her Box Brownie. But she'd insisted that they say nothing about it until the film could be put through the police laboratory, to be developed and printed, and they could be sure that the snap turned out okay. This entailed a delay. It would be quicker to hand it over to the local Boots, of course. But the counter assistant might find the picture of a small boy's buttocks a little confusing. Even worrying.

"But listen, "Matt pushed on. "I'm a damn fool. I forgot to ask the lad his full name. Dumb or what? Have you got it out of him yet."

"Yes. It's McKenzie."

"Terry McKenzie, okay. I'm on the case this morning. Get the gen on his background. Might drop back later on if I get some good results. Be okay with you?"

"Yes, fine. Be good to see you."

"Right. Oh, and by the way, I checked out your Beatniks last night."

"Did you now?"

"Yeah. Looking for these legendary children they're supposed to be abusing and neglecting. No sign of toys. No kids' clothes. No kids' food. In other words, no kids."

"I told you."

"I know. Still, got to check. As for the beatniks, I thought they were okay. I liked them. Especially that Lucy. What a great girl."

"Isn't she just! Fascinating."

"Uh-huh!" A teasing note crept into Matt's voice. "Fell for her a bit, did you? Going to try your luck there?"

"Matt! I'm a happily married man."

"Good. Leaves the field open to me. I might just check back on her later on. Not that she gave me any encouragement. Plays it very cool, she does. But you know, faint heart never won fair Sheila, eh?"

"Good luck." Derek sighed quietly. Of course he hadn't seriously expected anything to happen between him and Lucy. For a start, he loved Mary with all his heart. For a start. And for a finish! And there was no room in between for any other girl. Of course there wasn't. And yet... There had almost been something between him and Lucy. Hadn't there? The way she'd looked at him in those final moments in the chapel porch. Her eyes glowing. The touch of her fingertips on his lips.

"And did she show you her knives?" Matt asked, interrupting his treacherous thoughts.

"Her what?" Derek decided to play dumb for now.

"She's a knife thrower mate. Would you believe it? Amazing, yeah? She's got these two dirty great knives in a box. Does knife throwing displays, apparently."

"Did you do it?"

"What?"

"I mean, did you stand and let her throw the knives at you?"

"What? You got to be kidding. No, she suggested it, but I said no way baby. Not this boy. But listen..." Matt's tone of voice now typically changed entirely. "What's all the panic about, Derek? Why all the objections? They're not doing anyone any harm. It's only an old wreck of a place. Why all the fuss?"

"You won't credit this, Matt," he told him. "But I think it's all coming from one source."

"Oh, right. I suppose that figures. Who exactly? Some tight-arsed gentleman farmer, thinks they're polluting the atmosphere and nicking his chickens?"

Mental pictures of Colonel Critchley and Joshua Voden flashed up in Derek's mind. The Colonel had wished the beatniks gone. And Mad Harry had stolen Voden's chickens. Was Matt psychic or something?

"No. I've got no proof, but I think it's one of the village's upstanding citizens. The chapel minister."

"Aah. Holy roller, eh? Makes sense." Matt's tone was now oddly flat. "Bit of a stickler, is he?"

"Yes. He says they're on holy ground, that it's sacrilege."

"Does he keep going on about being washed in the blood of the lamb.?"

"Well. Yes, he does." That was odd. Maybe Matt knew his non-conformists. "Why, what makes you?"

"What's his name?" Matt snapped, overriding him.

"Er, not sure I should. Oh why not? It's Simpson."

"Thompson?" Matt's tone was suddenly accusatory.

"No. Simpson. With an 'S'"

"Simpson. I thought you said..." Matt's voice faded. Derek waited for him to finish what he was saying, but he didn't. Such silence was odd from a man normally such a chatterbox.

Finally, he said: "Matt? "You still there?"

"Sorry, sorry, miles away." Another brief silence, and then: "Listen. Got to rush. I'll be on Terry's case today. Are you in this evening?"

"Oh. Yes. Sure."

"See you then." There was a small crash on the line, presumably Matt putting the phone down with some emphasis. Then the dialling tone resumed.

Derek stood still, gazing at the faintly humming receiver. Then he slowly, gently, replaced it on the rest. He remained standing there, quite still. His mind was buzzing. What had just been said? What had he said, or Matt said, which had suddenly thrown everything a little off-key? He struggled to focus, to remember. Something important. No, not important, perhaps, but strange. Off kilter. Odd. What the hell?

Niggle, niggle.

Mary came out from the kitchen with a pile of laundry in her arms, smiled at him, and went up the stairs. Through the open door came the happy sounds of Terry trying unsuccessfully to teach Blondie to beg for toast. Derek didn't see her, didn't hear them. He took a deep breath. This was a real niggle. Forget the others. Or was it one of the others? Anyway, it was there. And niggling. Hard.

Slowly he entered the front room that served as his office, and sat down automatically at the table that served as his desk. And at last something clicked. He reached into his breast pocket, and pulled out the newspaper cutting he had filched from the Minister's house. He opened it and spread it out on the table. He did so with great care. The cutting was very old and yellow-ish in places. His casual treatment of it had not helped, and the folds were in danger of splitting. Fortunately the text remained legible. So far, he had only taken a very brief look at the report it contained. Now he looked again.

It was a report of a court case. Involving someone called Thompson.

Not Simpson, with an 'S'. Thompson, with a 'T'. And an 'o'.

CHAPTER SEVENTEEN

Indulging in its predictable and frequent habit, the phone rang at an inappropriate time. Equally inappropriate, it was Sergeant Welbeloved.

"Has that whatsisname school, Havenhill is it? Have they missed one of their pupils? Cos they should have told someone by now. And if they have missed one, why haven't they told us.

"You'd have to ask them." Derek began, but the Sergeant told him abruptly to wait. There was a moment or two of confused muttering at the end of the Okehampton line, more sounds of paper shuffling, even the slam of a book on a desk, a second voice telling the Sergeant something unintelligible, but hopefully intelligent. Then Welbeloved came back on the line.

"Apparently, they have reported it. It's in the book. Honestly, some of you people's handwriting!" This was clearly aimed at some poor constable in the office.

"Now Martin," the Sergeant was audibly getting himself into gear once more. "What's happening with this Child Welfare chap?"

"Mark, you mean, Sergeant? Matthew Mark. Well, he's digging into the lad's background, finding out where his parents are, who they are, why they dumped a nine-year-old in a school for tough teenage boys, that sort of thing. He says he should be up to speed by this evening."

"Good. Then I'm calling a meeting. Tomorrow morning. Friday. Nine sharp. Here in the office. Him, that Matt chap I mean, and you, me and Inspector Reed, of course. Okay? High time we did some proper police work on this case. There's been too much messing around with soppy dogs and stroppy women." Welbeloved clearly hadn't forgotten his confrontation with Mary and her rolling pin. "Time we remembered we are the official custodians of the law. Tell your chap Mark about the meeting, won't you?"

"Will do, Sergeant."

He replaced the receiver, and within two seconds it rang again. Derek looked at it. On his desk he could sense the ancient newspaper cutting, waiting patiently to reveal its secrets, and he was tempted to let the damn phone ring. But then, if he did, Mary would grab it. She loathed the sound of an unanswered telephone, and then, assuming it was for him, he'd have to answer it.

"North Tawe Police?"

"Oh, Derek, sorry, it's me again."

It was Matt. Derek felt a quick surge of relief. It was not some footling complaint, not even from Joshua claiming another missing chicken. He realised that he rapidly come to look on Matt as a friend, a mate. Someone he could talk to, on his own level. A scarce enough quality around here, he sneered to himself. Though there was John at the pub, of course. And the Colonel. And the vicar. And Neville's dad, Clive Parsons, he of the doubtful reputation. There was even Neville himself at a pinch. And of course there was

Mary. What was he thinking? He had loads of friends. Nonetheless he was relieved that it was Matt on the line.

"Hey Matt. What can I do you for?"

"Little thing. When I was out your way yesterday, I don't know if I was dreaming or half asleep, but I swear I saw a man taking a couple of goats for a walk."

"You probably did. That's the man we were talking about, the one complaining about the beatniks. The Reverend Simpson."

"Oh that's him, is it? I mean, him." Matt sounded hesitant, at least in comparison to his usual confident style. "Um, Simpson, yes?"

"Yes."

"Oh. Right. Big feller, isn't he. Stands tall."

So do you, Derek thought. But he said: "We always say, if he stands more upright, he'll fall over backwards."

"Ha!" There was little humour in Matt's voice. He went on: "Okay, just thought it was a bit weird, goat on a lead, like it's a dog. Thanks mate. Don't mean to bother you."

"Actually. Christ, I nearly forgot." Derek gabbled. "I'm glad you did call. Are you getting plenty of gen on young Terry?"

"No worries there, mate. The international phone lines have been buzzing. London's in an uproar. Matt the investigator is on the warpath." Matt was recovering, and sounding more like his usual flamboyant self. "Do you want to hear what I've got so far?"

"Better not," Derek cautioned. "Not over an open line. But listen, my sergeant, Welbeloved wants a meeting tomorrow, nine o'clock. Sort it all out, official-like. You, me, him and the Inspector."

"At the Okehampton cop shop? No worries, I'll be there. Now, gotta go, things to do, places to see, girls to... what I can get away with."

With a click the line went dead.

Derek carefully replaced the receiver, and dared the phone to ring again. It chickened out. But as he turned to go back to the study, and the waiting newspaper cutting, the front door opened, and Mary, Terry and floppy-eared Blondie all tried to come in at the same time. They were giggling, grinning, nudging each other, chattering, and Derek was struck by a thought. They looked like a family. Mother, son, pet dog. All it needed was Dad. And that's' what they'd be. A family. His family.

He brushed the thought away. The dog wasn't theirs. Terry wasn't theirs. Don't be foolish.

"I didn't know you were out," he said to Mary. "Been anywhere nice?"

"I popped Terry round to see Jean. Another quick check-over. And before you ask, he's right as rain and fit as a fiddle and smart as paint! Aren't you, young man?"

"I'm alright," the boy said brightly, but then his mood darkened. "But not alright enough to, you know, leave. Or go back." His dread of what might be done with him shortly was palpable.

Mary shooed him and Blondie into the kitchen, on a hunt for biscuits, then turned back to Derek.

"We owe Jean a couple of quid, I'm afraid. I've been using her phone."

"But we get this one free..."

"Oh don't fuss. You're always on it, anyway. I just rang a couple of mates from teacher's training. See if they know anything about Terry's school. This Havenhill place.

"And do they?"

"Not much that we didn't know already. Apparently, the original idea behind it was to be somewhere for ex-pats to send their boys there, as boarders. To get an English education. Headmaster's a chap called Raymond Jeeves. Bit of a seedy type, apparently, though his qualifications sound pretty impressive. Strict disciplinarian, mind you. As poor little Terry possibly knows to his cost."

"And then there's that other something, that Terry won't talk about," Derek mentioned hesitantly.

"I'm not nagging him about that. He'll tell us more in his own good time."

"There's a fair bit of bullying going on, isn't there? Anyone hear anything about that?"

"Well, they say it was okay when most of the boys were from overseas. Children of middle-class ex-patriots, mid-level civil servants. But then lots pulled their children out. Big hike in fees, I think. And a dodgy government report. Anyway, as we know, Jeeves compensated by agreeing to take in tough cases from County. You know, the sort of kid being given one last chance before being packed off to an official Approved School. County pay the fees."

"So now it's a case of a load of louts, beating up the little kids."

"They're not louts!" Mary said, displaying a teacher's professional ethic. "They're boys with difficulties. Single parents. Or alcohol problems at home. You know the sort of thing. They've got to go somewhere."

"Mmm." Derek wasn't sure he agreed but decided to leave it. "What about his staff?"

"Well again, the decent ones have mostly gone elsewhere. Others are said to be walking wounded from the War. Physically and mentally. Listen, do we know any more about Terry yet? His mum and dad..."

"Matt's on the job. There's a meeting tomorrow, in Okehampton. With Welbeloved and Inspector Reed. He says he's on top of it. And I'm sure he is."

Mary gave him a shrewd look. "You like him, don't you?

"Yes. I love my Sergeant Welbeloved."

Mary punched him on the arm. "Matt, I mean. You weren't so sure at first, I know, but..."

"Yes. He's a good mate. Very committed, you know."

"Yes." She wasn't so sure. "Not too hyper, too emotional for you? You have to admit he's a bit, well, mercurial."

"Well. That's a good thing, isn't it? Better than the alternative, the time-servers, sitting on their fat arses, not caring, waiting for their pensions."

She grinned. "We're back to Welbeloved again, aren't we!"

* * *

Alone again in his office, Derek took a deep breath, trying to clear his mind of the issues around Terry and the school. Then again, he read the headline on the now rather tattered clipping:

> "Plymouth Gangster Ronald Thompson Freed
> 'Washed In The Blood Of The Lamb'.

He looked at the date. April 1924. Nearly 30 years ago. The Minister had kept this report for nearly 30 years. Not forgetting the flick knife. Why? Had he just forgotten about it, or...? He read on:

> Noted member of the Plymouth under-world Ronald Thompson escaped a lengthy prison sentence yesterday, when local magistrates decided that his conversion to Christianity was a genuine change of heart.
>
> Thompson had been facing charges of affray, intimidation and living off immoral earnings. He pleaded guilty to all offences.
>
> The bench heard that there was strong evidence that Thompson had turned his life around, after a religious experience on Plymouth Hoe in the weeks following his arrest, which had occurred while he was out on bail.
>
> Social reports seen by the magistrates indicated that Thompson had reformed his behaviour considerably. He had stopped drinking and gambling. His wife, a convicted prostitute, had suffered mental breakdown and was now permanently hospitalised, and

> Thompson had taken on the care of his young son. It was pointed out that if Thompson was given a custodial sentence the boy would be taken into care at the local orphanage.
>
> Thompson was fined £50 and bound over to keep the peace for two years.
>
> After the case, Thompson made the following statement:
>
> "I had an epiphany on the Hoe. God and his Angels rose out of the foam, and enveloped me. I was washed in the blood of the lamb, and became re-born in the service of the Lord. From now on my life will be dedicated to all that is good and worthy, under heaven. Bless you all."

Derek read it twice. Whoever this Thompson chummy was, he was a lucky bugger. Today's magistrates in the 1950s surely wouldn't be so easily persuaded. And what did it have to do with the North Tawe minister? Why had he kept the cutting. Probably nothing, he told himself. Coincidence. Happenstance. At which stage of his mental whirlwind the niggle, which had been circling his brain in a wide orbit, now came crashing in. Niggle, niggle, niggle. Something was still bothering him. His head ached, and he put the cutting away in the wire tray on his work table.

From the back of the house he heard happy family noises. Mary's voice, raised in admiration at some youthful exploit by the child, the giggle of that child, the excited woofing of the family pet.

They're not your family, Derek told himself. Now concentrate.

CHAPTER EIGHTEEN

The meeting to review the Terry situation, scheduled for the following morning, was a pantomime. Nearly as much fun, Derek decided, as the forthcoming annual village trip to the Bude panto, and that was high praise indeed. The Bude show, with a retired veteran comedian in charge, was always a riot.

The panto meeting was held in Inspector Reed's room in the Okehampton police HQ, and presided over by a reluctant Inspector, who made an unlikely Widow Twankey. On either side of him appeared Prince Charming, in the shape of Matt, facing up against a belligerent Baron Hardup, personified by Sergeant Welbeloved.

Derek himself, he decided as they made their entrances, would be Buttons, keeping out of the firing line while making the occasional contribution to help the plot along.

In Matt's free-wheeling style, it didn't need much helping. Invited by the Inspector to kick things, off, he began with a bombshell. "The mother is a non-starter. Hopeless. Terry is better off without her."

"Better off without his own mother?" Welbeloved was scandalised. He was unwisely ensconced in the room's second-best chair, which had arms, over and under which his midriff bulged uncomfortably. "Every boy needs his mother. Of course young Terry needs her.

She should be informed of his situation at once. For heaven's sake."

Wellbeloved's attitude to Matt, Derek decided, was as dismissive as Matt's attitude to Welbeloved. Was this still panto? Or perhaps Victorian melodrama.? The two men were chalk and cheese. Sweet and sour. Beauty and the Beast. He wasn't quite sure, Derek thought, which was which, and he hid a secret grin in a cough.

Matt, with what might be described as a beastly gleam in his eye, proceeded to reinforce the mutual resentment.

"My dear Sergeant," he began. Then again, watching Welbeloved bristle at the endearment. "My dear Sergeant, perhaps you would care to inform his mother of her maternal duties. Personally. A colleague of mine has endeavoured to do so. He found her in a bombed out building in Hammersmith, along with some twenty others who sleep, eat and defecate within the ruins. Locally she is known as Cocaine Katy, though her name is Anita. The drug itself, cocaine, is widely available in London now, thanks to the continuing presence of American troops in the UK. Otherwise she is referred to as that drunk bitch with the posh accent. When contacted face to withered face, and told about her son, she told my colleague to perform an indecent act upon herself." He turned deliberately away from the Sergeant, and spoke directly to Inspector Reed. "She is, Sir, as I said, a non-starter. And this is one case in which we should certainly not let romantic sentiment cloud our judgement."

The Sergeant, on the retreat, said weakly," I was just saying..."

"And I'm glad you did, Sergeant," Matt told him. "It gave me the opportunity to make my point with, I think, sufficient strength. I thank you."

Welbeloved stared at him, not knowing whether to smile with gratitude or glare with resentment. He did neither, just sweated a little. He shifted his bottom, and his chair shifted with him.

Inspector Reed cleared his throat. The Inspector had always slightly dreaded formal meetings. He much preferred cosy one-to-one chats. Meetings could be so confrontational. Just like this one. But the Sergeant had wanted it. Demanded it. Insisted on it. He'd felt, he'd said, that the whole situation of the runaway boy and this rather grim-sounding boarding school was being dealt with in an unprofessional manner. In particular the lad should be under official care, not left in the arms of someone with no professional qualifications in that respect.

Balls, the Inspector thought privately. He had come to know Constable Martin's wife over the past few months, and had conceived a high opinion of the girl. What's more his own daughter, a 17-year-old pupil at the local Grammar where Mrs Martin taught, had told him that her teacher was "fabuloso", a word which he needed translated, but which subsequently endorsed his own opinion. So he had been inclined to let Constable Martin, Mary Martin and this chap Matt something-or-other from Child Welfare, handle things.

But then the Sergeant had dug his heels in, shifting his considerable weight towards a suggestion that County should be informed, perhaps asked for help in what might develop into a delicate situation, young children being what they were. So additional help from H.Q. might be of some...

Well! The last thing Inspector needed was a bunch of ambitious young pink-faced parvenu policemen tooling down the A30, waving their spiral notebooks and their shiny propelling pencils under his nose, finding fault with this and that and the other, and him now only a few months before retirement with a spotless record.

So he partially gave way. This meeting was a compromise. And he had to chair it. He sighed, masking his sullen resentment with a show of deep thought.

Then he said: "And the father?"

"Ah. Different kettle of fish." Matt dragged a new set of notes from a floppy leather briefcase. "Let's see. Yes. Brigadier Austin McKenzie. Military attaché to the Hong Kong authorities. I managed to exchange a few cables with him yesterday, and, with a certain amount of reading through the lines, this is the gist of what he told me.

"Apparently, he and this Anita, not sure of her maiden name, were wed back in the Thirties, but his wife hated and resented military life, especially when in 1943, she was left behind with a baby boy in some crumbling military accommodation. In any event, the couple were divorced in 1946, as soon as possible after hostilities ceased. She got custody of Terry. You know what the courts are like about mother-child relationships."

Again Welbeloved stirred for a moment, and Matt stopped to allow him to speak. But the Sergeant subsided.

Matt went on: "She, plus sprog. returned to the UK. McKenzie claims he gave his wife a generous allowance, and for a while all seemed to go well, as far as he could tell from halfway around the world. But then disturbing reports of his ex-wife's habits began to filter back to him, and it was with some relief that she informed him that she had placed the lad in a good boarding school, where he was well and happy." He looked up briefly at the other three. "Well and happy," he repeated bleakly.

"I conveyed more exact details of the boy's so-called fitness and happiness to the Brigadier, and he was naturally appalled. As he was when he learned of his ex-wife's state of being. I think he blames himself for neglecting his son. Anyway, he's getting emergency leave, should be on his way as we speak. That's if he can get a flight. Otherwise he'll get on a boat. But it's no short journey from Honkers to Blighty, is it? I'd say at least two weeks, to be sure. So, in the meantime, my recommendation will be that the lad remain in the home of Constable and Mrs Martin, where he is happy, where he can keep up with his education thanks to Mrs. Martin, and where," Matt smiled at Derek, "he will most certainly not be beaten."

The Inspector gave Matt an almost formal nod, thankfully remembering his name as he did so. "Thank you, Mr. Mark."

Matt produced his most extreme variety of Australian accent: "Call me cobber, mate. Or, if you prefer, call me mate, cobber."

The Inspector blushed.

Derek decided that, although it would be great fun relating this meeting to Mary, it was time to move things on.

"Sir, if we are all in agreement with Mr. Mark's recommendation, and I take it we are", (a blatant contradiction of the true situation, but never mind) "Can I suggest that we release him from this meeting at this point? I believe he has further important issues to attend to."

What these important issues were, Derek knew not. But Matt had primed him to make the suggestion.

"Of course. And thank you again, Mr. Mark." The Inspector meant it. Reducing a meeting from four to three met with his full approval.

Left as one of a trio, Welbeloved was clearly more comfortable in his mind, if not with his posterior.

"Sir!" He addressed the Inspector directly, ignoring Derek. "Now that the wishy-washy welfare section has had its say, perhaps we can get down to some genuine police work. Specifically, it is hardly necessary to point out that there is evidence of a crime having been committed."

The Inspector held up a restraining hand. "Precisely what crime, Sergeant? This is a very tricky area, you know. It is not a crime to punish children with a caning. Heavens, can you imagine what state some schools would degenerate to if it was? There'd be chaos. Teachers would be afraid to teach, standards would drop... no, no, no, you have to have caning. For boys only, of course."

The Inspector was a kindly man, he would never cane his own children, but Derek knew he was only voicing the general attitude to corporal punishment.

He went on: "From what you told me, however, it seems that this lad has been treated with unnecessary severity. But I've no doubt that those in authority over him thought it appropriate. To maintain discipline, you see."

There was a silence in the room. Then Welbeloved dropped his officious tone. He also abandoned all his usual creepy obsequiousness towards the Inspector.

"You didn't see it!"

Surprised, Derek glanced at Welbeloved. The man's face, usually rather mobile, was set.

"What was that, Sergeant?" The Inspector also seemed a little perturbed.

"I said," the Sergeant didn't modify his tone, but rather reinforced it: "I said, you didn't see it!"

"Yes. Or rather, no." Reed felt the meeting, rather than getting easier, was going very wrong. He searched for reassurance. "Constable? Any thoughts?"

Derek had no hesitation: "You didn't see it!" he told the Inspector. His emphasis echoed Welbeloved.

Perhaps surprisingly, Inspector Reed relaxed. There was going to be no clash of opinions, no row, no recriminations. Sergeant and Constable were of one mind, they agreed, and the Inspector hastened to join in that agreement.

"Very well," he said, hoping he was putting a note of decisive command into his voice. "Constable, this has occurred on your patch At least, that's where the boy was found. I suggest you launch an investigation, perhaps commencing with a visit to this school. Havenhill, is it? Tomorrow morning, I would suggest. Don't tell them you're coming. And, most important, you should secure an interview with the Headmaster. Agreed?"

Derek exchanged glances with Welbeloved. The fat sergeant didn't seem inclined to argue.

Derek stood up and came to a formal attention. "Yes Sir!".

The meeting was over. The Inspector was happy. He rose from the seat behind his desk. Derek rose from his chair. The Sergeant rose and his chair rose with him.

* * *

In all her years running the North Tawe sub-post office, Miss Phyllis Parker had never, to the best of her recollection, ever delivered any mail to the ruined chapel at Fursdon. But the address on the official-looking sturdy brown envelope was quite clear. The thing was franked. It was marked urgent. It had been sent out to her on a special delivery van from Okehampton, to both her and the driver's bewilderment. And it needed to be signed for.

So there was only one thing to do. She stashed the package in her Official Post Office satchel, got out her new Official Post Office bicycle, the old one now in pieces and forming a part of a hedge near Holesworthy, and rode to the chapel in the teeth of a biting wind. "Typical of old Phyllis," people would say, she thought. "She's a tough old bird." At least, that's what she hoped they would say.

Was there just a hint of apprehension in Phyllis's mind, as she leaned her new Official Post Office bicycle against the hedge, and approached the old place? After all, she, in common with the rest of the village, was aware that the building had been taken over by a bunch of weirdos, beatniks, devil-worshippers and whatnot. Did she feel just a tremor of nerves as she knocked on the double-doors? No, of course she didn't. Phyllis feared no-one.

And quite right too. There was nothing to fear. The tall girl who came to the door had a nice smile, and was very polite. Another girl looked over the shoulder of the first one as she used Phyllis's pencil to sign for the package, and she too smiled warmly. Equally warm thanks were offered, even a cup of tea which was declined, and Phyllis rode home pleased to have done her duty.

Back in the chapel, the others crowded around as Lucy opened the envelope. They were not accustomed to getting mail.

The contents changed the mood abruptly. Lucy read it through, then broke the news.

"It's a copy of some deeds. And a threat. The chapel people do own this place. No argument. And they're sending in the bailiffs to clear us out." She sighed.

"What do we do now?" Jennifer asked. She asked on behalf of the others. They all knew that Lucy would make the big decisions, she would lead them. Even if they were all equal.

"We go. Simple as that." Lucy shrugged. "I agreed if they could prove ownership... So, let's get packed. Harry, go and sort out the pony, bring the cart up to the door. We'll find somewhere."

As they dispersed, a sports car drew up, and a tall figure got out. It was a man, and he stood for a moment, posing, Lucy thought, standing up so straight. Then, with something of a swagger, he walked slowly up the path.

Him again, Lucy said to herself. Then aloud: "It's all go today, isn't it!"

CHAPTER NINETEEN

The previous evening Derek had unwisely told Mary about his plan next day to visit the school whilst in the hearing of young Terry, who had reacted by immediately dropping the hunk of pasty he had been in the process of conveying to his mouth. Blondie, lurking below his chair with dogged dog patience for such an eventuality, got it before it hit the floor.

Derek briefly wondered whether he too could dispose of his pasty in such an efficient manner. Not a chance. Not under Mary's sanguine gaze. God, these things the country people ate... he had doused his pasty in brown sauce, the only solution he knew to the challenge of making its consumption acceptable.

But Terry's reaction put paid to any such speculation. He had risen with a jerk, sending his chair clattering to the linoleum. His face was red and furious. Tears might be close.

"I'm not going!" he said, his treble voice shrilling with alarm. "No."

"Of course you're not going," Mary rushed to assure him.

"You're never going back there, I promised you that," Derek added, cursing his clumsiness.

"No! I'm not!" And then, abruptly, "Can I take Blondie for a walk? Just round the garden?"

Derek watched him go. He was struck by how Terry had stood tall and talked with new vigour. It was, he thought, an indication that the boy was recovering from whatever ordeal he had undergone at his school, and from his nightmare journey across rough countryside in the dark. What had been an almost silent pathetic little child was slowly revealing himself now to be a spirited young lad who could speak for himself. Mary had told him the previous evening that her youthful charge was starting to exert himself, and Derek and she now exchanged knowing glances. Their visitor was beginning to feel his strength, demonstrating his character. Which was good. Wasn't it? Mary might disagree. From the start, and out of good judgement, she had treated Terry as if he were five years old, not nearly ten. But now he was no longer a waif to be cuddled and tended. He was a ten-year-old kid. Possibly a slightly stroppy kid. A kid who would see his own way forward. Derek saw a brief shadow of imminent loss cross his wife's face.

And there was something more. She seemed to make up her mind to something, and there was another shadow, something more painful. "He talked to me again," she said. "About what happened with the headmaster."

Derek felt a chill in the small of his back. "What?"

"Well, Terry doesn't really have the words for it but, well, I think the man interferes with him."

"Oh Christ...you mean?"

"Yes. They call it abuse, you know. Stupid word, sounds like he just calls him names. But no, he, he..." She was close to tears, holding herself tightly together.

"He uses him?" Derek suggested, trying to make it easier for her. "Sexually?"

"And then he canes him for doing it. Can you believe it?" Now she was crying, and Derek put his arms around her. She raised her face to him: "You'll get him, won't you? Won't you?"

* * *

"Right. Whistle, truncheon, handcuffs, notebook, pencil and helmet." Derek struck a pose in the early morning kitchen. "How do I look?"

"Your flies are open."

"Oh sh... shoot! So they are."

Derek silently congratulated himself on his restrained language in front of a child. But from the enthralled look on the face of said child, he hadn't fooled anyone. Young Terry was well aware of what he had and hadn't said.

So was Mary. "Well done. We'll have you house-trained yet." She was boiling eggs, Terry having apparently developed a fondness for boiled eggs, or rather for dipping into them with soldiers.

Derek turned his back and struggled with his buttons. The thick serge of the uniform trousers was welcome in cold weather, but the buttons had to be wrestled into their holes.

"Where are you going Derek?" the boy asked. And then, fearfully, "You're going to the school, aren't you!"

"I am. But you're not." After what Mary had told him he could say it with extra emphasis. "You're never going back there. Never."

Even Mary seemed a little surprised at his tone and raised an eyebrow.

"The niggle," he told her. "It's worse."

Outside he fastened the chinstrap to his helmet and fired up the bike. If everything Mary had learned from the boy was true, then this would be his first case of child abuse. He would get the man for the offence if he could. Trouble was, as he had learned in training, this sort of thing was so bloody hard to prove. Sometimes courts, ruled by naïve country magistrates, simply didn't believe such a crime existed. And there was rarely any real proof. Put a small, scared child in a witness box, with his tormenter glaring at him from the dock and most times not even the kindest magistrate could coax the truth out of him.

No, it would be a battle of wills, he imagined. He'd have to be strong. Was he strong enough? He remembered his fumbling terror when, with Mary, he was trapped in a blazing barn in the battle with the people-traffickers. And his dismal despair when facing the loaded shotgun of Bucky, the drug-using tearaway, who had so abused Sandy, his friend's daughter. And then just a couple of days ago, there had been his panic as he raced from a pursuing Blondie down the field and into the marsh. No, he wasn't as mentally strong as he might wish to be. He offered himself a feeble excuse – that he was only human. He had a right to seek the truth, and to be appalled when it proved to be unacceptably repellent. And the thought of the damage that little Terry had suffered from the hand of someone in authority at this so-called place of education...

His route to the Havenhill school was by no means straightforward. It soon veered off the usual Okehampton road, became a mostly single-track lane, and twice twisted its erratic way over two unmanned crossings of the rail line that ran west to the coast. The purple hills of Dartmoor rose before him, as did a sign reading "No Through Road". Another sign, rusted but legible, read "Meldon Quarry. No public access." And yes, there it was, the quarry itself, a huge gouge into the rising slopes of the moor. Through gaps in fencing Derek could see and hear all the activity and noise of a major industrial plant. It was quite a sight and he knew that it was a source of well-paid employment for local Devonians who didn't fancy a life washing cow dung out of shippens, and the county was grateful for it.

And then, a few yards later, and dominating even the vast quarry, was the Meldon Viaduct, the extraordinary Victorian structure, built brick on countless brick, rising ever higher, topped off by the rail line, and bridging the enormous gap beneath it. The tiny road track ran under it and there was a small lay-by to stop in. Derek let the motorbike dribble to a halt and made himself look up at the structure. It was a magnificent sight, but he didn't look for long. He would admit to himself, and to Mary, that he and heights did not get on well together, neither looking up them or looking down. The viaduct looked even higher from the ground than from the window of a train crossing it. Derek loved trains, but he didn't like viaducts, and when he was on a train crossing it, which was frequently, he would keep his eyes inside the carriage until they reached the other side. Now, looking up at it, he felt a little dizzy, a little sick even.

He revved the bike up and continued on the safely earth-bound tarmac.

* * *

A short drive in a semi-circle past some untidy shrubbery brought Derek and motorbike to a halt in front of the forbidding stone-walled structure that was Havenhill School. He climbed off, ditched the helmet, and looked around. Nothing moved, no-one was in sight. Certainly, no search parties seeking the whereabouts of an absconding nine-year-old.

He approached what appeared to be the main door of the building. This was a magnificent piece of Victorian woodwork, with prominent black iron hinges and a large globular metal knob in its centre. To one side, embedded into the brickwork of the walls, was a circular doorbell frame, with a white enamel button protruding from its centre.

He pressed the button. He waited. Nothing happened. He tried again. Again, there was no response from inside the imposing building. He tried giving the button three sharp jabs. Again, nothing transpired.

Was it possible that no-one was at home? At a boarding school with at least one hundred pupils and staff?

Then a thought occurred. He grasped the white button between thumb and two fingers and pulled. It slide neatly out, and some sort of bell jangled in the distance. Almost immediately he heard the click-clack of heels on tiles from behind the door. Finally, with a creak, even a groan, the thing swung open.

The figure that greeted him was small, rounded and feminine. She was the sort of woman you find beaming at you from behind tea urns in railway buffets. She was perhaps fifty-five, with a head of permed grey hair, steel-rimmed spectacles and an ample bosom protruding perhaps a little too blatantly amongst the folds of a fluffy blue sweater.

She was smiling warmly as she pushed back the heavy door, but she lost that look as she reacted to the police uniform, and what had been a welcoming expression became one hinting of resentful suspicion.

When she spoke, however, she seemed non-committal, even friendly. "Sorry for the delay," she told him. "Most people use the side door."

"Apologies, Madam," Derek responded, and reached to show her his warrant card. "I'm Constable Martin."

"And what can I do for you Constable?"

"I'd like to speak to Mr. Raymond Jeeves, please."

"Well, I'm Mrs Jeeves. Can I help?"

"I'd prefer to speak to Mr Jeeves, if I may, Madam. Routine enquiries, you understand."

"Very well." She stood aside to let him in. "I'm afraid there may be some delay. The Doctor is currently taking the sixth form in Advanced Mathematics."

Derek blinked. Advanced Mathematics was not exactly his field. Come to that, he wasn't sure he could cope with Advanced Anything

He closed the door behind him, catching a whiff of an institutional smell. Sweat, cabbage, pipe tobacco, drains, and something else one would not wish to identify. The woman led him through a neglected porch, to join a long wooden-floored corridor leading to the left.

"Perhaps you would wait for the Headmaster in his study," she suggested. Then, as he kept pace with her, "I suppose this is about that dreadful little McKenzie boy."

Derek said nothing, startled at the notion that Terry could be described as "dreadful."

"Wretched boy. Been giving us trouble ever since he got here. I assume you have him in custody?" It was a question.

"He's being cared for," Derek told her, then as an afterthought, "we're keeping an eye on him."

"You better. He'll run off again, given half the chance. Not our fault."

Why was she so defensive? Derek wondered. Why be so bitchy about a ten-year-old? "May I ask," he began, "why did he run off on this occasion?"

"You'd have to ask him," Mrs Jeeves was predictably matron-like. But was there a slight quiver in her voice, a note even of fear? "I believe he was subject to disciplinary procedures. You have to understand, officer, that some boys do run off from an institution such as Havenhill. We demand high standards of behaviour, a culture of independent development, of, as Mr. Jeeves likes to put it, grace under fire. Boys leave here as self-sufficient young men, strong and independent, natural leaders."

And go straight into the Hitler Youth, Derek thought. Or, on the other hand, they hate the place so much, they rise from their beds and endure a terrifying scramble into the wild darkness of the unforgiving Devon night.

They had come to a stop by an oaken door nearly as impressive as the entrance, and the woman led them in to what was obviously the Headmaster's study. Derek had the impression of lines of leather-bound books, shaded lighting despite it being in daylight, formal photographs of school rugby and cricket teams on the walls, a thick Turkish carpet, and a new and more pungent smell, another one which he couldn't identify. There was a large leather-topped desk placed centrally, with an impressive swing chair behind it. An antique armchair stood to one side of the desk, and there were two more upright conventional chairs facing it. Mrs Jeeves not-too-subtly made sure that Derek took one of the latter two.

A boy of about sixteen, without seeming to be summoned, had joined them. There was a terse whispered conversation between Mrs Jeeves and the boy, who then disappeared. She then turned and faced Derek.

"I've sent a message to the Headmaster. I'm sure he won't keep you long."

She got to the door, hesitated, stopped. She turned back, and her previously quasi-aggressive manner, seemed to have been replaced by a certain more conciliatory anxiety.

"You know," she began, "you don't want to believe everything little scraps like the boy McKenzie might tell you. They make things up, these boys. They even write home, telling tales of this and that, all made up."

Derek stopped her. "How do you know? How do you know what they say?"

"We read their letters of course."

"You read the letters they send home? Really?" Derek wondered if he was being too rude, too inquisitive.

"Of course we do, young man. We are responsible for our boys, for their welfare, their mental state. They are in our care. We would be neglecting our duty if we allowed their silly fantasies to be taken seriously."

Yes. Otherwise, defenceless little boys might tell their parents about how they received severe abrasions to their bottoms - and add precise details of what perverted activity led them to be punished, Derek thought. The woman hovered by the door, she clearly thought there was more she should say.

"The, well, the truth is, my husband, struggles sometimes. They tempt him, you know. Especially the little ones, with their piping little voices and their devious ways. Wicked little imps. He struggles. He prays for them. But they tempt him!" Her voice had risen by almost an octave, and there was malice and disgust in it. "They tempt him."

She left him. He heard her footsteps clacking hurriedly away. Then silence. Derek thought about what he had just heard. By heaven, what *had* he just heard? An excuse? A confession? 'They tempt him...' What did that mean?

He waited some more, worried some more. Then, fretfully, he got up and began, almost automatically, to examine the bookshelves, reading the spines of a number of large serious-looking volumes. After a moment he realised that the majority of them were credited to "Raymond Jeeves". Impressed, he looked at the titles – and then realised that each book bore the same title. He was looking at a line of the same edition. The headmaster seemed to collect copies of his own book. Or perhaps he just couldn't sell the thing.

Amused, Derek pulled one of the volumes off the shelf and opened it. The pages seemed full of diagrams, together with some sections of small prose. None of it made any sense to Derek, and he closed the thing. He was putting it carefully back in its place when he saw that behind it and its neighbours was a large buff envelope.

He hesitated. None of his business, leave it, his conscience told him. But no, hang on a minute, this man was his business. This man might be a sadist, an abuser. This man was hiding something behind his books.

He listened for footsteps. Still nothing.

The envelope wasn't sealed. The flap opened easily. The contents seemed to be photographs. He drew one out and looked at it.

The blood roared in his ears. His stomach lurched. He nearly dropped the envelope. He was looking at pictures of small boys and adults, at nakedness, at perversion beyond his knowledge, beyond his imagination.

His fingers trembled as he pulled a few more stills from the envelope. They were different but the same. More scenes of something so horrible... and scenes too of sadism, of pain...

Footsteps. He pushed the book back in its place tidily. Then he realised he was still holding the buff envelope with its disgusting content. Panicked, he sat on it.

"Thank you, Mummy!" It was not a strong voice, more of an insistent whine. Mrs Jeeves had opened the door, and through it strode the man himself – clearly Headmaster Jeeves - tall, immaculately suited, with a black scholar's gown slipping theatrically around his shoulders.

"Sorry to keep you, constable. Don't get up."

At that moment 'don't get up' was, Derek thought, the best thing he could have said. The envelope crackled slightly beneath him.

"Thank you, mummy!" The words were dismissive. The woman almost scurried away, closing the door behind her. Jeeves casually strolled behind his desk and relaxed into his chair.

"So you've met Mavis. My wife of thirty years. We call her Mummy," he gave a genial smile, "because she's like a mother to the boys. Now how can I help you, young man? About the boy McKenzie, I assume."

"Yes. The boy your wife, mummy, called him wretched, and dreadful."

"Just a manner of speaking," Jeeves said smoothly. "All in the rough and tumble of a boys school, you know. Now, McKenzie. Is he here? Have you brought our wandering lamb back to the fold?"

Where the wolf is waiting? Derek wondered

"Not yet," he told Jeeves. "Not while he is still healing."

"Healing?" Jeeves was puzzled. "Has he hurt himself? I'm not surprised, mind you. Foolish child, running off into the dark like that."

"Mr. Jeeves..." Derek had enough of the man's airy remarks. "Perhaps you might care to give us an explanation for the lacerations on that boy's body."

"Lacerations?"

"He'd been assaulted with something," Derek was insistent. "On his behind. With a stick or rod. A cane, perhaps. Leaving distinct marks of a flogging."

"Flogging? I think that's putting it a little strongly, young man," Jeeves said patiently. "He may have been smacked for some misdemeanour or...

"Misdemeanour, Sir? Smacked? The boy had been flogged." Derek found he was breathing quickly. Jeeves was flushed, and he too seemed to be having trouble keeping his expression calm and serene.

"Hmmm." Jeeves appeared to consider. "Sounds bad, I admit. And we do have certain elements in the upper school who might indulge in such condign punishment of their juniors. Something I must deal with. Thank you for bringing it to my attention."

Derek took a deep breath: "He says it was you, Headmaster,"

"What?" A rather wobbly reaction intended to convey startled and innocent disbelief. The man pulled his academic gown around himself, in a protective gesture.

"Terry McKenzie says it was you. That you personally inflicted these wounds on him. He was bullied by the bigger boys, yes. But you personally administered the corporal punishment."

Now Jeeves seemed to sit back, putting a finger to his cheek, apparently searching his memory. "Ah, yes. Well. It is true, as I recall, that the lad did need some personal correction. But you know, young man, it was not undeserved."

"Are you saying that Terry McKenzie, aged nine, did something so appalling that he deserved to be thrashed until the blood ran?"

"I'm saying...well, what did the little liar tell you? What am I supposed to have done with this wretched child?"

Derek braced himself. No more prevarication. No more beating about the bush. He leaned forward in his chair, the envelope beneath him rustling slightly. "He told me what you did, Headmaster. And now I'm going to tell you precisely what you did."

CHAPTER TWENTY

Timex watches were relatively new on the market in the early Fifties, but Clive Parsons, the patriarch of the ill-famed Parsons collective family near North Tawe, got his hands on one quite simply. He bought it from one Private First Class Wilson, an American serviceman in the USAAF based in Wiltshire - Clive's contacts could be found at extreme distances - who had in turn purchased it from the PX, the USAF retail store on his base. Clive himself had no use for it. He sported a fob watch that had belonged to his father, and which still told the time more often than twice a day. Instead, silently, almost casually, Clive had presented it to his son, Neville.

Neville didn't ask why he deserved the gift. He knew it was to acknowledge his deeds in the affair of the Polish people being trafficked from a barn in the locality. He had saved Clive's friends Constable Martin and his wife from being baked in a metal animal feed container, and several innocent Poles from being burned alive while imprisoned in cattle restraint chains. Neville didn't flash the watch in front of his mates, because, for no reason he could quite understand, he didn't like talking about the fiery episode and the ensuing escapes. The watch itself served as a sustaining reminder of how he had coped. It was a treasure. A treasured possession. All his.

But now, was the bloody thing running slow?

Friday had taken an age to arrive. Thursday evening had frozen in time. In his lonely bed, Neville had waited and fidgeted like a kid on Christmas Eve. But then Friday did come. And with it would come Sandy. And all he had to do was wait for was eleven o'clock. Eleven was the appointed time. Sandy would be there at eleven. He too would arrive at eleven. And not before. Not stupidly early, like some over-anxious over-eager virgin, condemned to hang around the place with a red face and a butterfly stomach. So, with enormous self-restraint, careful time-planning, and almost God-like patience, Neville arrived at the Chapel at what his Timex told him was – no, it couldn't be, but it was – an unbelievable only twenty past ten.

He stacked his bike around the back of the building, telling himself that, although the hands of the Timex seemed to be on a go-slow, the time until eleven would pass. He strolled around the village, popped into the shop for a Penguin (Nev liked Penguins), then went to the telephone kiosk and pretended to make a telephone call. Yes, he felt, the time was passing at a routine speed, and he held off checking the Timex until he was sure it must be five to eleven. Then he checked the Timex. It told him it was twenty-nine minutes to eleven.

He held the thing to his ear. It ticked vigorously.

Okay, he told himself, do something. Make the bloody time pass. He dropped down the Okehampton road, on down the hill some four hundred yards to the bridge over the Tawe, then climbed down the bank to crouch by the big pool just below. The water here ran with an icy clarity, and something caught his country-boy's eye. It was a large brown trout, basking in the shadow of some weed. Just feet away. Neville recognised it. Old Grandad. A senior denizen of the pool. The fish had been a target for him and his friends from their early teenage years, and they knew Old Grandad well. Yet all the squiggling worms on hooks, the lumps of dough nicked from the bakery, the night lines, the flashy artificial flies - none of them had ever captured the prize. Old Grandad swam serenely on.

But now there he was. Only a couple of feet from where Neville crouched, and lazily unaware of the proximity of any threat. Behind Neville a cloudy sky, with no sun casting shadows, gave the fish no warning. Moving with infinite deliberation, Neville first pushed his watch up his left arm, to keep it dry, then lowered that hand slowly into the water and onto the gravelly bottom. This arm would serve as a support. God, the water was cold! But the Tawe, which began its short life amongst the rocky hills of Dartmoor, was always cold. Again, with snail-like speed, Neville now leaned forward, and slid his right hand into the river with all the surreptitious cunning again of a true country-boy. Slowly, slowly he edged his fingers forward, until they were lurking with evil intent beneath Old Grandad's fat white tummy. Now was the moment. Neville slowly curled his first and second fingers and raised them infinitesimally. The fingertips registered the slightly scaly surface of the underside of Old Grandad. Neville gave the fingers the merest wiggle. Old Grandad rolled over them in piscine ecstasy.

Then a cloud above them split, a ray of sharp winter sun cut through, it zipped across the shiny metal of the

Timex, it flashed into Neville's eyes, and, quite unlike a true country-boy, he jumped, he turned and he looked.

"Jesus!"

Old Grandad leapt, swirled, and disappeared, possibly muttering "That was a close one" to himself.

And Neville scrambled to his feet, gazing in horror at the face of the Timex. The hands said five to eleven.

"Christ! I'm late!"

It takes the average walker some four minutes to climb the hill from bridge to village square. Neville did it in one. At the top, sweating and breathless, he gave himself another two minutes to calm down and dry up, then spent his last minute in a casual stroll across the square, and down the small side road to the chapel, noting as he did so that the village streets were predictably and blessedly deserted.

He walked up the path to the porch of the building. No Sandy. He placed himself on the other side of the porch, shielding himself from inquisitive eyes. Five long minutes he waited, motionless. Five long minutes in which he became convinced that Sandy had either forgotten their appointment, or had changed her mind about him, or even that she had told all her friends about him, and a whole crowd were hiding nearby, poised to burst out and direct streams of derisive laughter at him.

Then, at exactly five minutes past eleven, wearing a short coat with a hood to keep off any drizzle, Sandy came.

CHAPTER TWENTY-ONE

"You abused him, Headmaster. You sexually assaulted him. Here, in your study, night after night, you used that innocent child for your own sexual gratification."

Jeeves stared at Derek, his face turning red, and he raised an arm to stop him. Derrek ignored it.

"To be more precise, you brought him in here, in the middle of the night, in his pyjamas. You sat him on your lap. And you abused him."

"Nonsense!" The man had almost leaped out of his chair and began to walk stiffly back and forth on the deep-pile carpet. "Absolute rubbish."

"You abused him, Headmaster. You put your big hands inside his pyjamas. You fondled him. You touched his genitals, you made him touch you, and you continued until you achieved your disgusting..."

"No!" It was a cry of anguish, almost a bellow, and it rang around the room. In its aftermath Derek heard the door behind him open, and someone enter. He ignored it.

"Do you deny it?" he was determined to get his voice back to an even level.

Jeeves visibly struggled with some self-control and slowly succeeded. He sat back in his chair. "Of course I deny it. I deny every word of it. What nonsense!"

He sat up straight, ready to say more. Derek waited.

"Now look, young man. How long have you been a police officer?"

Derek shrugged and said nothing.

"Not long, I'll be bound. And I can tell that you have yet to learn how wild accusations, based on nothing, can damage someone's life. Some people will believe anything, especially about figures in authority, such as myself. And not just me. Your own career will be blighted if you should continue to allege such nonsensical rubbish."

Derek said nothing, and his silence seemed to encourage Jeeves.

"You need to understand, Constable, that young boys are fantasists. They make things up. Stupid things. Those of us in education are aware of this. Indeed, it sometimes threatens our careers. That isn't fair. Any teacher will tell you the same."

Derek wondered if Mary would agree. He thought not, though she was aware that she was an object of admiration amongst sixth form boys – and probably of their fantasies.

"And. And..." Jeeves's voice had a growing note of desperation about it. "You've got to understand. It's not a one-sided thing, you know. There is a link, a connection, between boys and men. They know it, and they take advantage. They tempt us. They do!"

Derek kept strict control of his hopefully implacable face. He remembered the man's wife saying much the same thing when he first arrived. Was it some kind of rehearsed excuse? A justification?

Jeeves now lost any of the dignity he had struggled hard to maintain. "Christ, man, if these rumours, which is all they are, if they get out, I'd ruined. Disgraced. I'd be destroyed. I'd have to kill myself. Jesus." The man was in tears.

"Just one moment!" It was his wife, Mrs. Jeeves, who had entered behind Derek, but who now moved across the room to stand by her husband, who had half-collapsed across his desk, his head in his hands.

She spoke directly to Derek: "Young man, I don't think you know who you're dealing with here. This is Headmaster Jeeves, a distinguished educator, a man of position, a respected man, indeed, a published author."

She indicated the row of books on the shelves. Then, she sank to one knee and whispered urgently in Jeeves's ear. Derek struggled to hear what she was saying but failed. Whatever it was, it seemed to put a little new life in the man.

Jeeves raised his head, sat up, and glared at Derek through his tears.

"Yes. Quite so, my dear." He got to his feet and Mrs. Jeeves joined him. "As my dear wife says, go ahead. Do your worst. "Put me in the dock, if you must. You won't get a conviction; I'll tell you now. Who are the jury going to believe, eh? Me, a man of position and note? Or a snotty little ten-year-old? And where's your evidence? Where is it? Truth is, you have none. Not a shred."

The man snorted with contempt. His wife looked suitably defiant and echoed her husband. "Not a shred."

"I think you may be wrong there." Derek stood up carefully, reached behind him, and picked up the buff envelope. It was slightly creased from his weight, but the flap opened easily. "I think we might describe these photographs as evidence."

He pulled out two of the prints and held them up. Jeeves stared, stricken. From Mrs. Jeeves came an anguished squawk.

"Oh God, Raymond! I told you not to keep those."

Jeeves was visibly trembling, but still desperately defiant. "Those, those are private. You stole them. Give them to me!"

Derek didn't.

"No, you see... They're not mine." Jeeves was babbling now. "I... I... I confiscated them. From some of the big boys. They'd smuggled them into school. I had nothing to do with them, I hid them, to protect the school."

"You're saying these photographs are nothing to do with you?"

"No, nothing, nothing."

"That's funny. You're in some of them."

It was enough. Jeeves broke. He collapsed onto the desk in front of him. Mrs Jeeves put a comforting arm around his shoulders, tucking his academic gown more securely around his heaving shoulders. Both of them were weeping, Jeeves in big despairing sobs.

Derek spoke clearly and loudly: "Raymond Jeeves I am arresting you on suspicion of physical child abuse, and of sexual activity with a minor. You are not obliged to say anything unless you wish to do so, but what you say may be put in writing and given in evidence."

* * *

"Sorry I'm late." Sandy's face wore the cheeky grin of a woman who doesn't really have to apologise for being late. Or for anything. "Been waiting long?"

"Me, I only just got here too," Neville told her. Which, he thought, was almost true.

"Come on then. Let's get inside." She took his hand and pulled him into the chapel porch. The solid oaken door dared them to enter. Neville took a deep breath, found the big iron catch, and cautiously pushed the door open. According to his observations of the past few days the place had to be empty. Certainly the small vestibule, with its lines of coat hooks, was. And when he listened, he could hear no sound of movement. Everything was okay. Nothing was happening.

But now, 'everything' was about to happen. He turned to Sandy, and there was a look on her face that he could have died for.

"Sweetheart." he began, automatically reaching to hold her, but she put up a gentle but restraining hand.

"Couple of things we got to talk about first, you know."

"Oh yeh, right."

"Well only one thing, really." The girl giggled briefly. "Did you remember to bring a thingy?"

This was a major moment for Neville. A turning point in his day, in his week, perhaps in his life. Sandy had never promised anything. She had never specifically outlined the purpose of their meeting like this. And then, neither had he. He hadn't dared. Her intention might be just a necking session, nothing below the waist, like so many of his previous girls. Or worse, perhaps she just wanted to talk. But now there was no longer any doubt. A thingy itself was a statement of intention. And he did have a thingy, too. In fact he had three. Three in their thin shiny metallic envelopes. He'd had to make a special dash into Okehampton to get them. His previous stock of three had been loaned out to one of his Parsons cousins, who'd met a girl on holiday, and, as he explained, the girl was from Swindon, so he needed at least three of them. The only place to get them in town was one of the two local barbers. And that took a bit of a nerve. Derek had entered the premises, which was inevitably crowded, with one barber, one client in the chair, and four or five more waiting patiently for their turn. The barber had paused in his snipping, and raised an eyebrow at him. Neville murmured his request, handing over, as he did so, what he knew to be the correct purchase price. He hoped that the waiting queue would ignore him, but they didn't, of course, because there was nothing else to distract them apart from old copies of the Farmers' Weekly. "Here we are, young man!" the barber announced cheerfully. "One packet of three gossamer. Have a nice weekend." And Neville left the shop with two burning ears and a lusty chorus of "Aye, aye!" from the benches.

"Yes," he now told Sandy. "I got a thingy. Fact, I got three."

"That's ambitious," Sandy giggled, then laughed more as Neville extracted the items from his pocked, clumsily juggled with them, and dropped them on the floor. Embarrassed yet again, he bent to pick them up, and when he straightened up, he saw that she now wore a more serious expression.

"Nev." she said quietly, as she put a hand to his cheek. "There's no need to be nervous. We've both done this before, right?"

"Yeah."

"Yeah. So. Why don't you go on through to that side room you were talking about, and sort out them cushions? I'll just hang this up..." she indicated her top coat, "and I'll be with you."

"Right!" Neville took two paces to the double doors with frosted glass, that led into the main body of the chapel, pulled them open with slightly shaky hands, and walked through them, letting them swing shut behind him.

Then he stopped. And looked. There was only one thing to see, and it was an unforgettably horrific thing.

Neville clapped a hand over his mouth, in a desperate attempt to stop himself screaming, then turned and burst back through the doors.

CHAPTER TWENTY-TWO

Did Headmaster Jeeves have something to say when he was formally arrested? Something to be taken down and used in evidence? Apparently not. He remained with his head sunk in his hands, sobbing, and doubtless his tears were running off his cheeks and soaking into the immaculate leather-bound blotter on his desk.

Derek waited, then notebook in hand, he wrote, 'no reply' in it. He felt a little self-conscious but told himself not to be so pathetic. This was a routine arrest, nothing to be overly concerned

Eventually Mrs Jeeves gathered herself together sufficiently, to ask: "What happens now?"

"Your husband will be taken to Okehampton police station, and then, I expect, to Exeter H.Q. for more formal interrogation."

"But you can't take him."

"Mrs Jeeves, please. I think you'll find I can. This is a serious charge."

"No, I mean you personally. You can't take him. You came here on a motorcycle. I saw it."

Oh Lord. Derek tried not to look taken aback. Of course, the woman was right. He didn't have a car. And he could hardly expect the headmaster, a detainee, to ride pillion.

"I shall telephone for back up." He tried not to sound like the detective in some cheap Hollywood film. He reached for the phone on Jeeves' desk.

"You can't use that!" Mrs Jeeves's spirits were clearly on the rise. "That's our phone. You don't have permission to use it."

"Madam, allow me to remind you that there is such an offence as perverting the course of justice. And obstructing the police in their duties. And aiding and abetting an offender before, during and after a..."

This was enough for Mrs Jeeves. Her little rebellion was over. She sank to her knees by her husband and mopped her tears in the skirt of his academic gown.

Derek took the phone. Fatty Arbuckle should be his first call. He dialled the Okehampton number. The phone rang out. And rang out and rang out. Where was Welbeloved? What the hell? Were they all asleep in Okehampton?

* * *

Neville ran. He ran with all his might, all the power of his muscular cyclist legs. Sandy ran too, but she had to run backwards, at least at first, because Neville had grasped her two arms just above her elbows, virtually picked her off her feet, and rushed her across the vestibule, out through the porch and down the path, only allowing her to turn and run properly, although physically propelled, when they reached the street and sped back towards the square and the Dragon.

Sandy wasn't the kind of girl who would stay silent whilst enduring this kind of thing.

"Nev! Stop. Wait. What you doing? Neville, for God's sake. What's the matter? Stop it. Christ."

But Neville paid no attention, his breath was coming and going in fearful bursts, and when she did make out a few words that somehow escaped from his mouth they didn't tell her much.

"No. Not you. You can't. You can't be here. Come on! Come on!"

When Neville had first burst back through the interior doors, to grab her, his expression was so desperate, his eyes so fixed and wide, that she thought for a finely split second that desire for her had overwhelmed him, and that whatever the two of them were going to do, they were going to do it right there in the entrance hall, on the tiled floor beneath the coat hooks. Or even up against the wall. She realised almost instantly that she was wrong, and with a faint sense of disappointment mingled with total confusion, she allowed herself to be bundled out.

In no time, it seemed, they reached the forecourt of the pub. Neville took her to the front door – still firmly closed until opening time at noon - stood her with her back to it, and moved his hands to her shoulders to hold her still.

Now his eyes grew bigger still, his face set rigid. "You weren't there. Get it? You were never there. Never. Understand?"

"No." she shook her head.

"Doesn't matter. Just say. If anyone says anything. You weren't there."

Faintly: "All right. But..."

"You'll find out. You can't be mixed up in this. Just remember. You weren't there."

"Oh Neville." she turned her face, now slightly tear-stained, up to his, and he thought for a moment that she was going to say something romantic, something passionate, perhaps "I love you."

What she said was: "My coat – I left it on the peg."

"Shit!" and then: "Don't move."

Neville ran again, across the corner of the square, back to the chapel, into the porch. Then he stopped. He remembered what he had seen. He felt afraid. He tried to stop panting, to be calm. He had to get her coat, he couldn't leave it there, people would know. Probably had her name inside the collar, that's what girls did.

He opened the outside door, and peered in. Nothing. Of course not. And there was the coat, on the peg, just as she had left it. He crouched, not knowing why, and half-crawled across the tiles, reached up to grab the garment, then scuttled back to the porch, pulling the door to behind him.

Then he ran again, down the path, along the road, back to the pub, and to Sandy who, obediently, had not moved.

"Got it." He handed the coat to her, and she looked at him appealingly.

"What is it, Nev? What happened?"

"Not now. You'll hear about it. But remember. You weren't there. Now go on in, I got things to do."

They hugged briefly, then she was gone, and Neville stood alone, and thought. That was the main thing, done. To protect Sandy. He couldn't have her see the thing he had seen. It would mean she'd be involved. He couldn't have that. It would be too much. It was nearly too much for him, and God, he was a man! And no-one would know she had even been to the chapel with him, no-one would know what they were going there for. She was safe.

Job done.

Only not job done. He felt giddy. He wanted to go away somewhere, and hide. But he had to do the next bit. He had to tell. Tell someone. Of course. Tell his friend. The Ginger Copper. Derek. He'd know what to do.

He ran again. By now one or two villagers had seen him running. None were concerned at the sight. That was just that Parsons boy. He's a bit "mazed", people said. Typical Parsons.

* * *

The phone rang on and on. Derek found himself counting the unanswered buzzing. He reached twenty and disconnected. Maybe he'd mis-dialled. He re-checked the number that in truth he knew by heart. At the back of his notebook, he kept a short list of numbers he might need. He redialled the Okehampton number. It rang and rang and rang. They couldn't really be asleep... could they?

He was aware that both the Jeeves had recovered some composure during the time he'd been dialling, that they were straightening up and looking at him. Almost angrily he dialled the number for the Exeter Police H.Q. There had to be somebody there.

There was. A girl's voice, young and slightly nervous.

"Hello...?"

"Exeter Police?"

"Well, yes."

"Give me the duty sergeant please."

"He's not here."

"Well. Anyone from the front desk."

"Putting you through." At last!

"Hello?" Another young voice.

"Hi, this is Constable Martin, North Tawe. I need a car, please, soon as possible, to..."

"Hold on, hold on. Who did you say you are?

Derek a deep breath and patiently repeated his name. "And I need a car, pronto."

"You'll be lucky."

"What?"

"You can whistle for a car mate. None left."

"What are you saying?"

"Every patrol car's in use. You should see the car park. Naked as a jaybird."

"Then. Give me CID."

"Well, all right. But they won't answer. They're all out too. In the cars, I suppose. Ha, ha."

Christ... "What, all of them?"

"Yep."

"They can't be."

"They are."

Derek disconnected. What the bloody... what did he do now? Mary, she'd know what to do.

He dialled his home number.

It was engaged.

He put the phone down. The world had gone cuckoo. It wasn't possible that there was not one, not a single solitary police car available. Anywhere. He'd have to go, go somewhere where he could borrow a car or something, find someone to help. Which would mean leaving Jeeves here, in the school. But the man was under arrest. For serious crimes. He could run off. Bloody hell.

"Young man." Jeeves was making a steady recovery from the emotional pit he had fallen in only a few minutes ago. He now stood, and at his full height. His face was dry despite the recent sobs. His eyes were clear and steady. He adjusted his academic gown firmly around his shoulders, as if it were a badge of authority. "Young man, you seem to be experiencing some difficulty."

Derek shrugged. "Problem with transport."

"You mean, you can't immediately haul me off to your cells."

"No."

"You can't raise assistance."

"Apparently not."

"But having arrested me, you can't abandon me here. You fear I might abscond."

"Well put." The man had indeed summed things up succinctly.

"You could chain me to a radiator, perhaps. But I believe that would lay you open to a charge of kidnapping."

Derek nodded, wearily.

"Then allow me to make a suggestion." Jeeves resumed his seat and waved his wife away with a dismissive hand. "Let me put it this way. When I do come to court, I intend to establish my innocence of any charge. You will be aware that such cases often result in a not guilty verdict. A good lawyer will make mincemeat of any so-called evidence." He nodded at the photographs that Derek had carefully stacked in his uniform pocket. "Fakes. Nothing more. But it is not in my interest to antagonize the authorities during any pre-trial procedures. In other words, when transport does arrive, I will, as they say, come quietly."

"Well. Good, but..."

But Jeeves wasn't finished. "I will, I assure you, have a full answer to any charges you may bring against me. And as you are undoubtedly aware, charges such as these often collapse under more forensic examination."

"You mean you'll wriggle out of it. Not if I can help it."

The man gave a theatrical sigh. "You may not have much of an opinion of me. That I understand. And when you are older, I would suggest that you will become aware that us men, we are not all made the same. And that, while an individual might have certain proclivities, certain needs, this does not make him any less of a man, who in other circumstances can and will behave honourably, properly, and in an accepted and approved fashion."

"All right, but..."

"And thus I can say to you, Constable, that in these circumstances I shall endeavour to, as they say, do the right thing. I shall remain here. I shall not abscond. I do not intend to be hunted across the South West. Nor held at foreign ports. Not my style. No, I shall still be here when the Black Maria comes to take me away." He paused. "And on that you have my word of honour."

"Your... what exactly?"

* * *

The bike started first kick. As he straddled it, Derek felt relieved and relaxed. The Headmaster's "word of honour" was enough. He would keep it. Jeeves had seen him to the door. The man had sufficient insight not to offer a handshake, which, Derek realised, he would have had to refuse. He knew what the man's hands had done. Still, at least he had his word of honour.

By the time he had ridden around the short semi-circular front garden, and out into the narrow lane, a queasy feeling spread up from his groin to his chest, to his brain. What the hell was he thinking? Word of honour? From a sadistic child abuser? How much did that mean? Something? No. Bugger all. Nothing. Worse than nothing. Christ.

And yet what else could he do? What? He shouted the word to the wind.

He trundled on. There was the quarry and now came the towering viaduct. Feeling sick to his stomach already, Derek didn't dare look up at it. He accelerated away from under it, then had to tread hard on the brake to wrench the bike around one of those typical Devon corners. Yes, have a crash now, he told himself. Make the day complete. What had he done? What could he do?

He drove on, on down and up the twisty West Devon lane, then back out onto the more open Okehampton road, and on into North Tawe, and into chaos.

CHAPTER TWENTY-THREE

Neville hadn't run a long distance, when he thought about it, but he couldn't have run another step when he reached the police house, such was the intensity with which he had hurled himself around the village. His breath was raw in his throat, his legs felt like bales of hay, and the image of what he had seen in the chapel flared vividly behind his eyes.

There was no knocker on the door of the police house. It was another thing that Derek and Mary would get round to, once they'd got round to a lot of other things. Nor was there a doorbell. Doorbells were rare in North Tawe. So Neville banged on the door with his knuckles, as hard as he could, and it hurt.

The door opened. Mary, Mrs Martin, that is, who Neville looked up to, even idolised, stood there. Behind her trotted Terry, and behind him, the lolloping Blondie.

"Neville! Good God."

She was staring at him, as he stood, wild-eyed and panting, on the door step. For a long moment he couldn't speak.

"Hello," he said at last.

"Whatever is the matter?"

He hesitated, looked at her, then at Terry, then back to her, and Mary understood. She turned to the boy.

"Terry love, would you take Blondie out the back, to the garden. See if you can find the football, eh? Blondie would love another game. I'll come in a minute."

The boy plus dog dutifully disappeared. Mary turned back to Neville.

"Right. Tell me." And then after a terrified pause, "Is it Derek? Oh God!"

"No. It's not him, no."

"What?"

"Murder. He's dead, I know he's dead. Cut up. Murdered."

Mary reached across the door step, grabbed Neville by the front of his jacket, and pulled him, even jerked him, across the threshold. Once he was inside, she pushed the door shut, then let Neville go. The lad swayed a little, briefly leaned against a corridor wall, but stayed on his feet.

"Tell me!"

"It's the Minister. Simpson, you know. Someone's killed him. In the chapel. Stabbed him, all down the front. He's dead."

"Neville. Wait now. Are you...? that is, are you sure?"

"Oh, yes, Missus. Mary. He's all cut up, his innards are out, gutted like a rabbit he is, there's blood, loads of it, all down him and his big chair and on the floor and..."

"Okay, Neville. Calm down, it's all right. Have you told anyone else?"

"No. Come straight here."

"Then that's the first thing we do, right? We must tell people." She picked the telephone off its stand. "You get your breath. And well done, you've done the right thing."

She dialled 999. Later she would wonder that she did so without hesitation, without any feeling of drama, or over-excitement. It was almost routine.

"Which service please?"

"Police."

She waited. "Police. Can I help you?" It was the Birmingham-tinged voice of a bored constable, no doubt with his feet up on a desk in the Exeter H.Q.

"My name is Mrs Mary Martin."

"Hang on. Get a pencil. Yeah?"

"I am Mary Martin, I am the wife of Constable Martin, the village constable at North Tawe, village the other side of Okehampton." She paused.

"Got that. What can we do for you, Mrs Martin?"

"I have just received information that a man has been killed, in the village chapel."

"What?" She imagined feet hitting the floor in Exeter. "Hang on. Say that again."

"I have just been told that there's a body in the chapel here. Possibly murdered. No, definitely murdered."

"Wait please."

A series of clicks, some muffled voices, then the more confident West Country burr of a mature voice: "Hello? Mrs Martin? Could you please repeat what you have just told the officer?"

Mary did so.

"Are you at the scene at this moment?"

"No." How could I be? Unless there's a phone in chapel. "Someone who has been there, and seen the victim, has just come to tell me."

"Is the witness reliable?"

"Yes."

"And is he sure that the victim is dead?"

Mary looked at Neville. He was no longer standing, instead he'd found a seat on the second step of the stairs, and was sitting with his head in his hands. As Mary turned, he looked up at her. She saw his eyes. In one way, they were blank. In another, there behind them was all the detail of what he had seen – the blood, the slashes, the guts, the lolling head...

"Yes," she said into the phone. "He's sure. The victim is dead."

* * *

Derek sat on his bike, motionless, astonished. So that was where all the police cars were. Mystery solved. They were all parked in and around the North Tawe square. Police vehicles everywhere you looked. Possibly every damn one in the entire South West of England, including squad cars, minor patrol vehicles, motorcycles, vans (including Langdon's dog van), bicycles... every single one of them appeared to have been parked in the thankfully extensive village square. Some, those that had them, were continuing to ring their alarm bells which had cleared their way in the race to reach the village, and had caused two cows to give birth while grazing in adjoining fields. Others, equipped with the new-fangled flickering blue lights, continued to flicker, even though they had come to an untidy but unthreatening full stop. Out of these vehicles had spilled some of the most determined, energetic, and frankly thrilled police officers, young and middle aged, men for the most part, but including a pair of women constables, who, as ever with pairs of women constables, consisted of one grossly overweight bully, and one so beguiling in her tight uniform that she could wring a confession out of the Pope. All these representatives of law and order milled around the village like a disturbed crowd of maggots that you find when you overturn an aged cowpat.

Altogether it was a scene of semi-organised confusion. And no wonder! This was a murder case. Murder for sure - a rare enough crime in the western peninsular of the country, true. But this one – wow! What a murder! Not your usual killing, not by a hundred miles. Not some drunk kicked to death in a late-night pub fight. Not some violent husband, lying on the kitchen floor with a weeping little woman in a blood-stained housecoat standing over him and still gripping the carving knife, and with the Sunday lunch still half-sticking against the scullery wall where he had thrown it. Not even the greasy lover found naked and bludgeoned on the floor of the bedroom of his best friend's wife. No, this was a real murder. A movie-type murder. A who-dun-it. A murder par excellence. No domestic upheaval, no casual and unintended fatality, no, this was an upstanding citizen, a respected man, a Minister of Religion for heaven's sake. And the recipient of a bloody assault with some sharp instrument which, according to the first couple of bobbies who entered the chapel – a House Of God, for God's sake – had filleted him into something more resembling what arrives at the end of the mechanical line in a slaughterhouse.

Yes, every cop, helmeted, capped or plain-clothed, wanted to be in on this one. And they were all there. Them and their police vehicles. This was a real murder.

So Derek's inner turmoil, the mixture of guilt and misgiving swishing around in his brain after his encounter with the dreadful Jeeves, faded away into infinity as he stared at the scene. He wondered what on earth had happened. He saw some official faces he recognised, but many of the police he had never seen in his life. But there of course was Welbeloved. Large, slow, and getting in the way. And somewhere in the square, no doubt parked to create a traffic jam, would be the rickety Okehampton squad car that he had needed so badly less than an hour or so ago.

What on earth was going on? A pretty obvious question to ask, and one undoubtedly echoed by the villagers witnessing the scene, some hovering on their doorsteps, others peeping through net curtains that hadn't been parted with such dusty alacrity since the War.

Derek decided not to ask. If he did, he decided, he might tip himself into an emotional brainstorm. Enough. The day had been too much. He put the bike into gear and slowly rode out of the square, into the side road, and home.

What he thought of in lighter moments as his newly acquired family, wife, kid, dog, plus Neville the love-struck teenager, were all in the kitchen. But this was obviously not a lighter moment. Only the dog looked cheerful. Terry sat at the kitchen table, eating a marmalade sandwich and reading. His expression was one of controlled excitement. The book he had was Derek's own copy of Treasure Island – a much-loved volume. Derek hoped Terry wouldn't get marmalade on it.

It was the other two occupants, Mary and Neville, sitting at either end of the table in front of cold cups of tea, who together promoted a grim and chilling atmosphere that seemed to envelop Derek as he entered. He attempted to lighten it.

"I leave the village in your hands for a single morning, and look what happens to it!"

Mary tried to speak, but her words were trapped in her throat.

"Well come on then," Derek insisted. "Half the police on earth are charging around out there. What the hell is going on?"

Mary sighed, as if shouldering a burden. "It's Simpson. Your friend. The minister."

"Him again! No friend of mine, the jumped-up little ... Or rather big..." he remembered Terry's presence and held back the appropriate word.

Mary didn't smile. "He's dead."

"Wha..? Dead? Really?" Weak words but they were the first to come.

"Dead. Murdered. Stabbed. In the chapel."

"Good God. Well, that would account for all the chaos. Have they got who did it? When did it happen? Who found the body?"

Mary clearly decided to answer only the last question, and pointed an accusatory finger at Neville.

"You did it, Nev?" He stared at the lad, aghast.

"No, no, no." Mary's exasperation was mingled with shock and strain. "Of course not. No, Neville found him. In the chapel. In his, whatever you call it. His special seat."

"There was all this blood," Neville told him, in a small voice. "He was all opened up. Bits out, like when you gut a rabbit. You know?"

"Christ."

"Neville did the right thing," Mary sounded more in control. "He came straight here and told me."

"I ran like buggery," Neville put in.

Derek glanced at Terry. The boy still seemed deep in the treasure island jungle with Jim Hawkins.

"And I rang 999," Mary finished. "Asked for the police."

"That certainly worked," Derek told her. "They're all here."

"I heard the bells. But I thought I should stay here. Wait for them to come to us. "

"Yeah, right." He nodded reassuringly. But where were they? They should be here, he thought. They're everywhere else. Another thought struck him.

"Nev, what were you doing in the chapel? In the first place?"

Neville's face, up to now looking pale and strained, began slowly to be coloured by a reddish flow, starting at his open neck, and flooding up past his cheeks.

He was saved from providing any kind of answer to the question by a loud and authoritative bang on the front door.

CHAPTER TWENTY-FOUR

Detective Chief Superintendent Paul Anderson was not a man to mess about. "I'm not a man to mess about," he told his team members, and they all knew that he wasn't a man to mess about. Or to be messed about. No way.

And today Anderson wasn't either being messed about or messing about. He was getting on with the job. By the time he reached North Tawe the remainder of the Devon constabulary had arrived in the village. He was late because he had insisted on directing his driver too far down the A.30 and thus missed the most appropriate turn-off. But he was there now, and now there'd be no messing about.

Smart-suited, smart booted, it was sometimes commented that Anderson looked much smarter in his plain civilian clothes than the Chief Constable did in his uniform. The Detective Chief Superintendent strode through the square like a titan. A small titan, barely five feet six even when he stretched. But he thought of himself more as a bullet, an explosive-tipped bullet at that, whizzing through space to detonate on target. As he walked, a small retinue joined him, falling in beside him and trailing behind him. Inspectors, senior Sergeants, one of the two women constables. All of them trying to keep in step with him, which always proved rather difficult for the taller ones with longer legs, because the Detective Chief Superintendent's legs were short even in comparison to his short body, so while he strode out with purpose and style, behind him came a slightly stumbling and hesitating tail.

Anderson encouraged an entourage. He believed it gave him a sense of command, a sense of mission. He preferred to be called "Commander". He believed that his people were relieved that he had come to take over, that they were saying to themselves: "The chief's here. The boss man. All right!" In truth, none of them ever said anything like that, to themselves or anyone else. What some of them said to themselves, and one or two actually whispered out loud, was "Oh God, here we go again!" in tones verging on professional despair.

Anderson strode on, down the side street to the Chapel. He strode up the path. That fool of a doctor in his flapping white coat was hovering, but Anderson brushed him aside, and strode unflinchingly into the chapel, where a couple of white-overall-clad technicians stood aside to give him a clear view of the victim. Two minutes later he strode out equally confidently. Some of his entourage had waited outside, some had accompanied him inside, and now straggled out with him. He told them all to wait. He then strode importantly around the chapel to a patch of grass where he could not be seen, and brought up both his breakfast and last night's supper. Then he strode on round the building to take the entourage rather by surprise from the rear. He surveyed them all for the first time that morning. Some of them, those who had entered the chapel with him, looked a little pale and unsteady.

"What's the matter with you lot?" he demanded. "Never seen a stiff before?" And then, without a pause:

"Now, where's my incident room? We do have an incident room set up, don't we? We don't? All right. Bloody incompetence. What are we going to do for an incident room?"

"The tent?" The suggestion came from an Inspector - actually Inspector Reed from Okehampton, feeling awed by the company but also anxious to help, and apparently also being the only one present who remembered that the force did have a portable incident tent for just such situations.

"In this bloody weather?" Anderson sneered. "Talk sense!" A gust of January wind off the North Atlantic made his point for him. "Any sensible suggestions?"

"The village hall?" someone else tried, and accordingly Anderson led his people back up into the square, and on down the lane that led to the pre-war concrete-constructed Victory Hall, which, with its multitude of chairs, its small stage, its running water, electricity and toilets, was an ideal site for an incident room.

No-one had the key. And no-one knew who had the key. Anderson made a decision. "The pub!" he announced.

At the Green Dragon John the Landlord put up what opposition he could to the proposal that he had to close down for the duration. "I'm not sure I can legally close down," he told Anderson "The law says that..."

"We are the damn law," Anderson told him, and the damn law duly moved in. John slipped upstairs to explain and comfort his dying wife, and Sandy hid in her bedroom. The bar tables were scraped, with much clattering and screeching, into the vague formation of a big company board room. Phone lines were installed by technicians, in the process of which the pub's own telephone connection was ruthlessly disconnected. Anderson took his rightful place at the head of this ad hoc reconstruction, seating himself on the highest available chair. Under the table he sat at, his smart city boots dangled some three inches from the floor, but he put up with that because no-one could see them. Outside the pub a constable pinned a hastily written notice on the front door. It read: "Public House Temporarily Closed", words which one regular would subsequently describe as the saddest four words in the dictionary.

"Right!" Anderson announced, his hard voice penetrating the noise of subordinates hurriedly finding chairs for themselves. "First question. Who is the victim?" There was a pause. Then he answered himself. "Oh yes, someone said. The Minister. Simpson. Okay. Second question. Who found the body?"

A Sergeant from Exeter knew, or rather, knew after he consulted his notebook. "The first report was made by a Mrs Mary Martin."

"Who she? And where is she? She should be here!"

Welbeloved saw his chance to shine. He was a little out of breath, having been left behind in all three of the Superintendent's surges across the square. But now he could contribute – and to better effect than Inspector Reed.

"I know her, Sir," he volunteered.

"Who you?"

"Sergeant Welbeloved, Okehampton station."

"Oh God, yes. I remember you." Anderson raised his eyes to the pub's nicotine-yellow ceiling. "Well?"

"Sir, Mrs Martin is the wife of Constable Martin, the North Tawe bobby. Martin is under me, you see."

"Poor bugger. Must be squashed." Anderson sucked in some sycophantic appreciation of his joke, then said: "Well? Is he here? Where is he?"

"Well, Sir..." Welbeloved felt an urgent and unfamiliar need not to drop Derek in it. "He's been otherwise..."

"Oh for God's sake!" The Superintendent's famous temper was beginning to blossom. "Go and get him. And his wife. And his bloody cat if he's got one."

Welbeloved turned to go, but was stopped.

"Not you, fatso. We haven't got all day. Please! Someone who knows where to go. Go!"

A young constable raised his hand, then turned and left in a hurry.

"Right," the Superintendent said. "Where's my tea?"

CHAPTER TWENTY-FIVE

Derek vaguely recognised the young constable at the door. They'd served together at Exeter. Neither liked the other.

"Superintendent wants you," the constable told him on the doorstep, showing no sign of wishing to enter.

"Right. About the..?"

"About the murder. What else?"

"Yeah, I've only just heard about it."

"You're the village copper and you've only just heard about it. Half the cops in Devon are here, and you've only just heard about it? You're really on the ball, aren't you, mate!"

"Look, I... Never mind. He wants me, does he?"

"You and your missus. Get your skates on."

"He can get lost!" It was Mary. She startled Derek. He hadn't been aware that she'd followed him to the door. Now she elbowed him aside. "I'm not going anywhere," she told the constable. "I have a child to look after. If he wants to speak to me, he can come here." Mary didn't exactly explain that the child she had to look after wasn't actually her child, and the constable didn't query her assertion. Instead he said:

"But you discovered the body! The victim. The crime."

"No I didn't. I just reported it. Someone else discovered the body. They told me."

"Who? Anderson will want them as well."

Mary hesitated. Don't be silly, she told herself. Of course they will want to speak to Neville. But...

"It was me." As Mary had surprised Derek, so Neville surprised her, speaking over her shoulder to the man at the door. "I discovered it. In the chapel."

"Right. Come on then," the constable said, "you can help us with our enquiries." He turned to Derek. "You too."

Derek found his helmet, Neville found his plimsoles, and they joined the Exeter constable in the street. He looked at them pityingly.

"Christ, Old Anderson is going to eat you two alive!"

* * *

"Old Anderson" ate Neville alive first.

"What's your name?"

"Neville."

"No, Sonny. Not what your mummy calls you. Your proper name."

"Oh. Parsons."

A slight frisson ran through a couple of the entourage, and Anderson, always ready to seize on something that didn't need to be seized on, picked up on it at once.

"Hello?" he asked. "That name mean something?"

Neville, who had been placed before the Superintendent, looked much like a recanting sinner hauled before a Spanish inquisitor who was trying to fulfil his quota of burnings for the day. He attempted to say something, but a keen sergeant got in first.

"Well known criminal fraternity in these parts," the man said. "Bunch of rapscallions."

"Oh! Ah! So we have a rapscallion here, do we?" Anderson was delighted. "So, Mr Rapscallion Parsons – why d'you do it?"

"Um." Neville looked around, desperately but trying but failing to catch Derek's eye, "I just ran to Derek, Constable Martin's place and..."

"No, no, no." Anderson shook his head with mock sadness. "Why did you do it, Sunshine? Why did you kill the Minister?"

"But I never killed him..." Neville sagged at the knees. "I never... I just went in and saw him and..."

"Caution him, someone."

A plain clothes detective started to recite the familiar words to Neville, who gaped at him like a rabbit in the headlights.

Derek pushed his way forward through the scrum of policemen. "Sir, if I might. I think you might have the wrong man here."

"Oh you think so, do you, Constable? You know better, do you?"

Derek took in a breath. Then: "Sir, I'm the local Bobby here, PC Martin, and I do know Neville Parson quite well. I believe him when he says he discovered the victim, that he's not the killer."

"Hmm. He seems a bit upset. A bit guilty."

"Sir, I think he is in shock from witnessing the deceased. I understand it is a little distressing. And if he was the perpetrator, wouldn't he be covered in blood?"

Neville looked down his own front, as did everyone else.

"What's that stain?" Anderson demanded, pointing to the boy's shirt. "How did you get that then?"

"I spilled me tea."

To Neville's surprise this got a laugh. The Superintendent changed tack immediately. "Forensics tell me the damage was done with a large hand knife. You, boy, do you possess a large knife?"

Neville shook his head but tried to be helpful. "I got a hook. For hedging."

Anderson ignored a secondary laugh. But by now even he knew he was following a dud trail. He lightened his tone. "But not for killing chapel ministers, eh? Well, don't go anywhere. We'll deal with you in a moment.' He turned back to Derek. "Who did you say you are?"

"Constable Martin. The local bobby."

Anderson narrowed his eyes. "You're the one they talk about, right? Something of a hero?" Then before Derek could react: "Well we want none of your heroics here, laddie. Just plain proper police work. You know the local peasants. Get out there, do some house-to-house."

He rose from his chair, looking smaller than ever, but retaining his chronic self-possession, and his strident voice: "Same goes for the rest of you. House to house. I want everyone in this god-forsaken dump spoken to this morning. All of 'em, all the yokels, all the peasants, even those that can't speak English. Let's do some policing by the book, shall we? I need to know why anyone would want to kill this poor bugger in the chapel. Who wanted him dead? Because quite obviously someone, someone with a big knife, did. Come on, out of here!"

The roomful of police dispersed with haste, taking Derek with them. The Superintendent sent one constable into Okehampton to arrange for a mass delivery of sandwiches. He sent another to find John, who had been hovering in the backrooms of his beloved pub, and to tell him to open up the bar for him, the County would pay. It was lunch time.

Neville was left standing. Police uniforms flowed around him. It is debatable whether any other member of the Parsons heritage had ever been in contact with so many representatives of the law in one place at one time, even though the tribe's relationship with the force was long and complex. As the rush to duty began to die down, Neville turned, hopefully on his way out to clean decent Devon air untainted by officialdom. But a burly sergeant caught his arm with one beefy hand, picked up a chair with the other, and sat both down, the chair first and Neville on top of it. He was told firmly to stay put. He looked up and found he was sitting immediately under the pub dart board. It somehow seemed significant.

Derek walked out onto the square, feeling a little dizzy. A sergeant was organising the house-to-house, allocating certain streets to pairs of constables. Derek ignored him.

Instead he walked slowly across the tarmac, heading for home. Thinking hard, then trying not to think. He didn't like the way his thoughts were leading him.

And then, as he walked on, someone was waving at him, someone over by the phone kiosk. Someone in a long gabardine raincoat, buttoned to the neck, even though the rain had threatened but not fallen. Then he recognised him. It was Matt. Christ; he'd forgotten all about him in the last few hours. He wanted badly to break off, to go and see him, relish his jovial if high-octane company.

But, no. No, he'd have to wait for the pleasure of his friend's company. Something else was pressing in on him. A niggle, a heavyweight niggle, that he was afraid to face. The significance of it appalled him.

So. They wanted to know who would kill the poor bugger in the chapel. Who would want him dead? Who had a motive? And he knew who. She'd virtually said so. She had motive. If the minister died, her little tribe would be secure. She had the opportunity too, in that she accounted to no-one for her movements. And she had the necessary knife.

But she wouldn't, would she? Kill someone? No of course she wouldn't. Never. Not a girl like that. Not Aphrodite Wondergirl. Not Lucy.

But the thought boiled up like a storm cloud. It wouldn't blow away. She had said so. He heard her voice again. Talking about Simpson. "Honestly, I could kill them." "Them," not "him", of course. But that was just, what was it called? Semantics. And it was just an outburst, anyway. Words that were just said, in the heat – or rather the mid-winter chill – of the moment, meaning nothing, just casual hyperbole. Anyone might say it, might just mutter "I could kill him..." husbands and wives said it about each other. Meaningless talk. Teasing. Exaggeration. Just chatter. Surely, she didn't mean it. Surely not.

And then there was the knife...

* * *

"You've got to go straight back and tell him. Tell him everything." Mary was taking no prisoners.

"Yes, but... Look, I don't have to tell them. Someone else will. Someone else will say, oh, Simpson was having a row with the Beatniks." Actually he wasn't sure anyone else knew, but...

"Makes no difference. You're the police, for heaven's sake. You've got that duty you're always on about."

They were in the kitchen. Terry sat at the table, doing schoolwork Mary had found for him. He was exhibiting a surprising ability to concentrate on his studies when all around him adults were flaying each other with moans, groans and accusations. At this moment he was concentrating on the complexity of compound interest. At his feet, Blondie was concentrating on compound disinterest.

"It's just that I can't quite get it into my head that she'd be capable of something like that. Not killing someone..."

"Ha! Why not? They're beatniks. I've read about them, in America. They're weird, those people. They're said to be immoral. You don't really know them. You don't know what they might do. Well, do you?"

"No, true." Derek sighed. "But it sort of feels wrong."

"I don't know what's the matter with you," Mary shot back. "You're usually so straight, so decisive. You know what's the right thing to do. Have you started giving flipping criminals the benefit of the doubt or something? Letting them off?"

"Look, I just think..."

Mary wasn't finished. "And now just because you've got a thing about this woman."

Derek stood up so abruptly that the table jerked, and both Terry and Blondie looked up briefly, before going back to what they were or were not doing before. Derek went to the door to the hall, then turned back.

"Let's get one thing clear," he told his wife. "I do not have a thing for that woman, as you call her. Her name is Lucy, and she is a friend. And if I can't have a friend who happens to be a woman, then I don't know what I'm doing in this job. Or, come to that, what I'm doing here. With you."

He felt his face burning, as he headed for the front door. It had never been like this, not in their two years of marriage, not since the day they met. God almighty, what had he just said? Why did he say that last bit? Oh Jesus.

She caught up with him before he reached the door. "No, no, no. I'm sorry, I'm sorry, I didn't mean it like that," she wailed, wrapping her arms around him. Derek did similar wrapping on his own account.

"I suppose I'm jealous," Mary said weepily. "Of course you can have friends, of course. I've just been silly."

"No, I'm sorry, I shouldn't have shouted, it was stupid." he told her. They kissed; each kiss full of instant forgiveness.

"They'll want me back soon, you can bet on it," he told her.

"Stay a little bit." And she pulled him down to sit beside her on the bottom stairs.

They smiled at each other, and smiles turned into more kisses and hugs.

Terry appeared in the hall, holding up his exercise book

"Finished!" he crowed.

"I haven't," Derek told him. And they hugged some more.

CHAPTER TWENTY-SIX

"All right, Sherlock. Tell us the tale."

There were just three interrogators. Anderson himself, sitting between two other individuals, one in the familiar shape of Inspector Reed, presumably there because the murder had happened on his 'patch'; the other a detective in plain clothes that looked extremely shabby when compared to the Savile Row stylings of the Detective Chief Superintendent. Welbeloved hovered, or rather sagged, somewhere in the background.

Before the three interrogators stood Derek and Neville, the former fresh from hugging his wife, the latter relieved to be freed from his chair under the dartboard, especially as one of the two police women in the Superintendent's entourage, both of whom had been retained for tea-making duties, had picked up a set of pub darts and pretended to begin a game.

Derek wasn't sure which of them was the 'Sherlock' in Anderson's opening remark, finally deciding it must be him.

"Sir," he began, "can I suggest that we hear from Neville, Mr. Parsons, first. How exactly he found the victim, and so on?"

"Sir, can I suggest that we hear from..." The Superintended produced a ludicrously inaccurate mockery of Derek's words, then sighed heavily and sarcastically. "Go on then, Neville. Tell us about it."

"I already said."

"Say it again, laddie."

"Well, I went in the chapel, and I saw him and then I ran like buggery."

Anderson turned elegantly to his Inspector Reed. "Write that down, man. He ran like buggery."

The inspector wrote industriously on a pad, mouthing the words: "He... ran... like... buggery..."

The plain-clothes detective now spoke up.

"Sir, can I ask a question?"

"Ask away."

"Son," the man turned to Neville. "Why did you go in the chapel?"

Derek felt Neville twitch. Neville himself had a brief vision of Sandy, smiling at him, asking if he'd remembered to bring a thingy.

"About time someone asked that question," Anderson snapped, giving the impression that he'd been deliberately waiting for it. "Answer him, Parsons," And then, when Neville opened his mouth but said nothing, "Come on. You must remember. It was only this morning. Middle of the morning, a week-day. What were you doing in the chapel?"

Neville stuttered, but the words, such as they were, made no sense. "I wanted something."

"The poor box?" The Superintendent made it more of an assumption than a question.

"No!" Neville managed that with some emphasis. Then, in injured tones: "I would never steal from a church. The house of God. Never!"

Derek remembered how, back in the autumn, he had first met Neville when he was trying to wrench a sheet of lead off the porch of a House of God, namely the parish church. Well, he thought, that wasn't actually inside the House of God. Just outside. Mentally he forgave Neville.

"They ain't got no poor box," Neville managed.

"How disappointing for you. One more time, Mr. Parsons," Anderson told him. "One more time before we stick you in the cells and throw the key away. Why did you go into the chapel this morning. Why?"

Neville glanced at Derek. Derek could only look back, he couldn't help. Indeed, he too wanted to know why Neville was in the chapel.

After a long hesitation, Neville answered the question.

"To pray."

Derek couldn't quite manage to stifle a snort of laughter, but covered it up with a cough. The detective was staring at the desk in front of him, his shoulders shaking. The inspector had his eyes turned to the ceiling. Anderson, visibly fuming, simply glared.

"Get out of here, boy. Before I kick your arse to Bideford and back."

Neville literally ran for it, and found himself out in the village square, out in the open fresh crisp West Devon air. He took a deep breath. It tasted of petrol, supplied by the host of police vehicles.

* * *

Derek knew he must speak. Despite the Superintendent's obvious contempt for and dismissal of rural cops, he'd be in trouble If he didn't report all he should report as soon as possible. So when Neville escaped, he stood his ground and waited.

Anderson looked up. "You still here?"

"Sir, I do have some knowledge of, well, I know some things which might help in your investigation."

"Some things, eh? Go on then. What things?"

"Well." A deep breath. "I have recently had contact with the deceased. The victim. The minister."

There was a short silence. Anderson's face creased, as if puzzled. He turned and held a whispered conversation with the detective, lasting several sentences. Then he turned the other way, and whispered to Inspector Reed, again for a surprisingly long time.

"Of course, Constable." The Superintendent now managed to sound bored. "We are well aware of the victim. He is a Mr Dermot Sim..."

"Donald." the plain clothes detective corrected.

"Mr. Donald Simpson," Anderson continued blithely, "the vicar, or rather, the minister of the village chapel. A single man. Very much respected, apparently. And known as the man who..." He paused, turned again to the detective, and another whispered chat took place. Finally he turned back to Derek. "Known as a man who takes his goats for a walk."

His voice tailed off in disbelief, and Derek came to his rescue. "Yes Sir, that's him. What I should tell you is..." He hesitated, collecting his thoughts.

Anderson's patience was reducing to a bare minimum: "Well? What?"

"Well, it started because he asked me to visit him just after Christmas. I did, and he showed me some cards – printed cards – which had been distributed amongst the graves in the chapel cemetery."

"What cards? Playing cards?"

"No Sir, specially printed cards. With writing on them. The Minister was very annoyed, he said it was littering, and he insisted that I get it stopped. The same cards also appeared amongst the graves in the Parish Church, but the vicar wasn't that bothered, to be honest."

The detective raised an eyebrow. "The writing on these cards, what did it say?"

"It asked whoever read it to remember three women."

"What women?"

"Um." Derek dredged his memory. "Mary Trembles. Susannah Edwards and Temperance Lloyd," he managed, not without a sense of achievement.

"Who are they? Know them, do you? Names sound familiar?" Anderson asked bluntly. And when Derek shook his head and shrugged, he turned to his colleagues. "Those names mean anything to us?"

Getting no positive reply, he turned back to Derek. "So." And with heavy irony, "This was a case of criminal littering, was it?"

"Yes Sir. But..."

"Well go on, sunbeam. Don't leave us in suspenders." He laughed at his hackneyed pun, but to their credit, neither of his colleagues reacted.

"Sir, at around the same time a case of chicken-stealing was reported to me, by a small-time local farmer."

"The plot thickens!" the Superintendent. "And, and..." He glanced around to make sure everyone was paying attention... "and did this lead you to suspect fowl play!?" He nudged the detective. "Get it?"

If he'd hoped for what comedians called a "woofa!" he was disappointed. Instead he received an ovation of indifference, broken only by a sycophantic chuckle from the Inspector.

Derek told himself it was funnier the first time. Perhaps it was in the way you tell them. He waited for a moment, then continued: "Yes Sir. I reported the thefts, and..."

Welbeloved broke in: "Yes, Sir, he did. I can confirm that."

"Just as well he did, for his sake," Anderson remarked. "All thefts must be reported." He looked severely around at everyone, and Derek blessed the elderly sergeant and his advice. "Always cover your..."

"Yes Sir," he went on. "The owner of the chickens claimed that the thieves were part of a group of Beatniks."

"What!?" It was both a question and an exclamation. "What Beatniks? More of those grubby parasites" He turned angrily to the detective. "That the same lot we got rid of in Brixham?"

"No, Sir," came the reply. "New ones. We had a little group of them, camped out in the Cathedral Close, the cheeky buggers. Had their pony grazing on the grass. They did a bit of busking, but we moved them on."

"Did they have a woman leading them?" Derek asked, despite an irritated look from Anderson. "Wore a long cloak."

"That's them," the detective said. "A bossy one, that one. Bit of a mouth on her."

"Then it is the same group, Sir," Derek admitted.

"Beatniks. These people are scum," Anderson pronounced, a vein visibly throbbing by his right eye. He made a brushing motion with his hand on the table in front of him. "We need to get rid of them. So, where are these people? In the village?"

"No, Sir. They were camped out in a ruined chapel near here. But I think by now they may have moved on."

"Hmmm." The Detective appeared to consider. "From Exeter. Here. Probably heading for the coast. Bude. Sort of place these people like to infest."

"Sir." Derek cleared his throat. He knew what he had to say. He hated the prospect of saying it. It felt like betrayal. Fortunately the Inspector said some of it for him.

"Did these so-called beatniks, were they responsible for the cards?"

"Yes, they were. Some campaign or other."

"And the victim, Simpson, did he have contact with them?"

"Well, yes. But not so much about the cards." I'm betraying her, Derek thought. But it had to be said. "It was because they were in the old chapel. Holy ground, he said. He had them thrown out, got some sort of court order, and they had nowhere else to go. There was a bit of a row. Between the girl, their leader, and the Minister."

The Superintendent, who had been unusually quiet for the last few moments, virtually pricked up his ears. "A bit of a row? A shouting match?"

"Yes, Sir," Derek had to agree.

"Were you there?"

"Yes, coincidentally. I was there about the stolen chicken, but..."

"So you saw the row. You witnessed it. Were threats made?"

Derek nodded.

"Well?"

"Yes. It became a little heated. But I can't think..."

Anderson looked at both his colleagues in turn. "There you have it. Motive. Get after them. Specially the woman. Bring her back here. She shouldn't be hard to find. Probably smell her, that sort never wash." And, when the other two hesitated, reverting to his sarcastic mode, "Now, gentlemen. If you would be so good, I want some lunch. What's happened to those sandwiches?"

"Sir, can I just say..." Derek asked reluctantly.

Half out of their chairs, the three men stopped, and listened, though Derek wished that they hadn't. But this was a case of murder, he had to say it, because...it had to be said.

"When, If you find her, she has a flat wooden box. You'll need to have that."

"Why? What's in it?"

"A couple of rather large knives."

CHAPTER TWENTY-SEVEN

A sleek, shiny and purring Jaguar saloon, the class of car that rarely graced the tarmacked square of North Tawe, now made its entrance, and a more fanciful mind than Derek's might imagine that the other more common police vehicles, parked in haphazard confusion, might now shuffle to one side to allow the Jag to take pride of place in the centre of the square. Derek, not being of fanciful mind, instead watched with envy as the car drew to a halt with the same smooth grace that he had seen it achieve in the Colonel's farm yard. Out of it stepped the glossily uniformed figure of the Chief Constable, Sir Arthur Beer.

Derek had expected that Sir Arthur, being the County's top cop, would immediately stride with official confidence into the Dragon, to take personal charge of the case. He didn't. Instead he plunged headlong into the branch of police work that, in retrospect, Derek would realise was of equal importance. It was termed Public Relations – or PR as he would learn to call it. There'd been a minimally brief lecture on the subject of Public Relations during training, and Derek had either been absent, or absent-minded, and it had passed him by. Now here it was, in all its shining glory.

Sir Arthur's craggy face bore an entirely appropriate expression for the occasion – a trace of compassion for a murder victim, a touch of resolution to catch the evil doer, and a smear of reassurance which would convince the local yokels that they were not all about to be murdered in their beds, all of which was somehow conveyed through a shiny-eyed beam. He stood for a moment, looked around, increased the beam factor, even gave small waves of his hand as if recognising certain individuals. If he did, no-one beamed back. But Sir Arthur didn't mind.

Members of his team had been to work on his behalf, and a small stand had been put together in the centre of the square, consisting of some empty beer bottle crates from the back of the Dragon, covered by a length of green material from the stage prop store in the now belatedly unlocked village hall. Others, mostly those doing door-to-door enquiries, had encouraged residents to leave nervous doorsteps and assemble in front of this ad hoc stage, About thirty of them had complied. Standing to one side – but undoubtedly, in the Chief Constable's opinion, the most important person within hearing range was a photographer from the Western Morning News, who arrived in a newsroom van so battered and rusted that he hid it down a side turning.

Sir Arthur, having acknowledged a few more fictional greetings, now strode towards his rostrum. As he did so he passed Derek and, with what must have been a moment of considerable relief, he saw someone he actually knew.

"Hello there, young constable," he cried. A busy man like Sir Arthur could not be expected to remember names of course. "How did you get on with those hounds from hell, then? Did they catch you?"

"More or less, Sir," Derek managed.

"Jolly good, jolly good." Sir Arthur's laugh, like his beam, was expertly crafted to signify good will while not detracting from the serious nature of the situation.

Mounting his green platform, the Chief Constable looked out gravely at the crowd. He saw various expressions looking back at him, some of serious concern, some vacantly curious, and not a few of eager anticipation of watching one of them highfalutin toffee-nosed buggers from Exeter make a fool of himself. One of the latter group made himself heard.

"Golly-gosh! Look at his ribbons. Looks like a Christmas tree!"

Sir Arthur did indeed wear a three-decker display of military decorations on his chest. When did he win those? Derek wondered. 1914-1918? Wherever, however, he deserved respect. Not heckling.

What Derek didn't see, and neither presumably did Sir Arthur, was the group of Sunday-suited men, plus a few rather dowdy women, who came together in one corner of the square, where they remained watching events in grave silence.

"Good morning, everyone." Sir Arthur began, but his voice was lost in the general hum of conversation. With an irritable gesture, he turned to officers nearby, one of whom reacted almost violently with the guilty realisation that he had forgotten to give the man his megaphone. This he now did, and when the Chief Constable now spoke his words echoed around the whitewashed cottages lining the square.

"Good morning, everyone. My name is Sir Arthur Beer, I am your Chief Constable, and I am here today to speak to you about the tragic event of the last twenty-four hours."

Which means, thought Derek, that they still don't know exactly when Simpson was slaughtered. But it must have been some time in the previous night.

"First of all," Sir Arthur continued, "I am here to reassure you that our finest detectives are at this very moment conducting a thorough investigation, doing all they can to bring the perpetrator of this despicable act to book. We are currently following up several lines of enquiry – one in particular would seem to be very promising - and of course I will personally bring you news of any developments, as and when they occur. Secondly, I would like to offer you my personal sympathy for the loss this community has suffered. I understand that the victim, the Reverend Doctor Donald Simpson..." Derek noted that at least Sir Arthur had troubled to get the name and title right "...was a much loved and respected Minister, and will be sorely missed."

Derek found himself warming to the Chief Constable. Yes, he was mouthing clichés, but they were mouthed with sincerity. And sometimes clichés say it all. Good for the old boy, he thought.

The Old Boy now continued, in a more conversational style. "Now I know how some of you probably feel, about people like me, stuck up in our ivory towers, thirty miles away in Exeter. You probably – and possibly with some justification – feel that we don't really care too much about you, over here in the west. Well if you think that, let me assure you, you are quite wrong. The life you live here, in these villages, is as important to us as it is in any of our bigger towns and cities. I came into policing – many, many years ago now of course, ha, ha – but I came into it to help people. To protect people. All the people. In the smallest hamlet to the biggest city."

Derek felt absurdly touched. That was why he'd taken the job too, wasn't it? Or had recent events rubbed his sensibilities raw?

"So I would ask you now to return to your homes, to your places of livelihood, feeling that your safety is in good hands."

Nicely put, Derek thought. He decided he liked Sir Arthur.

"Look at that supercilious old bastard. Someone ought to shoot him!"

The Australian accent, the derisive voice, it was Matt, of course. Derek grinned up at the tall man, who loomed over him in his buttoned-to-the-neck raincoat. Somehow it was always good to see him.

"Come to see the fun then?"

"Well, I'll tell you what I haven't come to see – some old fart like him, chuntering on with his fatuous garbage. God, he's typical, isn't he! Another one of these old fools, the Thirties people, the windbags...cluttering up the bloody country... I mean, did you hear him just now? A load of paternalistic twaddle, designed to fool the credulous..."

"Oh come on." Derek was a little alarmed at Matt's vehemence, and the man's raised voice was drawing some curious looks from those nearby. "He's not so bad, you know. He means well. "

"He's a bastard," was Matt's reply. "They're all bastards."

This, Derek decided, was getting a bit much. Change the subject, he told himself. "So, what's the latest on young Terry and his Dad?"

"All good. Except some old fool of a ship's captain tried to do a U-ey in the Suez Canal, got stuck halfway across it, so it'll be another seven days before they get here. Typical, eh? Anyway Daddy seems a decent sort from his telegrams, and he's bringing a new wife with him. Hong Kong girl. New mum for Terry."

"Excellent. Mind you, me and Mary, we'll be sad to see the lad go."

"Course you will. Kids. It's what life's all about. Or should be. I mean to say, Derek mate, this is the 1950s. The New Age." He seemed to give the term capital letters. "We're the New Elizabethans, mate. It's our turn, our children's turn. All these ministers and politicians and councillors, they're the Thirties people. They failed. They killed half of us off in the war, didn't they? Their time has come and gone. They got to step aside, or be put aside."

"What are you going to do?" Derek decided to joke. "Shoot everyone over forty?"

Matt had the grace to give him a slightly maniacal smile. "It would be a start," he said.

A skittering of rain swept unexpectedly across the square, and Derek wished he'd had the sense to wear his police waterproof. Matt grinned at him, snug in his mackintosh.

Now several things happened at once. The Chief Constable finished answering a question from his audience about dog licences., climbed off his makeshift platform, and was whisked away into outer Devonshire in his shiny Jaguar. The group of soberly dressed men and women in the corner of the square – now identifiable as the core of the chapel congregation – began singing a tuneful version of "Jesu Lover Of My Soul", complete with harmonies, and a police patrol car nosed its way into the square and, slowly, found its way through the other cars and the crowd, towards the Dragon.

In the back seat of the vehicle, all alone, sat Lucy. There was no mistaking her. The long slightly sallow face, the fine profile, the pose of dignity, even arrogance. Derek felt his heart lurch, but quite why he wasn't sure. Not love, not fear, just something. And then she turned, and looked straight at him. And she smiled, but what sort of smile it was, again he wasn't sure.

The patrol car, despite penetrating the muddle of parked cars, was still obliged to pull up some twenty yards from the pub. Lucy was hauled rather awkwardly out of the rear because she was in handcuffs and couldn't help herself. Several of the dispersing villagers noticed this, and behind him Derek heard a voice saying triumphantly: "I knew it would be one of them beatniks! They nicked my chickens, you know."

Derek glanced back. Of course it was Joshua. He turned back to Matt, to avoid eye contact with the squalid little man, and found that his tall friend had somehow disappeared. Just as well, he decided. He would be needed back inside the pub. Detective Chief Superintendent Anderson would be poised for action.

CHAPTER TWENTY-EIGHT

The seating arrangements in the bar had undergone another re-arrangement. There were still three chairs behind a main table, but now there was one chair set out on its own, facing the table. To Derek, allowing his imagination full rein, it looked even more than before like the preparation for a formal Spanish Inquisition, with the equally formal sentence of death by torture waiting to be pronounced, all done and dusted by tea-time.

Lucy had been placed in the solitary chair. She sat there proudly, her handcuffed hands in her lap, her spine rigidly held away from the back of the chair, her chin jutting cleanly, her eyes unblinking. Her three inquisitors, Anderson, Inspector Reed, and the so-far unnamed detective, took their respective places, with only the Inspector showing any sign of reluctance, as he sorted out a writing pad and pens in front of him. Anderson waved Derek down into a spare chair at the end of the table. He tried not to look at Lucy, but found he had to, because she was looking at him. There was a question in her eyes. What exactly was all this about, she seemed to ask. In reply he gave her the ghost of a shrug.

"Right. So there you are. We found you. The Queen of the May!" Anderson said, rubbing his hands vigorously. "Now then. I am Chief Detective Superintendent Anderson, of Exeter. This Is my colleague, Detective Inspector Dawson. And this is Inspector Reed, from Okehampton. You are?"

"I seem to be your prisoner," Lucy said tautly.

"Not at all. You have not been arrested. You are helping the police with their enquiries."

In answer, Lucy lifted her shackled hands.

"For God's sake someone take those things off her," Anderson said brusquely. "She's not going anywhere." And then as an afterthought, "Stand by the door, someone, in case she makes a run for it."

A constable unlocked the handcuffs, and Anderson, with a laborious show of effort, began again.

"Would you now tell us your name, please? For the record."

"I am Aphrodite Wondergirl," Lucy replied, to Derek's hidden joy. Good for you, girl, he thought.

"Your real name, if you please?" Anderson said, flushing a little.

"My real name is what I say my real name is," she told him, to Derek's increasing satisfaction.

Anderson gave a sigh to indicate the sort of perverted scum the police had to deal with these days, and turned to Derek.

"Constable, do you know her real name?"

Derek felt himself stepping off a virtual ledge, into a maelstrom. "I know her first name, Sir."

"Which is?"

"Lucy."

The girl now looked directly at him, and her previous glances, which had been neutral at worst and warm at best, were now replaced with one of sudden and shocked scorn. Her lips moved, as if she was saying something, and Derek was momentarily glad he didn't lip-read.

"So. Lucy. Do you know why you're here."

"I have no idea."

"Allow me to inform you. Do you know of a chapel minister, by name Donald Simpson?"

"Yes."

"He objected to you and your followers occupying his chapel?"

"He did."

"He got a court order and threw you out, with nowhere to go."

"Yes."

"So that night you lured him to the village chapel, where you stabbed him to death."

"What?" It was almost a scream. Lucy lost all her poise, rocking back in the chair, her eyes wide, her fists curling up into a ball. And Derek felt a surge of hope. All along it had been possible, if not probable, that Lucy was guilty, was the murderer. Now he knew for certain she wasn't. And surely everyone else in the bar could see it too. Couldn't they?

They couldn't. The atmosphere remained full of accusation, even condemnation.

"Make a note, Inspector," Anderson instructed. "She denies it."

"Of course I deny it!" She was recovering fast, but the words still came out hot and spiky.

Anderson smiled benevolently, evidently pleased that he had destroyed her poise. "Of course you do. Cold blooded murder. Always denied, even by such as you."

"What? Such as me? What does that mean."

"It means your sort. You, with your so-called alternative life-style, your flouting of all standards of decency, your rejection of Christian principles, your decadence, your filth, undermining everything decent people stand for..."

Anderson ran out of breath, to the obvious relief of his two colleagues, who clearly thought the man was going too far. But he recovered fast from his outburst.

"Allow me to sketch out the events which occurred yesterday, and which led to the death of Mr. Simpson. You and he had become mortal enemies. He was throwing you out of this tumbledown chapel of yours. Or rather, of his. So that night you probably telephoned him. You pleaded with him. You probably made certain suggestions to this lonely 60-year-old man. You persuaded him, quite easily, I imagine, to meet you in secret. And once you'd got him on his own, alone in the chapel, in the darkness of the night, you knifed that good man to death. And may God forgive you."

There was silence. Derek thought Anderson's account was so outlandish, it would crumble under its own weight. But again, everyone else seemed to think it not only plausible, but chillingly accurate. He knew why. He knew Lucy, he liked her, he almost had a kind of relationship with her. But everyone else saw her as weird, different, even perverted. Perhaps Lucy realised this, and now she spoke out with some determination.

"You have no evidence. No evidence at all."

"Oh, haven't we? I wouldn't be too sure about that. Constable Martin. I believe you were a witness to the confrontation of Miss Wondergirl here and the Reverend Simpson."

"Part of it, Sir, yes."

"Tell us, were angry words exchanged between the two? Words of insult, of threat?"

"Words were exchanged, Sir."

"Such as?"

"Oh, bigot. Um, blasphemer. Witch." Surely none of these words that he had selected from his memory amounted to serious threats. As he stopped, Derek risked a glance up at Lucy. He wished he hadn't. The old cliché was true. If looks could kill, he'd be dead. Those eyes of her, the eyes to which he had been so easily drawn, they blazed with bitter disappointment, with contempt, with pure poison. He hoped to God his part in all this was at an end, that what could yet be quoted would be ignored.

Anderson was pleased with what he had heard. "Thank you, Constable. An excellent contribution to the case. Well, it seems pretty plain to me, and will no doubt seem equally plain to a jury, that..."

But Lucy interrupted him. Her tone was now falsely airy, almost light-hearted.

"No, please, wait, you, whatever your name is. Don't stop him now. Don't stop our chatty little Constable, I think he's got more to tell us." She looked at Derek. "Haven't you, dear Derek." Then back to Anderson. "You see, we got quite friendly, me and diddums here. Do let him go on, let him babble, you'll enjoy it."

"Well, Constable," Anderson began, but again she interrupted him.

"No, I've got a better idea. Let's not tax the poor lad's brain, as he struggles to remember something he'll never forget. I'll tell you. I'll tell you myself what he's dying to tell you."

Derek shut his eyes. This was a nightmare.

"Go on then. Tell us," Anderson said, with an aside to Inspector Reed: "Get this down verbatim."

"I said I could kill him! Didn't I, Derek? Didn't I, Mr. snake-in-the-grass? He'll confirm it. What I actually said was, I said I could kill anyone who tried to kick us off. And yes, I meant him, that bloody pillar of goodness, Mr. Simpson!" She turned to Inspector Reed. "Got that down verbatim, have you?"

"Yes, thank you," the Inspector told her.

"Right. Get this down too. I didn't kill him. Of course I didn't kill him. I don't believe in killing people. I believe in the sanctity of human life, of peace and love and brotherhood and sisterhood, and other things that you uniformed morons have never heard of. Of course I didn't kill Simpson. And what's more, you haven't got a single shred of evidence to prove I did." She turned again to Reed. "Did you get all that?"

"Yes, I've got that down verbatim, too," he confirmed before she could ask, earning a sneer from the Superintendent.

"We haven't finished," Anderson told her. "If you'd kindly stop raving like a fishwife, we can move on." He turned to an attending Constable. "Bring it," he snapped.

The officer produced the flat wooden box and placed it in front of Anderson. Derek caught his breath. He recognised it at once. So of course did Lucy.

"That's mine!" she exclaimed. "That's my property. What are you doing with it?"

"It's evidence," Anderson told her. "In fact, it could be that single shred of evidence you've been talking about."

He reached to open it, but she was too fast for him, slapping a hand on the top of the box.

"Leave it," she snapped. "Nobody opens that box except me."

"Very well. You. Open it. Please." Anderson smiled at her with hugely ironic politeness.

"I will. But I can tell you what's in it. Two knives. They were my father's knives, and he passed them on to me. I use them in my act."

"Act? What act?" Anderson was genuinely baffled.

"My act as a knife-thrower. Don't look so surprised. Ask Mr. Noddy Policeman here, he knows. And he'll only be too anxious to tell you about it."

Anderson turned to Derek. "Well?"

Derek stuttered. "Lucy... Yes, um, she does do this act. Throwing knives. It's called impalement." he heard himself saying.

Anderson interrupted: "Well, you certainly impaled our god-botherer, didn't you, love. He was carved up by some bloody great knife. Come on, girl, open the thing. And don't worry, if you're as innocent as a baby lamb, then forensics will clear you."

Lucy's fingers moved to the catch on the box. "Neither one of my knives has ever drawn blood," she declared.

And she flipped open the box lid.

One knife lay in the box. Only one. There was a space, an indentation in the velvet lining, but no second knife.

Lucy stared into the box, her pale face grew paler, then almost seemed to flush. For the first time since he met her, Derek saw that she was totally at a loss.

"Where's my knife?" she gasped. "You've taken it out, Christ, you're fitting me up. You bastards."

Anderson rose from his chair with an air of deep satisfaction at the successful end to a tiresome and ultimately unnecessary negotiation.

"We'll find the other one," he said casually. "It'll be in a ditch somewhere between here and where we found you. It'll have bloodstains on it. Simpson's blood. And probably your fingerprints. Bang to rights, that's what we call this."

He turned to Reed. "Charge her. Murder. Premeditated." And then a last malicious aside to a stricken Lucy. "That's the one they hang you for."

She looked blankly at him. But when an officer took her arm, to lead her away, she rose from her chair, turned to Derek, and spat at him.

CHAPTER TWENTY-NINE

The circus left town in a hurry.

Two hefty men in white overalls hefted an elongated bundle out of the chapel, then hefted it into a windowless police van, then drove off at high speed. All around the square drivers fired up their engines. Lucy, back in handcuffs, was driven off at another high speed. In the Dragon police telephones were disconnected, papers stacked away, chairs knocked over in the general rush to vacate the place, and John emerged from the back to start putting things in order. Car doors slammed. A couple of lowly constables just managed to scramble into departing cars, narrowly avoiding being abandoned in the hostile wilderness of West Devon. Stacks of sandwiches arrived too late from the Okehampton café, to be almost instantly snaffled by alert villagers. And then it was over, the square was empty as always, and the chaos and confusion of the last few hours had faded away like the proverbial bad dream.

Derek stood alone near the village pump. There were some traces of the occupancy strewn around the square; Cigarette packets, sandwich wrapping, someone's rolled up police cap, lost in the melee. He picked up the cap. He'd return it to the Okehampton office. If he remembered. And if he didn't, he'd give it to one of Mary's juvenile cousins.

He felt lost, alone, and stupid. And he went home.

In bed that night he tried to explain himself to Mary, who, despite ending their quarrel, still found the subject of "that beatnik woman" as she called Lucy, puzzling.

"Of course I'm not in love with her," Derek found himself repeating more than once. "But..." and this took some serious self-discipline, "But, perhaps I'm in some sort of thrall to her. She's got a very strong personality, she's a natural leader, you can see how the others respect her, and she lives her life the way she chooses. You'd know what I mean if you met her."

"Shouldn't think I ever will," Mary remarked. "Not if she's done for premeditated murder."

"Yes, but she won't be. There's no proof, not really. She can't be found guilty, not on the evidence. No jury would convict."

"I wouldn't bet on it. You know who makes up a jury? The stout solid conventional middle classes, just the sort of people who hate people like her. I don't know why. I can't see that beatniks and the like are any sort of threat. But people seem to think they're undermining society, or something. They won't like her. And they'll be happy to see her put away."

"What, you mean for life?"

"No. For death. They'll hang her."

"But not on such flimsy evidence, surely."

"Why not? They're going to hang that Bentley boy. Any day now. And he didn't kill anyone. Let alone rip them apart with a knife. We seem to be in the mood for hanging people these days. We hanged all those Nazis after the war, must have got into the habit."

"Yes, but not women. We don't hang women."

"Oh yes, we do. We hanged that woman Margaret Allen a couple of years ago."

Derek remembered. "Christ, yes. What am I going to do, love?"

"Well." She gave him an affectionate squeeze. "Someone killed poor old Simpson. If it wasn't your Lucy, who was it? You're a hot shot copper. And I bet you've got the appropriate niggle."

"God, yes. Size of a house."

The bedroom door creaked open. Terry stood in the doorway. "I had a bad dream," he said. "Can I come in your bed?"

"Just for five minutes," Mary told him with mock severity.

"And I've got some news for you, young man," Derek announced. "Sorry," he told Mary. "I forgot to say, I saw Matt earlier." Then to Terry: "You Dad is on the high seas, steaming in this direction. It won't be long now, he'll be here. And I'm told he's got a very nice lady with him, who'll be your new Mummy."

Terry muttered something agreeable, and snuggled down further between them.

"Yes, love," Mary added. "Back with your Dad, a new home, new school. It's all going to happen."

Derek heard soft padding footsteps on the stairs. "I'll tell you one thing that's not going to happen, young man. That damn dog of yours is not coming into bed as well.

* * *

Sleep took a long time coming that night, but when it did come, it stayed.

The phone rang shortly after eight. It stopped when Derek was half asleep and halfway down the stairs Five minutes later it rang again, and this time he got to it.

It was Welbeloved. At this time of the morning. Oh joy. And perhaps because he had been involved only peripherally in the shenanigans the day before, he was at his most acerbic, efficient and objectionable.

"So." Only Welbeloved could make that little word so meaningful. "That headmaster yesterday. Progress?"

"Um... Well, yes. It checked out. He virtually admitted to abusing the boy. Sexually and violently. And there were some incriminating photos."

"So. What did you do?"

"I arrested him. Charged him."

"Really? Did you?" Sarcasm began to seep down the telephone line from Okehampton to North Tawe. "Then if you arrested him, how come he isn't sitting in our little lock-up here, weeping bitter tears of remorse? What did you do with him? Take him home, tuck him up in your spare bed, cook him breakfast?"

"Sarge, I couldn't do anything with him. You didn't answer your phone. Exeter had no cars. They were all over here."

"So you just left him?"

"Well." Derek had to force the words out. "He assured me he wouldn't abscond. He, well, he gave me his word of honour."

"His what?"

"His word of honour." It sounded more pathetic every time.

"Jesus God you berk! His word of honour. Ha! He's probably halfway to Dover by now. Heading for somewhere where they don't mind that sort of thing. Thailand, or California. Word of honour, my arse!"

"But Sarge, what could I do? What?"

"I'll tell you what you're going to do right now, my lad. You're going to wait there, full uniform. I will pick you up in one hour's time. In the squad car. We will drive to the school, and in the unlikely event that your man is as dim as you and is still there, we'll nab him. Properly."

"Yes Sergeant."

"Word of honour! Word of honour, my..."

Derek put the phone down.

* * *

The Sergeant was still muttering the phrase under his breath as they drove through the bends of the little track that led them underneath the massive Weldon viaduct.

The Sergeant slowed almost to a halt, peering up at the structure. "Never seen it from down here. Big, isn't it?"

"Mmm"

"They don't build 'em like that any more."

"No." Derek's stomach was in knots, and there was no breakfast in it to ease the tension. If Jeeves was still there, everything would be okay. But if not... Christ what a bloody fool he had been. If it gets out, every copper in the county will be laughing at him. To accept the word of hour from a known sadistic paedophile.

The school grounds and front garden were in a state of mild uproar. The drive was crowded with parked cars, there was even a small coach, and adults and boys were bustling around, and there were large suitcases being loaded into car boots.

"Something's up." Welbeloved took his usual time in extracting himself from the car. Derek waited for him impatiently. What was happening? And where was Jeeves?

Through the confusion, looking bitter and angry, came Mrs Jeeves. "I saw you come. I knew you would. Haven't you done enough?"

Derek ignored her, searching behind her for Jeeves. The Sergeant didn't. "What's going on, Mrs..."

"The school's closing down, that's what's going on. I rang round this morning. This fine educational institution is finished. Thanks to you lot."

"Where is he?" Derek had no patience for her. "Your husband? Where is he?"

"Him? My nearest and dearest? Well he's gone, of course. Legged it."

"Where?"

"Somewhere you won't get him, sonny."

"But. He gave me his word of honour."

The woman laughed, or rather cackled, a sound of possible hysteria. "Yes, so he did. And you believed him. You fool. He wasn't going to stick around and let you sling him in jail and ruin his life and shame him before the mob. Did you really think he would?"

Derek didn't answer. He turned to Welbeloved, who was now looking at him with hard little piggy eyes. When he spoke Derek could hardly hear him. "Word of honour."

* * *

Welbeloved drove a scant quarter of a mile down the track before pulling into the small parking place. The viaduct towered above them.

"I'll have to do a report on this, constable. So will you."

"I know."

"I'm sorry."

"Are you?" Derek struggled to keep the bitterness out of his voice.

"Course I am. Me and you've been through quite a bit, one way or another. I'll try to say you couldn't help it, but..."

"Well, I couldn't, could I? What else could I have done? Tell me!"

"I wasn't there, I can't say."

"Oh thanks. Thanks a bunch."

"Now don't take it out on me, lad. And cheer up – we may nab him yet. I'll put out an A.P.B."

"A what?"

"An All-Points Bulletin. Like they do in America. Watch the roads, the railways, the airports..."

"Oh, for God's sake! I'm finished, I know I am."

"Check the hotels, boarding houses, bus stations..."

"Oh balls." Derek jerked the passenger door open and got out. The sergeant did the same, but as ever took considerably more time about it.

"Now look here, constable..." But he realised Derek wasn't listening. Instead, he was staring up at the viaduct and pointing.

"There's someone up there."

"Where? Oh yeah. There is!"

They both gazed up at the top of the structure, shading their eyes against any light.

"He's just standing there." The Sergeant bubbled with excitement. "What's he up to? Hang on, he's climbing up on the wall. The parapet. He's got some sort of cloak on. Llook!"

Derek felt his shoulders sag. He leaned against the car. "It's not a cloak," he said. "It's an academic gown."

"How did he get up there?"

"I think I know how he's going to get down." Derek spoke only to himself.

"Someone ought to stop him." The Sergeant waved a meaningless arm in the air. "He'll kill himself."

"Yes." Derek had seen the figure topple slowly forward, gradually over balancing. Then the man fell, and the gown swell out behind him in the wind, billowing, like a parachute.

Then it collapsed, and the man fell on down. He landed with an audible and sickening impact. On the side of the lane. Just fifteen feet in front of the squad car.

CHAPTER THIRTY

Derek had seen dead bodies in the past. But he found this one was not so easy to look at. Any damage to it was thankfully internal, but that didn't matter. A man he had met, known, confronted, was dead.

"He committed suicide." Welbeloved demonstrated his undoubted ability to say the obvious.

They waited, neither man quite knowing what to do next. A man in a hard hat came hurrying from the quarry. Welbeloved moved to meet him.

"Another one?"

"Not the first then?"

"Nope. Not the first. Jump off anything else round here, and you might sprain your ankle. But from up there, well..."

"I need a telephone."

"This way." The man led Welbeloved away.

Derek stood over the body. He wondered how he felt. His actions as a police officer had led to the death of a man. A vile man, but a man, nonetheless. Was it his fault? Did he feel blame? Regret? Into his mind came a poem. It was one Mary had read to him, several times, when she had first attempted to educate him in the beauty of literature. He recalled one line. That's all. That one line went: 'Every man's death diminishes me."

Every man's death. Every man?

Derek looked down at the body. And the words came in a rush. "You don't diminish me, Jeeves. Thanks to me you're dead and gone, and that doesn't dimmish me, it enhances me. The world's well rid of you, you creep. I made it happen, I'm bloody glad I made it happen, and now a multitude of little boys will thank me. And young Terry won't have to face you in a witness box, he'll be free of you, and safe at home. So, fuck you, Jeeves. Fuck you."

He got back in the car. He felt a little ashamed of himself. But not a lot. Just a little. In fact, he didn't feel one bit ashamed. He was sure of that – and sure of something else.

His niggle. It was gone. One less.

* * *

Neville found the knife. He arrived on Mary's doorstep with the thing wrapped in a copy of the Daily Express.

"I found it!" he crowed. "Place full of coppers, they couldn't find it, but I could. Tucked away down behind the telephone box, it was. I was just waiting around for a call, and there it was. D'you think I'll get a reward?"

He didn't. Instead, Exeter CID sent a car, and the knife was transported to Chief Superintendent Anderson who received it with undisguised joy. There were traces of blood on the blade which proved to be Simpson's, of course. Fingerprints? Well Neville had left a fine set of his, but not even Anderson could bring himself to put Nev in the frame for this one. There were faint traces of other prints, which seemed possibly to match Lucy's. But then there would be, right? She identified the knife. She admitted it was hers.

Anderson basked in the warmth of an open-and-shut case.

* * *

The press had a field day. The coverage seemed to assume that Lucy had already been accused, tried, condemned and even executed. There were the expected reports in the regional newspapers. In the wake of its factual reportage, the Western Morning News expressed grim disapproval of the presence of cultural drop-outs and rootless workshy scavengers invading the Christian and hard-working west country. The Express and Echo got itself worked up about the brutality behind the mask of the so-called peace-loving beatniks. The London papers picked up the story, and even found pictures of Lucy at the time she dropped out of University, abandoned her comfortable stock-broker home, and set out on the road. The Daily Mirror tried to nickname her "Loopy Lucy" but it didn't catch on.

After two days Lucy appeared before Okehampton magistrates. Derek attended, uninvited but determined to be there. Lucy spoke only to confirm her name. They'd found out what they believed to be her true name – Lucy Bellow. Asked for her address, she told them, "No fixed abode!" and laughed openly.

Brief police evidence was given, all quite unnecessary. There was no real decision or judgement to make. The case was automatically referred to the next session of the Assize Court in Exeter. Lucy was remanded in custody. The entire process took eight minutes. But it had given the bench something of a thrill to be so involved in such an horrific killing. And to witness such a striking defendant in the dock.

As she filed out, under escort, Lucy passed close to where Derek stood, at the back of the tiny courtroom.

Derek caught her eye, and was relieved to see that the venom she had directed at him before had dissipated, and instead he caught a flash of recognition.

Ten minutes before the patrol car arrived to take the accused to Exeter, and the Devon County gaol, Welbeloved opened the door to what passed as a holding cell in the Okehampton station.

"You can have five minutes," he told Derek.

"Sorry I spat at you. It should have been at that little bastard." Lucy told him. "And I know you had to say what you said, so don't bother apologising."

"No-one thinks you did it. Not anyone with any sense, that is."

"Anyone with any sense? Well, that rules out nine tenths of the population. Why do they hate us so much, Derek?"

"I'm sure they don't really." It sounded weak.

"They do you know. Enough to hang me." And then quickly, before he could react, "That reminds me, did you ever find out about the names on my cards."

"No. I meant to ask you, but..."

"Well. I'll tell you now. Now I have a chance. Or I will If you can remember the names."

"Oh." The memory came back, slowly but steadily: "Mary Trembles, easy to remember that one, and Temperance Lloyd. The last one's the difficult one, Susannah Edwards!"

"Well done." She clapped her hands.

"So who are they?"

"Who were they," she corrected. "They were three women who lived just up the road in Bideford, and in

1682 they were convicted of witchcraft and hanged in Exeter. I just thought they ought to be remembered. I decided to start a campaign to get some memorial for them, amongst the people of the west country who actually did the deed. Silly idea, I suppose."

"No," he protested. "I'll remember them, I'll never forget them, not now."

"Well, they call me a witch, don't they? So if they hang me too, you can remember me as well. Now you'll have four names to remember. If you can."

"Oh, I'll always remember Aphrodite Wondergirl," he told her.

Listening at the door, Sergeant Welbeloved wondered what on earth they could find to laugh about.

* * *

For the next four days Derek slept poorly. He went to bed with the niggle and woke up with the niggle. He constantly questioned himself. Not about Jeeves. That creep lay in the Exeter morgue, unmourned and soon to be forgotten. But Simpson's body lay in the next cold drawer. Could he, Derek, have stopped the murder of the minister? No, of course not. It had come as big a shock and surprise to him as it had to everyone else.

Could he have moved Lucy and her cohorts on, had he been too soft on her, because he liked her? If the group had disappeared, perhaps Simpson would still be alive. But no, to believe that, you had to believe that Lucy was his killer. And she wasn't. Of course she wasn't. That he knew without doubt. So who was? There had to be someone, someone with the stain of the Minister's blood on his hands and on his soul. Someone out there...

The whole oppressive puzzle sat on his shoulders, an incubus of mystery, anger, and sometimes despair. And Mary, listening as he went over and over the details of life since Christmas, began to fear for his sanity. She too had known how his so-playfully-named niggles could drive him on relentlessly to near destruction. But no niggle had ever been this dominant, this demanding.

For three of the blank days, he did little else but obsess over the problem. Luckily, everyone else, in both Okehampton and Exeter police stations, were so excited with events, so busy building a case against Lucy, that they paid scant attention to him.

On the fourth day, at ten in the morning, John the landlord appeared at his door. He looked weary beyond words, and his face was streaked with what might have been tears. There was a break in his voice.

"Derek mate, you busy?"

"No." It was the honest answer. Obsessed, yes. But not busy.

"Look. The ambulance just came. They need to take her to hospital. They say she's only got a couple of days. I said leave her with us, but they say the pain will be... Oh Christ."

He didn't have to explain any further. John's wife, Cathy, had terminal lung cancer, something that was known and grieved over throughout the village.

"We both want to go with her, me and Sandy." John stammered. "But I just can't leave the pub. Not empty. I locked all the doors and the windows, but, could you just keep an eye on it? Pop in if you like, make sure everything's okay. Sorry, it's such a rush. Here's the front door key." he handed over a large old-fashioned iron key, and if it seemed that he was taking Derek's help for granted, well, he was, and Derek was accepting the role with equal and willing assumption.

* * *

The pub seemed strangely quiet, and Derek, who couldn't resist unlocking the front door and going inside, realised that he had never known the bar to be empty. Always before, whenever he entered the Dragon, there had been the racket of customers, the smack of balls on the bar billiards table, or, at the very least, John's cheerful greeting. Now the place was a ghost bar, a monochrome version of itself. A tap dripped, there was a faint smell of stale beer, and disturbed dust showers sparkled in some surprising January sun. Nothing else.

At least the place once again looked like a bar, with the tables back in their familiar positions after the chaos of police organisation. He wandered around, wondered for a moment if he might pour himself a drink, just a small one, then remembered that it was not much past ten in the morning. Far too early. Instead he walked over to the bar billiards table, found a sixpence piece in his pocket, slotted it in, and jerked the handle to release the balls. He tried a couple of shots, knocked over the black pin, and gave up. It was no fun playing against yourself. And anyway, he had never encountered the game until he came to North Tawe, and when he'd tried it, he found he was no good at it.

He threw three darts at the board. One fell out. His total score was five. No, he reminded himself, he was no good at darts, either.

He wandered behind the bar itself, briefly imagining that he too could be a landlord of a country pub. It sounded like a welcome change from police work. No manic Sergeants. No crazy chicken farmers. He looked up at the row of bottles on the top shelf at the back. There stood the dusty drinks that no-one had ever been known to request. One label proclaimed that it was Green Chartreuse. What on earth was that? Another said Blue Curacao. Nothing on earth, Derek decided, would ever induce him to drink something blue. Or green.

He turned to the business part of the bar, where stood the mighty trio of beer pumps. And underneath them he noticed John's mini tape recorder, the device he had bought to entertain his ailing wife. Cautiously he pressed the "play" button. The little wheels span, and out floated the creaky strains of "Here come a blackbird." as sung by that elderly regular, Gerry the professional rabbit-trapper. Quickly, because it seemed as if he was fiddling too much, he pressed "stop", and then "rewind", and the wheels span back until the thing clicked off. For a second he was tempted to press "record", and leave a rude message for John to find, before he remembered why John was absent, and how he would be in no mood for jokes when he returned.

He left the bar, to sit at one of the tables, squarely in front of the room's main window looking out on the square. The niggle blazed. Who had killed the Minister? Who had slaughtered The Reverend Simpson? The bigot, the bully, the intolerant martinet. Yes, he was all that. But he was a man, and he'd been chopped down, or according to Neville, chopped up. By someone. By a murderer. And not, whatever Detective Chief Superintendent Anderson might claim, by Lucy.

He sat quietly, looking out into the sunny square. Technically the pub could open at eleven. But he doubted if anyone would come in, not even the early-morning cider addicts. Word would have gone round the village about Cathy. And the privacy of the family would be respected.

There was a drawer to the table in front of him. He'd never noticed it before, perhaps because he couldn't remember ever sitting at that particular table. Inside it was a dusty shove-halfpenny board. Now there was a game he did know, and what's more, he was good at it. He laid the thing in front of him, and began nudging the metal counters up between the lines, delighting in an old skill re-emerging.

And then he looked up, looked into the sun, and saw a ghost.

There, outlined against the sun, a black shape, a so-familiar pose. Simpson! Simpson the Minister. Simpson alive, Simpson back from the dead.

And then it wasn't Simpson, of course it wasn't. And Derek's heart lifted. It was Matt. Matt, his newly met mate. Yes, now he looked, it was clearly Matt, and he waved, and the tall man pushed his face against the glass, saw Derek, and waved back.

Derek sprang to the front door, turning the big key he had left in the lock. "Get in here!" he commanded, and stood aside to let the tall Australian enter. Great, Matt, his friend, someone to talk to. Brilliant.

And yet, it was funny he'd thought it was Simpson at the window. A trick of the light? Something in the way he'd been standing? Funny. He explained to Matt about John and his wife, how he'd been left in charge of the locked-down pub.

"Wow!" Matt grinned at him. "Me and you, locked up in an empty pub. No-one else can get in or out! Dreams do come true. Champagne, cobber?

"You'll be lucky," Derek told him. "Champagne in North Tawe? Sparkling cider's your closest bet."

"Well, let's have a couple of Double Diamonds, eh? While we're about it."

He tossed a ten-shilling note onto to the bar, pulled two bottles from a shelf, and skilfully used the opener permanently attached to the woodwork.

He handed one bottle to Derek, saying "Cheers", and swallowed half the contents of his own in one gulp. Derek, still feeling it was little early, took a sip.

Matt found a chair and sprawled back in it with overstated relaxation. Derek found his chair, they each drank again, and everything was all right.

Only it wasn't.

Matt's casual devil-may-care attitude was moment-by-moment becoming an act. A mask that was slipping. The man's whole body, spread-eagled as it was, was actually twitching. Jerking with nerves. He was swapping the bottle he held from one hand to another, trying to disguise the trembling of his hands, but failing to stop foam gushing over the neck. As Derek watched, he took another huge swallow of the beer, almost finishing it. His glance strayed wildly around the bar, focussing on one area, then another, and then abruptly back on Derek himself. His face was set in a weird glare, which, as their eyes met, he switched to a travesty of a grin.

"Well." the word was a croak, and Matt cleared his throat and tried again. "Well. This is great, eh? Me and you, in a pub."

The words, merely a weak repeat of what he had said as he'd entered, lacked all conviction. What's wrong? Derek wondered. Was he ill? No, perhaps it was drugs. Perhaps he had a source of cocaine, or heroin. Perhaps he was high on something. Or in a state of what Derek had heard described as "coming down." Whatever it was, it was changing Matt into someone he didn't recognise.

Yet It wasn't something he could ask the man about. He settled for something mundane to say instead.

"Take your coat off, mate. It's not raining inside today."

Matt ignored the remark, if anything pulling his long mac tighter around his shoulders.

Derek tried again. "Great news about Terry, eh? Well done on that, finding his father and so on. And the old school's packed up. Going to be a care home, they say. Care – ironic when you think about it."

Matt jerked his twitching frame into a conventional sitting pose. He seemed to get a touch more control of himself. "That's it! Get rid of the old, in with the new." His eyes shone with fervour. "That's our mission, Derek. Don't you see? It's our destiny. We're the new people, we're in control now, and it's up to us to protect children, and to get rid of the old lot, the bullies, the bastards who abandon children, bully them or hit them, kill the buggers off."

"Yeah, yeah, all right, calm down. I mean, you can't actually kill."

"Can't you? I can."

Derek forced a laugh, and it sounded bogus, even to his ears. "You Australians, you don't half exaggerate."

"I'm not Australian," Matt interrupted. "I hate bloody Australians. I'm as British as you. I was sent to Australia. On my own. Alone. When I was five, man. Five! You never hear of the Child Migration Scheme?"

"Vaguely. You were one of those kids?"

"One of thousands, mate. Some of us were orphans, but loads, like me, just given up by their couldn't-care-less families. Not wanted. Put away. My father... he put me away. My own bloody father. Said he couldn't cope now my mum had been stuck in the looney-bin. Ha! He could cope well enough to hit me when no one was looking. Not like in Oz. No, there they hit you when everyone's looking."

"It was tough, then, in Australia?"

"Going was all right. Had me little suitcase, dozens of us on the boat, good grub too. But over there – Jesus! They stuck me in a dump run by nuns, you'd think that would be okay, but it was worse than home. God, they beat the shit out of you every chance they had. One of them had a whip, man! A real whip! And then when I got out of there, I ended up on some farm out in the bush, more shit-kicking, and I lived on cattle food."

"Look." Derek suddenly felt an urge to stop the man talking. A dark and threatening feeling was descending on the bar, despite the sparkle of sunshine through the windows. Something bad was coming, something he didn't want to hear.

"Child Migration Programme, that's what they called it. Child Slavery Programme was more like it. And you know, it's still going on! Right now!"

"Really? That's..."

But there was no stopping Matt. Not yet. "But as I got older, bigger, I made a solemn vow. No, really, mate. A solemn vow, to God or whatever. I swore that I'd get back here, to Blighty, and find that so-called father of mine and..."

Derek cut in: "Your father. Did you remember him then? After all, you were only five when..."

"When he sold me off? You'd be surprised what a five-year-old can remember. He was always praying, I remembered that, out loud, usually when there were others around and could hear him. Claimed to have been washed in the blood of the lamb. Funny what you do remember."

And then Derek remembered something funny. The shape at the window, Simpson's ghost. Matt's upright stance. They both stood in the same way, so upright that you think they might topple over backwards. Why hadn't he seen that before? The stance must run in the family, in their genes. Father and son. Oh God.

"So you came back to England to find him?" There was no question of Derek stopping him now. It was all coming too fast, and he had to know what it was that Matt would say next. "Where did you start looking?"

"Around home, of course."

"Which is?"

"Plymouth."

Of course. Plymouth. The cutting, the one Simpson had kept, the court case, the man who had the epiphany. The man the magistrates let off. He'd had a small son. That was in Plymouth.

"Couldn't find him of course. Chased after dozens of Thompsons, none of them were him."

"Thompson – that was his name, right?"

"People said he was probably dead. Ha! Not him, I knew that, knew it in my bones. He'd have lived for ever. If I hadn't come along."

"But. Your name isn't Thompson."

"That convent in Oz, they said they already had two Thompsons. My name had to be Mathew Mark. Mathew and Mark, you see. Biblical. They thought it was funny. Nobody asked me, of course. Can I have another of these, Derek mate?" And he waved his empty bottle in the air.

Derek jerked his mind away from the grim revelations that the man's story was surely leading to. Instead he said "Why not?", and got up from his seat and moved behind the bar. He pulled another bottle of Double Diamond off the shelf, turned to fit the neck in the opener, and looked down at the shelf beneath the bar itself.

There was John's little tape-recorder. Without knowing why, but knowing he was doing the right thing, he reached down and quietly pushed the button marked "record". The tiny click of the machine was masked by the noise of the bottle opening.

"Go on," he told Matt, handing him the bottle, the foam bubbling up over both their hands.

"Oh. I got myself a job, with the Welfare people. Right up my street, looking after kids, making sure their god-awful parents treated them right. I knew one day I'd catch up with the bastard. And thanks to you, I did."

"Thanks to me?"

"Course. You found little Terry, I turn up, routine visit, and then, cos I'm to and fro to the village, I saw the sod. Funny how things work out. Fate, eh?"

He was relating a moment of triumph, Derek thought, and he watched as Matt now rose excitedly to his feet, and began moving jumpily around the bar, jiggling the lifeboat collection box, throwing a beer mat into the air and catching it, pulling the big key out of the door, poking his finger through the ring handle, and spinning it around in the air.

"I saw him. I knew him. And you know what he was doing? Of course you do. You told me about it. He was taking his bloody goats for a walk. His bloody goats! He never took me for a walk. Never. He stuck me on a boat, and washed his hands of me. Washed them in the blood of the lamb, do you think? Fuck off."

"But he was Simpson, not Thompson."

"Right. Clever, eh? Sounds much the same, could almost be a misprint, or something miss-heard. It's what they call in detective books 'hiding in plain sight.' You see? I reckon he must have wanted to get away from Plymouth, cos he had a criminal record down there. Yes, I looked it up in the court files, I get access to that sort of stuff in this job, yes, quite a teddy boy he'd been. Or the equivalent in those days. Thug, if you like. Tearaway. Cut someone up in a knife fight, once, though it never got to court."

The flick knife. In Simpson's Welsh dresser. Another clue cropping up, another puzzle solved. Bizarrely, Derek remembered how, as a small boy, he had frequently set up his dominoes in a long line, and if you tipped the first one over, the others all fell over in their turn. The dominoes that had led to the death of Simpson were now falling, one by one, in their turn.

"And then when they did get him to court, he pulled this religious conversion stunt, and the silly buggers believed him. Well. For all I know he did get God in a big way. Seems to have settled for the life, anyway."

Yes. The cutting told that story, Derek remembered.

"So. You found him. Listen, Matt. I'm a policeman. If you're going to tell me something now, you should remember that." Derek suddenly felt his head ache, but he pressed on. "In fact, I ought to caution you."

"Oh to hell with all that. I don't care. Yes, anything I say can be trotted out in court. Well, I'm not going to wind up in any court. I've got plans. And anyway, I've got to tell someone, I've got to tell the story. Think about it, we can't have our gorgeous Lucy topped for it, can we? Not when we've both got the hots for her, yes you have, admit it. So, I'm telling you, and then you can tell them. They won't believe you at first, course they won't, they want to hang Lucy, the blood-thirsty bastards, but you'll keep on at them, and in time they'll get it. They'll believe you. Eventually. Hey, then a grateful Lucy will fall into your arms, you lucky bugger. You'll thank me. Only you won't be able to by then, cos I'll be long gone."

"All right." Derek imagined he could hear those little wheels winding the tape through the sensors. Instant evidence! "Go ahead, then. Tell the story."

Matt posed grotesquely. "Once upon a time, listeners, I executed the bastard. Using, I might add, one of Lovely Lucy's knives."

"Yes, the knife. How did you get hold of that?"

"Oh, easy. When I turned up at the old chapel, to have another crack at her, they were all moving out. I helped. You know what moving house is like? Chaos, right. Lucy was all in a state about flitting. Women hate all that, don't they. Anyway, In the confusion it was simple enough to flip open that box of hers, nick one of the knives, chuck it into my boot rather than their cart."

"Christ, Matt, that makes it premeditated."

But Matt had paused for a moment, twiddling the key, looking, unusually for him, a little lacking in confidence. When he spoke, the words spun out of him wildly, almost hysterically.

"No, no, no. I wasn't going to kill him then. I just wanted to confront him. I called him up, suggested that we meet. In his chapel, I thought. But he was having none of that. Oh no, he didn't want to see me, he said I would ruin his life, he just wanted me to go away. But I told him he didn't have a choice. Either meet me, or I tell the world who he really is. Ha!"

"You blackmailed him."

"Call it what you like, he came. White as a sheet, he was. Trembling. I still had this pathetic idea that he could acknowledge me as his son, that I'd have something approaching a family at last. I mean, I could have forgiven him, even then. But he'd have none of it. Said I would ruin his life. But then, and, mate, this is what really did it, he offered me money. Cash. To go away. One hundred quid, he had it on him, in fivers. All he had in the world, he reckoned. And, you'll like this, he said he would pray for me. Pray for me. Well that did it. I went out to the car, got the knife, came back in, there he was in his chair, praying, out loud, and I carved the bastard up."

"Just like that?"

"Just like that. And I don't think anyone noticed this, but I did it in the shape of a cross. But upside down. Long stroke down, short one across below. Neat, eh? Symbolic of something, dunno what, but, Christ, that knife was sharp."

"Yes but..." A thought struck him. "Matt, take off your mackintosh."

"Ah! Who's a clever little policeman, eh?" Matt shrugged off the long coat, letting it fall to the bar floor. His suit, his sweater, all his clothes, were pristine. "Look, no blood! Of course not. It was days ago, wasn't it. I burnt those clothes, you bet. Straight after I saw you in the square, with the Chief Constable. But at the time the old mac hid a multitude of sins. And stains. I learned how to butcher sheep on that farm in Oz. It's a messy job, carving up a sheep. Or a preacher."

Derek took a deep breath. He felt his heart beating, pushing against his rib cage. He had to get himself on record too, he realised belatedly. "Matthew Mark, I am arresting you for murder" he began.

"Oh blow it out, Derek! You're not doing anything. Ha. By the time you get out of here to tell anyone, and they get round to believing it, and they'd probably tell you to piss off anyway, I told you, I'll be long gone."

"You're under arrest, Matt." It was all Derek could think of to say.

"And you're under a delusion, mate." Now Matt's manner faltered again. "You know, there's one thing I regret about all this. And that's you. I mean, we clicked, didn't we. We were mates." He grinned, suddenly the devil-may-care Matt he had once been. "Cheers, mate."

He finished his beer, got up, and backed towards the bar door.

"Stay where you are" Derek managed, his voice hoarse.

"Make me."

Derek tensed himself, then pushed his chair back violently and launched himself towards Matt. But as he did so the other man used his foot to tumble a chair in his path, and Derek sprawled over it, finishing on his hands and knees.

"Enjoy your trip, mate!"

He heard Matt laugh, then the door opened, slammed shut, and he heard the big key grind in the lock.

CHAPTER THIRTY-ONE

When you hit a crisis, when life goes suddenly askew, it's forgivable if your first reaction, before you have time to think, is to do the wrong thing. That was how, later on, Derek excused himself for what he now did immediately, that is, scramble to his feet, tug fruitlessly at the door, and shout.

"Matt! Come back! Stop him!"

A pointless appeal. If Matt heard him, he would laugh. And there was no-one else to hear. There never was. Not in this sleepy bloody village. What he did next was scarcely more sensible. He ran from room to room, trying the back exit, the windows, even the windows upstairs. But John had been as good as his word, everywhere was thoroughly locked, bolted, inside and out, and even, at the entrance from the cellar, barred. And no keys either.

Panic. Matt had his MG. He'd be going like the proverbial bat. Road blocks, they'd get him. If he wasn't already gone, which he would be, unless...

Derek paused on the landing. Oh of course. Phone! He tore down the stairs, rushed up the short passage, grabbed the receiver, and was already dialling 999 before realising the line was dead. No familiar dialling tone. Nothing. He looked down, following the cable. There it was – the little box on the wall, that linked the phone to the exchange – it was loose, lying flat on the floor. Wires hung loose from the wall. Disconnected.

The mighty force of Superintendent Anderson's men had ripped it off, to set up their own lines. And they hadn't put it back. John was probably waiting for a post office engineer to come and reconnect him. Derek, panic surging, found himself scrabbling on the floor with the box and its wires, but who knew what went where? He didn't.

Up and to the bar window. If he could shout, wave, attract someone's attention. But as ever the square spread itself vacantly in front of him. No-one in sight. Wait, there was someone... It was the vicar, Hugh Shelley, making his stately way home, a copy of the Times tucked under his arm. Derek shouted, gesticulated, but the Reverend Hugh, the kindly if slightly doddery figure, heard and saw nothing. His lunch, a kindly donated pasty, awaited him in the vicarage. He strolled on and disappeared.

Derek shouted again, but his bellow just echoed around the bar, mocking him with its futility.

Okay then. Come on! He told himself. Smash your way out. Break a window. John would never forgive him. God knows how long the brewery would take to give him a new window but he had to do it, had to do something. Nerving himself, he picked up a bar chair and flung it at the window. It bounced back.

Right, something better, something that would crack the toughened glass. Some sort of stick, with a point... A cue! Panting, he scuttled across to the bar billiards table, and grabbed one of the two cues hanging in the rack along the length of the machine. Then, setting himself by the window, he reversed the cue, so that its heavier end would do the damage. Using both hands, and feeling, in a mad moment, like a spearman in a Roman Legion, he drew the cue back and stopped.

His rescue, his freedom, his chance to stop Matt, was coming across the square in a little procession. There was Blondie, led on a bit of string by Terry, who's other hand gripped Mary's, and in who's other hand was what appeared to be a plate with a tea-towel covering it.

God bless her, she was bringing him some lunch.

He concentrated. His thoughts, for the first time since Matt's escape, were clear and cool. The tape recorder. Evidence. He'd need it. Take it.

He collected the thing, being careful with it. He'd never used one, never touched one before today. Now it would broadcast Matt's confession. His guilt.

And Lucy's innocence.

From the window he could see that Mary and her entourage had arrived. She was smiling at him, but her smile faded as she saw the frantic face looking back her, waving agitatedly, shouting muffled demands...

Now, crucially, had Matt taken the key with him? Or left it in the lock? Please God.

Mary gave up trying to make sense of her husband's antics. She shrugged, went to the front door. Derek craned his neck in an attempt to see but failed and then he heard the loud clunk, as the ancient lock was turned. Matt had left the key. Thank you, God.

The door opened inwards. Derek grabbed the handle and jerked it open at the same moment that Mary was pushing gently, from the other side. Startled, she stumbled forward. Derek caught her and pushed her back a little too firmly. The push sent the plate with his lunch high into the air. Terry caught the plate. Blondie caught, and consumed in one gulp, the contents. It was, or rather, had been, a pasty.

No loss there, Derek thought wildly, as he threw an apology over his shoulder, and ran out into the square, the tape recorder tucked under his arm. He ran for justice, he ran like a rabbit, he ran like Neville. Like buggery.

Home. In the door. Unlocked as ever. And there was the telephone. Connected.

Now, who to ring? 999? No, the system creaked, it would take hours to get through to someone who would take him seriously, to do anything to track Matt down. Welbeloved! Welbeloved would take him seriously. And Welbeloved could get the road blocks up and running, fast. Welbeloved.

He dialled.

"Sarge, listen to me. Listen please. I've got a confession, for the murder." A brief moment as he listened, then... "No, no, not me, you... No! Listen. It was that Matt chap. Matt Mark. I got it on tape, listen. No, don't talk Sarge. Just listen."

It was awkward, but he found a way. He slid down onto the hall floor, sitting with his back against the wall beneath the phone. On his lap he cradled the little tape-recorder. He held the receiver against the machine – the cord stretched just far enough – and pressed 'play'.

Matt's voice, a little squeaky but clearly Australian and his own voice, hummed into the phone and down the line to Sergeant Welbeloved.

> "Well that did it. I went out to the car, got the knife, came back in, there he was in his chair, praying, and I carved him up."
>
> "Just like that?"
>
> "Just like that. And I don't think anyone noticed, but I did it in the shape of a cross. But upside down. Long stroke down, short one across below. Neat, eh? Symbolic of something, dunno what, but..."

Derek was still sitting there, phone and machine in his lap, when Mary plus child and dog arrived, all three wondering if he'd gone mad. When Terry and Blondie were despatched to the garden, he told her everything. She listened until he finished.

"Blondie had your pasty,"

Derek tried to look regretful.

"But the good news is, I've got another in the meat safe."

* * *

But there was no more good news that early afternoon. Welbeloved confirmed that full road blocks had been mounted. With the help of neighbouring forces, every route leading in any direction from North Tawe in a fifteen-mile radius had been covered. It was, said the Sergeant, water-tight. And given the time between Matt escaping and Derek raising the alarm, the quarry must be within the cordon. The Sergeant was pleased with himself. He'd get the credit for chasing down the culprit.

So where was he?

"Gone to ground," The Sergeant pronounced, towards the end of the afternoon. "Though Lord knows where."

Derek put the phone down, and stood still in the hall. The niggle, his blazing, scorching niggle that had driven him on in these bleak January days, surged in his consciousness. The Sergeant just could be right. Perhaps the Lord did know where Matt was. And so did he.

* * *

"I knew if anyone could find me, it would be you, mate. Congratulations!"

Matt's voice, Australian, tired, strained, yet somehow full of his old spirit, full of his familiar mockery, echoed around the ruined chapel that stood in the otherwise deserted hamlet at Fursdon.

When Derek had allowed his motorbike to coast up the road towards the chapel, he thought at first that he'd guessed wrong. Where was Matt's MG? He'd expected to find it parked by the old building, but there was no sign.

Then he saw it. The overgrown and long-abandoned cottage was almost buried by the brambles and bushes that surrounded it and had spread themselves over it. So too was the ancient lean-to at its side. Somehow, Matt had driven or pushed his low-slung motor through the growths and into the lean-to's shelter. If you weren't looking for it, Derek told himself, you'd never see it. But there it was, which meant he'd guessed right. Matt was hiding out in the chapel.

Derek knew he should have raced on, to Okehampton or the nearest phone, and recalled the combined might of the Devon and Exeter Constabulary to apprehend the murderer. But he didn't. Matt was his friend. Perhaps now, with all hope of getting away gone, with no way of escaping the law, the man would, as the police phrase had it, come quietly. Come quietly with his friend, his mate.

He walked up the ancient path, ignoring the memory of past warnings, from Welbeloved, from Inspector Reed, from even higher authorities, never to 'go it alone', always to call for back-up. The hell with that. This had been his case, right from the start, and he was going to finish it.

He lifted the catch and pushed open the main door, which swung open smoothly, thanks to Lucy and her people's repair. He moved into the main room. When they'd left, Lucy and her hippies had not bothered to tidy up. Quite the reverse. The place was a jumble of overturned benches, litter, rubbish. No sign of Matt. But then, as he stood in the centre of the chaos, came the mocking and unmistakeable laugh.

Derek swung round. There was Matt, high up behind him, in the shaky-looking gallery, looking down over the rickety rail that still somehow clung on to the structure.

"You better come down from there," Derek told him. "It's not safe."

"It's safer than being down there, as far as I'm concerned," Matt said. "I come down there, and I'm on the way to an early morning appointment with your Mr. Albert Pierrepoint, right?"

"Not necessarily." Albert Pierrepoint was the country's notorious official hangman. "You can plead extenuating circumstances; the way Simpson treated you. It'll make a difference." Derek knew he wasn't convincing.

"Come off it!" Matt felt the same. "I killed my own Dad. Carved him up. And that's a terrible thing to do, no argument. They'll top me. If they get me. Which I suppose they will if I let them. I saw the road blocks. Two of them. Silly buggers left their blue lights flashing. I backed off, turned around. Fools."

Derek sighed heavily. "For Chrissake. Matt, what do you think you're doing? There's no way out. I told them where I was going. You could have a bash at me, if you like, probably kill me if you wanted to, but..."

"Christ! I wouldn't do that." Matt sounded genuinely shocked. "I wouldn't have a go at you, Derek. You're my mate."

He was doing something, fumbling with something, a rope? String? Then Derek remembered that, amongst the odd forgotten bits of farming life left or stored in the chapel there had been a half-used pack of binder twine. As Derek watched, Matt swung a double length of the heavy string over a beam above his head, pulled the loop down. Then he seemed to hook it on to something by his feet.

"What are you doing?"

"Listen, Derek. Got something to say to you. That's some girl you've got there, your Mary. I've seen her with that kid, Terry. She should be a mum herself, mate. I think she needs it. She'll be the best of mums. And you – you wouldn't make too bad a dad. Give a kid a decent home. Don't send him to Australia. Know what I mean? So you better get cracking, eh?"

He'd picked up the other end of the rope. It was twisted into the shape of a noose.

"No, Matt. Stop."

"And when you get your first-born, for God's sake don't name it after me. That would be a very bad idea." He laughed. "Especially if it's a girl."

He lifted his right leg and kicked the rail in front of him vigorously. It splintered out into the main room. Derek, who had been starting to run towards the stairs, had to duck, a bit of wood hitting him on the shoulder. He looked up.

"No, Matt, don't. You can get through this. Plead for mercy."

"I killed my own father, Derek. Don't reckon there's much mercy waiting for me in this life. Quite right too. It'll be interesting to see if there's any in the next world. Meanwhile... Cheers, mate."

In one unhesitating sequence Matt thrust his head into the makeshift noose, pulled it tight.

Derek looked up at the tall dark figure as the man posed for a moment. Then he toppled forward. For a moment Derek's brain short-circuited. He saw not one but two images as they fell, tall figures, Jeeves from the viaduct, Matt from the balcony.

There was a brief moment when the binder twine around Matt's neck might have snapped. It didn't. But the jerk gave to the high beam was all the rotting wooden support needed to free it from its ancient niche in the crumbling wall. It proved to be a seismic shock. Now the whole gallery began to crumble into the room below. Derek found himself scrambling out of the way of more debris. Dust swirled around the chapel, and it was seemed like five minutes before the dangerous creaking noise stilled, and odd bits of masonry and woodwork ceased to tumble.

But that first jerk had done the trick. When Derek managed to pull lumps of wood and rubble off Matt, he saw from the angle of the head that it had snapped the Australian's neck just as finally and efficiently as Mr. Pierrepoint, with all his macabre experience, would have managed.

CHAPTER THIRTY-TWO

It took the Devon and Exeter Constabulary and their lawyers three days before they were finally convinced that they had the wrong defendant banged up on remand, and Lucy Bellow, of no fixed abode, was exonerated. The tape recording did the trick, though John never got his recorder back. The charge of murder was dropped, as was a minor subsidiary charge of trespass, relating to Lucy's stay in the ruined chapel. Chief Superintendent Anderson was publicly congratulated on the success of his investigation and privately promoted to become Assistant Chief Constable of somewhere up north, anywhere, the Police Authority felt, other than the west country. And Aphrodite Wondergirl was allowed once again to enjoy the freedom she loved.

As she walked from the grim prison, several warders and a few other official personnel formed a group to applaud her, for during her brief period in the cells she had become popular. It was clear that others, as well as susceptible rural policemen, could fall under the spell of the "witch". There was enthusiastic talk about putting up a plaque commemorating the lives of Temperance Lloyd, Susannah Edwards and Mary Trembles, the three Devon women tried, convicted and hanged for the crime of witchcraft in 1682. There was palpable gratitude that they did not need to add another name to the tragic threesome.

Among those there to see Lucy step into freedom were PC Martin from North Tawe and Sergeant Welbeloved from Okehampton.

Lucy caught Derek's eye, and smiled. He returned the smile with a small shrug of apology. And before she was ushered into the patrol car, that would take her to Exeter St. David's station from where the Atlantic Coast Express would speed her and a couple of Fleet Street journalists to Paddington, and a new life, she hesitated. Then she went back to Derek, kissed the first two fingers of her right hand, then pressed them to his lips.

"What did she do that for?" Sergeant Welbeloved asked.

* * *

Cathy, beloved wife of John and mother of Sandy, died peacefully on the Saturday following her admission to hospital. Her husband and daughter were by her side.

Afterwards, having completed the tedious formalities that accompany a family death, John and Sandy returned to the Green Dragon in North Tawe and John opened the pub as usual. There was an expectation among some regulars of a big wake, with plenty of food and booze, jovial expressions of sadness, perhaps some singing. "Here come a blackbird."

But in the event, none of this happened. The wives left the food they brought in the pub's kitchen meat safe. The men accepted the glass of Johnnie Walker that John offered, shook his hand, and departed. The pub closed again at eight thirty. This wasn't Ireland, it wasn't Scotland, it was Devon. And it was the Devon way.

John accepted that his daughter had a right to a private life, and said nothing when she took Neville up to her room. The couple lay on Sandy's bed and held each other tight as Sandy sobbed. Slowly, over the night-time hours, her sobs changed to gentle weeping, and finally, sometime around four a.m. she slept.

Neville held her for another hour, warm in the knowledge that she trusted him, glowing with the realisation that she even loved him, wanted him. Then he slowly extricated himself from their wonderful tangle of arms and legs, crept out of the Dragon, found his bike, still parked behind the chapel, and rode home in the dawn rain, his heart singing.

* * *

Following protests from gardeners living near the now empty Manse, a new card was pinned to the announcement board in the village post office. It read in part: "Good home wanted for two goats."

* * *

At the police house in North Tawe the inevitable happened. They came to collect them at mid-day, several days later.

John Langdon came first, with his specialised police van. Terry and Blondie kissed and hugged each other immoderately, but Blondie then joined Dagwood in the van with apparent equanimity, while Mary mopped canine saliva off Terry's face and decided that, if either dog or boy were going to catch anything off each other, it was far too late to worry about it.

It was only twenty minutes later when they came for Terry. An official government limousine – apparently Terry's father was more important than anyone had realised – crept cautiously up the village street as if exploring a primitive jungle track lined by hostile tribes.

The hostile tribe awaiting it, Derek and Mary on their doorstep with Terry between them, watched as the car, it was a Daimler, Derek noted enviously, drew up almost soundlessly. A rear door opened, and a tall man in military uniform stepped out.

"Daddy!" Terry rushed forward, skidded to a stop in front of his father, then remembered he was ten, and held out a hand to shake. His father scooped him up and hugged him.

The pair were joined by another more graceful figure of a woman from the Far East, younger than the man, pretty, with a warm smile. Derek was standing too far back to hear what was said, but a sort of introduction took place, and all three seemed pleased and happy with each other.

Good manners were observed, of course, and thanks and invitations to come inside were offered, and a Devonshire cream tea was also offered. But time was pressing, and formalities were cut short. For one thing, Terry seemed anxious to go. He tugged his father towards the Daimler, and in no time all three were in the car, and their driver eased them away down the road with slow and elegant dignity.

On the doorstep Mary's body shook. A sob burst up through her throat. "He didn't even say goodbye," she cried, as Derek stood helpless.

Then, as they watched, holding hands, they saw the Daimler slow to a halt, then come gliding swiftly back up to them in a masterly display of reverse navigation.

A door opened, and Terry jumped out and ran to Mary and hugged her for a long tearful moment. Then he turned, and, slowly this time, got back in the car, and now it disappeared down through the narrow streets of North Tawe, across the square, and on out into the rest of the world.

Derek and Mary turned and went back into an empty house.

End

Printed in Dunstable, United Kingdom

72511907R00190